HOLD OF THE BONE

BAXTER CLARE TRAUTMAN

Ann Arbor
2015

Bywater Books

Bywater Books First Edition: June 2015

Printed in the United States of America on acid-free paper.

Cover designer: Bonnie Liss (Phoenix Graphics)

Bywater Books
PO Box 3671
Ann Arbor MI 48106-3671
www.bywaterbooks.com

ISBN: 978-1-61294-057-1

For Doc—*"Hurry, don't be late*

and

For Earl—*my Prince of Tides*

Chapter 1

The phone hums on the passenger seat. Lieutenant L.A. Franco picks it up and glances at her on-call detective's number. Frank frowns and holds the phone to her ear.

"Sister Shaft. Wha's up?"

Cheryl Lewis tells her, "Got an old one at an auto shop on Western. It's been here a while. Ain't much more 'an bone and rag. Forensics and the coroners are on their way."

"Hold on a sec." Frank grabs a pen and tells Lewis to give her the address. Steering with her knee, she writes the number on her palm. "A'ight. Give me about twenty."

"Ten-four."

Frank checks the time before stuffing the phone in her shirt pocket. With luck, she might make the tail end of her Saturday AA meeting. Traffic on LA's 101 Southbound is moving—but not fast enough. Frank clamps her police light onto the roof and flips the siren on. Vehicles part grudgingly.

She swings off on Slauson Avenue, slowing through red lights and stop signs until she gets to Western Avenue. She parks behind a patrol car, where a uniform she doesn't recognize greets her with the crime scene log. After Frank signs, he waves her through a gate in a chain-link fence topped with barbed wire. Near a small excavator, a muscular black woman steps daintily around a pile of rubble, directing a vaguely Asian female photographer. Frank notes that when she was a rookie everyone working an investigation would have been a white male. Now, other than Lewis' partner—wherever he is—she is the only Caucasian on the scene. And certainly the oldest.

Stepping closer to the broken concrete, Frank lifts her Ray-Bans to better peer into a hole in the ground. As she kneels, the excavation blurs. Frank puts out a hand to steady herself. She hears rattling, like sticks being clacked together. Lots of them, in unison, in a rhythm she wants to shuffle to with bare feet. She gives her head a sharp shake and the noise fades. Her eyes land on Lewis' shiny loafers and she wonders vaguely how her cop always finds time to show up at scenes buffed and creased. Frank stands carefully. The dizziness passes and she makes a note to drink more water.

"Morning, LT."

"Lewis."

"That's the kid over there, who dug it up." She points her chin toward a skinny guy outside the shop talking to an older man. "He was lookin' for a pipe and when he realized what he got into, he called his boss, that guy he's talking with. You know the first thing he says to me? Can't use his excavator unless we give him per diem on it." Lewis wags her head in sorrow at the human condition.

"City coming to dig up the rest?"

"On their way."

Frank looks back at the disturbed skeleton, bones and cloth barely distinguishable from the dirt. She notes there's little or no soft tissue to work with.

"How long's he owned this place?"

"Bought it in '98. Said it was a tool and die shop then."

"That body's been there longer than that," Frank thinks out loud. "Gonna take a while to get this sorted out and see if we got anymore in there. You talk to the owner about that?"

"Yeah." Lewis cuts an evil glare his way. "He say we can't search his property without a warrant, and when I tell him I'mma slap him with obstructing justice and interfering with a homicide investigation, and for all I know he put that body in the ground, he go all quiet, then start yapping about how the city gotta compensate him for lost wages. Blah, blah, blah."

Frank nods. They have consent on the body, but they'll need a warrant to search for more. "Where's Tatum at?"

Jerking a thumb at the unmarked, Lewis admits, "Ain't nothin' to door-knock here, so I got him working up the warrant."

Frank's gaze slides to the car. "You sure about that?"

Lewis squints. "That sum-bitch *sleeping?*"

Both women approach the unit from the rear. They needn't bother; Lewis' partner is asleep, mouth wide. Frank studies him through the open window. She probably shouldn't do what she's thinking of doing. It's old school, and the new breed of cops like Tatum have had all the fun bred from them. He'll probably report her to Human Resources and she'll have to go to Sensitivity Training. Again. What the hell, she thinks. Maybe next time, it'll take.

"Got a tampon?" she whispers.

Lewis frowns, then stealthily reaches inside for her purse. She rummages quietly and produces one. Frank takes the tampon and tips her head toward the shop.

"Go see if they got any Tapatío."

In LA, hot sauce is the condiment of choice, a bottle invariably in every break room in the city. Lewis returns with a full bottle and Frank douses the tampon. Spying a sweating soda cup on the console, she reaches across Tatum, dumps the contents, fills it with the rest of the Tapatío, and sets it back in place.

"Get your camera ready."

Frank gently inserts the tampon in Tatum's open mouth. Lewis chuckles and gets a couple shots before Frank raps her knuckles on the roof. Tatum bolts upright. He spits the tampon out and seeing what it is, gives half a scream before hurling it from the window. Lewis doubles over laughing.

Pawing at his tongue, Tatum grabs the cup on the console, chugs it, then spews all over the dash. His eyes tear as he yanks on his shirttail and swabs his mouth. "What the fuck?"

"Maybe that'll keep you awake," Frank tells him. "Lewis, when you're done being Martin Scorsese, send Sleeping Beauty back to the office. Get him started on provenance for this place. Find a concrete specialist to tell us how old it is where they dug it up. I'll be back at the station in a bit to see what he's come up with. Oh, and Tatum? Get this car cleaned. It's a fucking disgrace to the city."

Tatum searches for water while Lewis wipes tears from her eyes.

"You need anything?" Frank asks her.

"Not now. That made my day, LT. Hell," she grins. "Maybe my whole week."

Leaving Tatum whining and spitting, they walk back to the edge of the hole.

"Let me see your notes," Frank says. The Ray-Bans go back on her head, partly to keep her hair out of her eyes, but mostly because Frank needs to squint to read the tiny handwriting.

Cheryl Lewis has attitude, but she is Frank's most thorough detective. She scans the neat handwriting, checking that Lewis has all the who–what–when–where from the owner and the kid on the dozer. The how and why will be harder. There isn't much more they can do until after the coroner's people excavate the body. Even then, there might not be much to work with.

"Sure I can't get you anything?"

"Nah, LT. Just them techs."

"A'ight. They'll be here."

"In they own sweet time."

"I'mma take off. Holler if you need me."

"Ten-four."

Frank starts to walk away, but Lewis calls her. "Yeah?"

Her big cop grins. "Thanks, LT. That was fun."

Frank replies with a nod and parting wave.

Chapter 2

Frank keeps the strobe going on her way to the meeting. She drives with her sleeves up and windows down, gathering the sight, scent, and sound of her beat. She notes a Latino guy selling oranges on the corner, the smell of barbecue, splash of new graffiti on a storage building, an arthritic old man shuffling on the shady side of the avenue.

Frank is the rare cop who has spent a career at the same station. She registers day-to-day changes in the Figueroa Division, yet knows little has changed in the struggling neighborhood since big industry abandoned it in the 60s. With the jobs went the middle-class families, leaving an economic void that went unfilled until the crack epidemic of the 80s. The subsequent South-Central turf wars led to an unprecedented nationwide murder rate that peaked in the early 90s. Homicide numbers hovered around the all-time high throughout most of the decade until falling at the turn of the century to record lows. At Figueroa, Frank and her detectives have gone from a maximum caseload of 160 homicides a year to an almost giddy twenty-two.

Twenty-three, she corrects, adding Lewis' body. And a good thing, considering the budget cuts and reorganizations that have whittled her staff. Still, it's the first time in Frank's tenure at Figueroa that her detectives have what is procedurally considered a normal workload. So normal it's boring, and though she doesn't miss the 36- or 48-hour shifts, she pines a bit for the hectic adrenaline rush of getting called to one scene at midnight, another at 3:00 a.m., and a third at dawn.

Grabbing a parking spot, she jogs a half block to her meeting, tiptoes up the stairs, and stands at the back door. The room is packed with bright-eyed, freshly showered people starting their weekend with a healthy shot of sobriety.

"So that's it for me, and now I'd like to hear from our friend in the doorway who just turned five. Frank?"

Because she was late, she is surprised to be called on, but answers, "My name's Frank. I'm an alcoholic."

About forty people chorus, "Hi, Frank." Except for three or four of the faces turned her way, she recognizes them all. "Welcome to any newcomers and visitors. I got here late—sorry—so I'll pass."

"Don't be silly," the man leading the meeting says. "Go on."

"Alright," she agrees, embarrassed to be standing instead of sitting like the others. "If you're new, stick around. Your life'll change. Mine sure has. First thing that happened to me was finding the man who murdered my father. Got that old monkey off my back, and did it sober. Then I got back together with a woman who'd left because of my drinking, only to lose her a year later to cancer. Managed to get through that, too, with your help, then a little after that I had, um, a very, unexpected one-night stand."

The people who know her well chuckle at the understatement.

"Yeah." Frank can't keep from grinning. "Ended up pregnant. That was a shock. I had the baby, but I gave her to her father to raise. He's a great guy and does a far better job raising her than I ever could. And right now—" she thinks about her abundance of riches "—I couldn't ask for a better life. I have a lovely girlfriend, lots of friends. My health. Mortgage is paid off, and I'm considering retirement. I'm comfortable in sobriety, but I hope not complacent. So like I said, stick around. Life gets easier. Doesn't mean tough times won't happen, but you'll learn how to get through them without drinking or making them worse."

She calls on the woman beside her and relaxes against the jamb. Across the room, Caroline Anderson sends a wink and a smile. Frank returns them. Caroline is not only a good friend but a companionable lover. They met in this room, and after her inexplicable one-night stand with Darcy James, Frank asked Caroline to be her obstetrician. They grew close during the pregnancy and after a gentle flirtation became easy lovers. Theirs is a tender relationship with few demands; recently out of a long-term relationship, Caroline is reluctant to enter another, while Frank doesn't need or want promises about the future, having learned that most of life occurs in the hollows between expectation and reality.

The meeting ends at ten sharp. Everyone chips in to pick up dirty cups and coffee pots, talking loudly over each other and laughing often. Frank is blocking the door, so she waits downstairs for Caroline, receiving cologned and perfumed hugs for her five years of sobriety. Caroline steps from the building, looking fine in jeans, boots, and a snug T-shirt.

Frank smiles and leaves the well-wishers to hook an arm through her lover's. "Coffee?"

"I'd love some, just give me a minute."

"Sure. How 'bout I grab a table and you get me a latte when you're done?"

"That's all? No breakfast?"

Frank grins and shakes her head. "Jeans are getting a little tight."

She crosses to the café across the street and threads past the line at the entrance to an umbrella-ed table on the back patio. Leaving the shaded seat for Caroline, Frank drops the sunglasses back into place and stretches her long legs into the sun. Stray hairs tickle her collarbone, reminding her it's time to get a trim. That makes her think how she always had to reprimand Darcy about keeping his hair regulation length, and she checks her phone. It's not unusual for him to ring on Saturdays to chat about their daughter, and sure enough, she's missed his call. She returns it, listening to the phone ringing two thousand miles away.

Conceived in a mutual confluence of grief, loneliness, and need, Destiny was quite the surprise to her perimenopausal mother. After Caroline confirmed Frank was indeed pregnant, she toyed with aborting the fetus, but the chances of getting pregnant in one shot at her age were astronomical enough to give Frank pause. The odds that she had slept with Darcy at all were so incalculable she couldn't help but feel that their brief coupling had happened for a reason. When she told Darcy, he begged her not to abort. She wasn't surprised; a few months earlier his beloved only child from a failed marriage had finally lost her grueling, lifelong battle with cystic fibrosis. Frank agreed to keep the baby, provided Darcy took full custody upon its birth.

7

She'd have it for him, which seemed right in a weirdly scripted kind of way, and she'd help with money but wanted no part of the day-to-day raising.

"Hey. How's it going?"

"It goes," Darcy answers in his grumbling diesel engine voice. "You?"

"S'all good. Destiny?"

He snorts, "She's your daughter. Intractable as hell."

"Yeah, like you're such a pushover."

"We had to buy shoes last week and she saw a pair of moccasins. Had a fit until I let her try 'em on. Now I have to bargain with her every night to take 'em off and they're the first things she puts on in the morning. That and her bone necklace."

"Bone?"

"Yeah, she found some old vertebrae and strung 'em together with baling twine. She wears 'em all day and if anyone tries to take 'em off she has a fit. Didn't I send you a picture last week?"

Darcy sends so many videos and photos she honestly doesn't look at them all, but she recalls one of Destiny smiling under a platinum tangle of hair, naked but for underwear and what she guesses now were the moccasins. "What kind of vertebrae we talking?"

"I don't know, some old possum or raccoon. They're harmless. But here's the queer thing."

Frank rolls her eyes. Darcy loves saying that to her.

"She was crying the other night when I was trying to talk her out of 'em and when I explained that they'd be right by her bed and that she could put 'em on first thing in the morning she said that Gran'ma Marioneaux told her to never take them off."

"Who's that?"

"Pearl Marioneaux was my mother's grandmother."

Darcy gives her time to do the math. His mother's in her seventies. Her mother would be at least in her nineties, making her grand-mother—"She's *still alive*?"

"Nope." She hears the grin in his voice. "Been dead sixty, seventy years. When I asked Dez how she knew about Gran'ma Marioneaux, she said, 'I knew her from before I came here.'"

It's not the first of her daughter's unearthly pronouncements, but each time Frank hears one her skin prickles. Caroline sets a foamy mug of coffee in front of her, and Frank mouths thanks. While Caroline scans the movie section of the local weekly, Frank listens to Darcy explain that his great-grandmother was a full-blooded Lakota.

"She and my great-grandfather married and got railroaded out of town and eventually settled here. You know the only two things she took with her?"

"Let me guess."

"Uh-huh. Mom said she was buried in them. Caused quite an uproar at the funeral home."

"Great. Our kid's channeling Sacajawea and you were worried about raising her in LA."

"Speaking of funny, guess who called yesterday."

"No idea."

"Marguerite."

"Oh, yeah? You two gettin' chummy again?"

"Nothing like that. Just seems since Gaby died she's been reaching out to me more. Probably because I'm her last link to her. Who knows, maybe she's softening in her old age. She said to say hi. Said she's been thinking about you."

"Oh, yeah?" She wonders why his ex-wife is thinking about her. Marguerite James isn't just a researcher at UCLA with a doctorate in quantum physics and half a dozen honorary titles; she is also a mambo, a Yoruban priestess who, along with Darcy, happened to save Frank's life years ago on a case gone bizarrely sideways.

"Are you there?"

"Sorry, what?"

"Your daughter. She's starting half-day care next week."

"Right, right. You got my check?"

"Yeah. It's all paid for. Mom and Tina took her shopping last week and she's already balking about having to wear clothes. I won't be surprised if she gets sent home naked before lunchtime."

"You're really raising a little heathen."

"You think you can do a better job?"

Frank laughs. "You know I can't."

"Damn right," he grumbles.

"Give me a call," she tells him. "Let me know how it goes."

"Will do."

She hangs up and Caroline asks without looking from her paper, "How's Dez?"

"Fine, I guess. Wearing bone necklaces and channeling her great-great grandmother."

"Again?"

"Hey, you're the one that told me it's not uncommon for kids to have past-life memories. Recanting your testimony, Doctor?"

"Not at all. I just find it fascinating she has so many."

Caroline nibbles her scone, catching the crumbs with her plate. "Can I have a bite?"

She neatly breaks off a piece and is about to put it on a napkin but Frank guides Caroline's hand to her mouth, taking the bite from her fingers and kissing them. Caroline is a delightful companion but lacks imagination in romance.

She stands and kisses Caroline's cheek. "I gotta go check on Tatum, drop off some paperwork. Pick the movie and let me know."

Frank kisses her again, on the mouth. She doesn't care who sees.

Chapter 3

Frank takes the long way to the station, veering east to drop papers off at Headquarters. It isn't a necessary detour, but a breeze from the ocean has cleared the air, cooled the heat, and made it far too nice to be inside. Frank smiles. It's a good excuse and she almost believes it, but she's been sober long enough to recognize her own shit when she's stepping in it, and though the weather is great it has nothing to do with avoiding the station.

Tapping the side panel in time to a Jay-Z rap, Frank pictures the retirement forms squared neatly on the corner of her desk. She filled the papers out once, then balled them into the trash. Now a fresh set beckons each time she walks into her office. Cop, detective, supervisor, bureaucrat—Frank is bored with it all. Not one aspect of the job excites her anymore. She can't even justify that bad guys still need catching. For every one they get off the streets, another takes his place. That's if they even get him off the street; handing the DA a live suspect and hard evidence never guarantees a conviction.

Automatically monitoring the sidewalks while she waits at a light, she decides pride is the only motivation she has left. Thirty years ago, as punishment for being women on an all-male force, Frank and her first lover were dumped into the worst division in the LAPD. Determined not to cave to harassment and cold shoulders, she persistently, quietly worked her way up from boot to detective, then Sergeant to Lieutenant. Under her aegis, cops sent to Figueroa for disciplinary action became detectives that closed record numbers of uncloseable cases.

But nowadays, except for Lewis, even her detectives bore her, the lot of them young and PC. She wouldn't be surprised if Tatum filed a suit against her for harassment or brutality or some other god-damned candy-assed complaint. Along with the rest of his colleagues, he looked at Frank like she was the last, thank God, of a dying breed. Like Frank had looked at the old-timers when she was new.

Frank sighs; she's hung around long enough to become a good old boy. Spotting a parking space, she switches lanes. There is parking below Headquarters, but the thought of being in her car when the next big quake hits makes above-ground spaces more attractive. She locks her old Honda and heads for the slick new Police Administration Building.

Thinking she's outlived even the old HQ, Frank glances at a dark bird turning circles high in the rare clear sky. She absently watches the faraway flight, knowing in her heart of hearts it's time to quit, yet each time she tries to fill out the papers she stumbles over the same old obstacle: being a cop is all she has ever been, done, or known. The job is wife, friend, mistress, mother, whore—and Frank isn't ready to explore the mystery of who she'll be without a badge.

"Lieutenant?"

Frank turns, shading her eyes. It isn't until the woman lowers her sunglasses that Frank recognizes Darcy's ex.

With a laugh she reaches for the mambo's hand. "Marguerite James. As I live and breathe. What brings you downtown on a Saturday?"

"A conference." Marguerite clasps her hand warmly. She tips her chin to the hotel beyond Frank. "I'm on my lunch break."

Keenly aware of the heat from the mambo's hands, Frank flushes and deliberately keeps her gaze from Marguerite's formidable cleavage. "I just talked to Darcy. Hear you've been asking about me."

"I have."

"Any particular reason?"

Marguerite lets go to check her watch. "I have some time before my next panel. Might we talk?"

"About?" Frank hedges.

"You, of course." Marguerite flashes an uncharacteristic smile. "Come. There's a seat over there."

She nods at a bench in the park across the street. Without waiting for agreement, she crosses to it. Frank waits for a car to pass. Marguerite has never told her anything she's wanted to hear. She should wave and

12

keep on walking. But curiosity impels her to follow. She sits next to Marguerite, who turns to face her.

"I'll wager you think this is complete coincidence, running into each other."

Frank admits, "The odds are long." Remembering the mambo as stern and severe, she is puzzled by Marguerite's second smile.

"Tell me how you are, Lieutenant."

Frank's brows shoot up. "I'm fine, but I don't recall you being long on chitchat, Marguerite. What's up?"

The mambo tilts her head to study Frank. Her hair, pulled into a bun, is shot with silver now, like Frank's, and the mambo has more wrinkles than she did at her daughter's funeral—also like herself, Frank concedes—yet still she remains powerfully attractive. And though Marguerite has been unusually cordial, her eyes can't hide her ferocity.

"Darcy is right. I have been thinking of you lately. I can't say why."

"Can't or won't?"

"Can't, Lieutenant."

Frank smiles, touches the tips of her fingers to Marguerite's bare arm. "Will you ever call me Frank?"

"I'll try."

Frank reluctantly moves her fingers. "So you've been thinking about me. Good or bad?"

"Good, I should say. At least, I think it's good, but I don't know that you'd agree. Are you sure everything is quite alright?"

"Far as I know. Do you think otherwise?" Frank braces for whatever the answer might be.

"I'm not sure. You keep coming into my thoughts, and when you do I feel a great restlessness, like a building storm that hasn't decided which way to blow."

Frank looks at the speck of bird still circling up in the blue. "I've got it all, Marguerite. The girl, the house, the job. I can even retire if I want."

"Do you want to?"

Frank turns into Marguerite's blunt gaze. It frightens her, but there's never been any bullshit in it, and Frank appreciates that. "I'd love to. I know it's time to move on, but I have no idea where to."

13

The heat in Marguerite's eyes melts into compassion so raw and unexpected it forces Frank to look away, down at the strong, dark hand that unexpectedly grips hers. A wave of dizziness hits Frank. She shuts her eyes against it. When she opens them, Marguerite's hand is old and wizened. Instead of the buffed French manicure, she sees broken fingernails rimed with dirt. Her hand is the extension of a gristly wrist poking from a grimy, ragged sleeve. Frank smells acrid smoke, like the chaparral above the city is on fire.

She jerks her head up. Marguerite watches her. Frank looks back at the mambo's hand. It is plump and brown, the nails round and shiny.

"Are you alright?"

"Yeah."

Frank takes a furtive whiff of the city air. It smells of diesel and asphalt, not wildfire. She mashes her eyes, vowing to drink more water and cut back on the caffeine. She probably should have had breakfast.

"Do you know why I left Darcy?"

According to him there had been a couple of reasons, but Frank shakes her head, unsure which one Marguerite means.

"He had remarkable gifts, but he refused to use them—at least, to any purpose—and I always thought it was such a waste. I couldn't abide it."

She gives Frank's hand a little shake, and Frank glances to make sure she's not holding the shriveled claw.

"You have the same talent. I told you that once, do you remember?"

Frank dredges up unwanted memories of the Mother Love case. Another priestess, but crazed with her own power, The Mother had taken to sacrificing enemies and dumping them in Frank's jurisdiction. Darcy had brought his ex–wife in to calm a terrified witness convinced he'd been hexed by The Mother. After "cleansing" the witness, Marguerite had taken Frank aside.

She had warned Frank that her powers were not to be ignored, but the plague of visions and *déjà vu*s Frank experienced during the case had ended when Darcy killed Mother Love, and Frank conveniently relegated the entire episode to a dark corner of her memory.

"It might not feel like it, but your life really is in order now, Lieu—Frank."

They share a short smile.

"I believe all the work you've done up to this point has been foundation for this, the second half of your life. I think you're finally ready to engage the real work, the work that matters here." She presses a hand between Frank's breasts.

Frank closes her eyes against the solid heat. In a voice that sounds too small to be her own, she says, "I don't know what that is."

"That's alright. You don't have to know right now. All you have to do is be open. It will come to you, I promise. It's been waiting a long time."

"You keep saying 'it.' What's 'it'?"

"Your life," Marguerite answers.

"What have I been doing the last fifty years?"

The mambo smiles. "Preparing."

Frank studies the buildings across the street. "What about this talent? What's that look like?"

"I'm not sure. But you'll know it as it begins to manifest. Which, I'm surprised it hasn't already."

"Hm. Like porn? I can't explain it, but I'll know it when I see it?"

"That's a crude analogy, but yes."

Frank nods. "I hope it's not going to manifest as traumatically as it did last time. I don't know that I've got another Mother Love in me."

Marguerite cocks her head as if listening. "It doesn't have to. You weren't prepared for that. It was a shock."

"Understatement."

"But now you know better. I think it will go much easier if you accept this. The harder you resist, the more difficult you'll make it."

"What if I just walk away, like Darcy?"

Marguerite shakes her head. I don't think you have that option. Even your latent ability is so much stronger than his."

"I hear you, Marguerite, I really do, but I'm not understanding a goddamned word."

"I know. I understand this is completely illogical, and irrational, but logic and reason will no longer serve you as they have. At this stage of your life, in this transition if you will, it is heart that matters most."

The mambo's hand slides to Frank's chest again. Warmth rises from Frank's groin but spreads. It confounds her, coursing through her belly and torso, shooting down her arms and legs, tingling out toes and fingers.

"You feel that?"

Frank nods. Marguerite removes her hand, but the heat remains.

"Trust that. Seek it. And when you find it, don't ignore it. If you come from here," she taps her knuckles on Frank's forehead, "you will struggle and inevitably lose. But if you come from here," she presses gently against Frank's breastbone, "I promise the path will be clear."

The mambo digs in her purse and presents Frank a white business card. "Call me. I'll help however I can."

Marguerite stands. Frank studies the familiar card.

"Oh. One thing I am certain of, you will always have help along the way. It may not look like you expect it to or even want it to, but it will always be there."

Frank offers a wry smile. "Like you?"

"Yes. Take close care, Lieutenant."

"Frank," she reminds, but Marguerite is already crossing the street. She considers the card in her hand, thinks about leaving it on the bench. Instead, tucks it in the pocket over her heart. Above, a lone vulture circles the City of Angels.

Chapter 4

Frank walks back to her car but doesn't go anywhere. She sits and stares down First Street. Two old Asian men argue past her. A black woman clicks by in heels, and a wino of indeterminate ancestry pokes through trashcans. She checks in with Lewis, who doesn't need her, then Caroline. "Hey. It's me."

"Hi," Caroline answers. "Where are you?"

"Headed to the station. You?"

"I'm at the hospital. I got paged right after you left."

"Anything serious?"

"I doubt it. Just a first-timer who's read everything on the Internet about what can go wrong during delivery and nothing about how often it goes right."

Recalling Caroline's steady presence throughout her labor, Frank says, "She's lucky to have you."

"What sort of case did you get?"

"Kid on an excavator dug up an old body. Not much to work with. Be a bitch to close. Plus Lewis' partner's an idiot."

"Tatum?"

"Yeah. I'm on my way to check on him. It's cops like Tatum that make me want to turn my badge in."

She considers telling Caroline about Marguerite but doesn't know how to begin explaining what even she doesn't understand.

Caroline says, "I think a movie's out, but I shouldn't be too late, if you want to spend the night. We could at least have the morning together."

The offer isn't wildly tempting, but with nothing better to do Frank agrees. After she hangs up she calls Lewis back.

"Damn, LT, what up? You gonna check in every ten minutes, you may as well come out and babysit the coroner your own self."

"Easy, girl. It's gonna be a long night and I was gonna send Sleeping Beauty back with some food. What do you want?"

"Ah, you sweet," Lewis relents, "but I ain't hungry."

"What?" Frank tries to think if she's ever heard Cheryl refuse food. "I was gonna have him get you a wet burrito."

"Nah, I'm good. But you know what? Tell him go by Takami's and pick me up a miso soup and side a rice. Tell him don't forget the damn spoon."

Frank teases, "You on a diet, girl?"

"Nah. Just not that hungry."

Frank shakes her head, surprised at the first. She pulls into the Figueroa parking lot and takes the steps to the squad room two at a time. Tatum actually appears to be working and she asks over his shoulder, "Whatcha got?"

They peer at tax rolls on his monitor.

"The address goes back to 1968. It's changed hands four times since then."

Frank grunts. "Ain't no longevity in the 'hood."

She fishes money from the wallet in her pocket. "Run over to Takami's and get Lewis some miso soup and a side of rice. Bring me the change. And don't forget the spoon."

"What about me?"

Walking into her office, she asks over her shoulder, "What about you?"

Tatum doesn't answer and she figures he is either waving his middle finger or juggling his crotch at her. Frank stands next to her scarred old desk, the retirement forms squared primly on the corner. She rests a hand on them, listening to Tatum stomp out. She returns to the quiet squad room and pauses at his desk. It was Bobby's before he promoted out to West Hollywood. She looks around the fusty room. Ghosts waft in the air like dust motes.

Noah, her best friend, best partner. Dead way too soon.

Gough. Nook. Taquito. Good old boys, all retired.

Murderous Ike Zabbo. Dead, too. No loss there.

Jill Denton, "Fire Truck." Red hair, chronically late, always screaming around the corner like she was on her way to a three-alarm.

Belligerent, drunken Johnnie Briggs. There were only three ways out for a hopeless alcoholic like Johnnie—hospitals, institutions, or death. Johnnie had chosen the latter, wrapping his car around an abutment on the 101. She always wondered if it had been deliberate.

Then there was Darcy. Demoted to Frank's squad for decking his last captain, he became not only an invaluable detective but friend as well.

She wishes he were here. He'd know what Marguerite was talking about. She thinks about calling, but doesn't want to bother him. She checks that the coffee pot is emptied and clean, studies wanted sheets posted on the bulletin board. Faces of Latino men, a couple black males, one woman, peek between administrative memos, posters for sexual harassment, workplace violence, influenza. The board is sterile, completely professional; there's not one badly printed sign announcing in bold letters, "WHEN YOU CHECK OUT, WE CHECK IN" or a bloody smiley face instructing "HAVE A GREAT DAY—IT MIGHT BE YOUR LAST!". There are no photos of Lewis superimposed over Brandi Chastain's classic victory pose. No pictures of departmental brass sprouting red horns and forked tails. Not even a crude hot sheet of one of the squad members, wanted for a lewd and lascivious, or worse, an "LOA" implying a detective wasn't working a case hard enough.

She considers making a "lack of activity" poster with Lewis' picture of Tatum, but surely someone will be offended and kick a complaint up the ladder. In the old days Frank wouldn't have cared, it would have been worth it for the morale of the squad. Now the squad finds its morale at home with family and kids, instead of at work with hi-jinks and after-hour highballs.

Back in her office she rummages in her top drawer and finds a crinkled pack of cigarettes. She shakes one loose and settles into her hard, wooden chair. She's had it so long the seat has worn into the shape of her ass. Every couple years an ergonomics expert comes along and tries to throw the chair away, and every couple years she hides it until the new chair arrives and they leave her alone.

One-handed, she opens the cover of a matchbook and bends a

19

match to the striker plate. The head spits and flares and she is glad for the quick, hot smell of sulfur. After lighting a cigarette, she shakes the match out, and twists it loose. She lets the hot end sizzle on her tongue, making sure it is dead before dropping it in the trash. She blows smoke toward the detector, hoping to set it off. She doubts the damn thing even works.

She reflects that cops today are different but in a good way. They don't smoke, for one, and if they did they certainly wouldn't in their offices. They are healthier and more balanced. They talk things out and exorcise with weights instead of alcohol. They seem purposeful and driven to succeed. She is sure most of them find the work satisfying, but wonders if it is *fun*. Frank loved her work for a long time. It was hard, but it was fun outsmarting and outplaying the bad guys. Even the desperate drudgery of back-to-back cases and three-day shifts had been play. She'd had a good crew back then, and they had played beside her.

Now all her playmates are gone. Crossing her ankles on the desk, she thinks how nice a glass of Scotch would taste with the cigarette. That's a bad thought for an alcoholic and Frank concentrates on the flavor of the stale tobacco. Its weight is a comfort in her chest and she recalls the heat of Marguerite's palm between her breasts.

Dropping her feet, she spins to dial the landline on her desk.

"Well, hiya," her sponsor answers. "Whatcha up to?"

"Sitting alone in my office, thinking bad thoughts."

"Why don't cha come over? I'm just folding laundry and watching *Dancing with the Stars* re-runs. That Kurt Warner, he's cute!"

Frank grins. Mary is in her seventies but hasn't lost her eye for a handsome man. "Better not let Ed hear you say that."

"Aw, he's off golfing. Besides, he couldn't hear me anyway."

"Can I bring you a Frappuccino?"

"Ooh, I'd love one. With extra whipped cream."

"You got it."

Frank switches off the office light and shuts the door. Her steps echo in the squad room. She pauses near the hall, tempted to look back, but afraid all she'll see are ghosts.

Chapter 5

"Hey." She pecks Mary's cheek and hands her the sticky drink.

"Thanks, you're a doll. Whadda I owe ya?"

Like Frank, Mary is from New York. Unlike Frank, she has retained much of her accent.

"Nothing. My pleasure."

"Well, thanks! Come on in. Let's go sit out back."

They settle on the oak-shaded deck overlooking Mulholland Canyon. A jay screeches and lands on the top rail.

Mary shoos, "Go on. You've been fed today."

To Frank, she says, "To what do I owe the honor? You never come by and see me no more."

"I know. I'm a terrible sponsee."

"Are you kidding? You're my easy one. You always handle everything on your own, then call me when it's all done and tell me how ya did it. I should have more like you."

"'Fraid I'm not gonna be so easy today."

"Why, what's going on?"

Frank hunches toward her sponsor. "I got it all, right? The job, girlfriend, a little sobriety. No bills. No debt. Can retire if I want. What's not to like about all that?"

Mary sucks at her frappé. "Nothing I can see."

"I know. And the god's honest truth, Mary? I'm about to come out of my skin."

Her sponsor's eyes narrow. "How many meetings you gettin' to?"

"It's not that. I don't want to drink. I just . . ." Frank gets up and leans against the railing. The shade is deep and cool and she has the impossible memory of riding up a narrow, bowered canyon where

21

evergreen boughs block the heat of the day and a horse's hooves fall soundlessly upon centuries of old, brown needles.

"You just what?"

She spins to face Mary. "Remember that case I told you about? With the Santeria priestess?"

"The one where you almost died?"

"Yeah, that one. There was a woman that helped me through it. Darcy's ex-wife. I ran into her today, and it was like she could see right through me. She says I'm ready to start the second half of my life, but I'm so damn dumb I don't even know what that is."

"Whoa, she said that?"

Frank offers a sheepish grin. "Not that last part. But that's what it feels like. My past has absolutely no attraction for me, but meanwhile I'm stumbling around in the dark trying to find the doorknob into my future."

"The doorknob? Have you even found the damn door yet?"

"No," Frank admits.

"Then quit looking for the knob! When you find the door, then you can start worrying about how to open it. 'Til then, relax."

Mary stands next to her at the railing. They lean on it, staring toward brown mountains thirsty for rain. She remembers scraps of a dream: a ghost-colored moon and black mountains rising to meet it; somewhere, running dark water and fish. Trout, she thinks, though filleted and fried is the closest she has ever come to a trout.

"She said I have talent."

"America's Got Talent. What kind you got?"

"I don't know. She didn't either. Says I'll know it when I see it."

"Like porn, huh?"

Frank chuckles. "That's what I said."

The jay scolds from a branch over the deck. It drops closer to Mary, dancing nervously for a handout.

"When I was involved with the Santeria case, I kept having dreams so vivid they seemed real. And visions, like the dreams, just as real, like they were happening in present time."

"What kinda visions?"

Frank takes a deep breath. She remembers Marguerite's warning that whatever's coming will be easier if she doesn't fight it. She tells her sponsor about the sandaled soldier on a battlefield littered with corpses, the scavenging women and children, the vultures and feeding dogs.

"Kept seeing it over and over."

"Why? What did it mean?"

Frank shrugs. "Marguerite said Mother Love and I had been adversaries through many lifetimes, that the latest battle was just one of many, and that the visions were carryover. Said being around The Mother's power woke up my own."

Mary looks indignant. "How come you never told me any of this?"

"Never had a need to. Not the kinda thing that comes up in everyday conversation."

"Geez. Ya can say that again."

"Marguerite said I'll be alright if I trust my heart over my head. Only the thing is, I'm not sure I know how to do that."

"That's about the only thing your friend's said that I understand." Mary sucks loudly at the bottom of her cup.

"How so?"

Mary raps her breastbone. "This is where God lives. Right here. The answers are always right here, kiddo. You know that."

Frank shakes her head. "I can think an answer, but I don't know that I can feel one."

"That's 'cause you don't spend enough time practicing. You gotta slow down, take the time to learn what an answer *feels* like. It's subtle, tiny at first, but the more you tune in to it, the stronger it gets. I promise, the answers are all there."

Looking at the dusty mountains Frank muses, "That's the second promise I've had today."

"What was the first?"

"Marguerite promised that if I keep my heart open my path will be clear, and that I'll have help along the way."

Mary chuckles and pats her back. "This lady sounded cuckoo at first, but I'm startin' to like her more and more."

"Yeah, she grows on you like that."

"Trust your heart and everything'll be okay—it don't get simpler than that."

"Easily said," Frank mutters, "but not so easily done."

"Like I said, it gets easier with practice. Are you trustin' or drivin' the bus?"

Frank grins. "Mostly driving."

"How's that workin' for ya?"

"Got me here talkin' to you."

"Ya see?" Mary grins and rubs a palm over Frank's back. "Relax, kiddo. You're ready for a change. You really are. But don't force it, let it come."

Frank narrows her eyes at Mary. "That's what Marguerite said. You two been talking?"

"Nah. We're just two broads that know a little more than you do. Am I gonna see you at the meeting Saturday?"

"Unless I got called out."

They walk through the house arm in arm. At the door Frank pecks her sponsor's wrinkled cheek.

"I love you, Mary."

"I love you, too, kiddo. Love you, too."

Chapter 6

Frank isn't particularly hungry but decades of odd hours have taught her to eat when she can. She gets a pizza and eats at Caroline's while watching Stanford beat USC, again. Caroline still hasn't come home by the time the game ends, so Frank takes a long swim in the condo pool. Because it's late she has a lane all to herself and in the rhythm of strokes she forgets about her day.

When she gets back upstairs, Caroline is in the shower. Frank slips in beside her. "Hey, you."

Caroline receives her nuzzled greeting happily if not wildly, and Frank proceeds undaunted. The water cools and Frank turns it off. Grabbing an oversized beach towel she wraps Caroline like a mummy and steers her, laughing, to the bed. Caroline is a Virgo, she doesn't like messes, and Frank judiciously lays a second towel under Caroline's wet head.

"You think of everything," she marvels.

"I try," Frank murmurs, caressing Caroline through the damp terry cloth. Caroline tries to free an arm, but Frank says, "Uh-uh. I want you all wrapped up. Like an early Christmas present."

"Sweetie," Caroline protests. "It's barely September and I'm bushed. Can Christmas wait at least until tomorrow morning?"

"Sure." Hiding her disappointment, Frank helps extricate Caroline from the towel. "I'm gonna hang this up."

She takes her time in the bathroom, letting her irritation fade. After all, she reasons coldly, it's not like she was that excited. Arousing Caroline is more an exercise in determination than passion. But to be honest, Frank concedes, she was into it more for the distraction than the pleasure. It's not fair to pick on Caroline's lack of enthusiasm when she can barely marshal her own.

Still, she studies herself in the mirror, it would have been nice. Frank eyes the extra inch at her waist, and gravity's relentless toll on her ass. The wrinkles that used to get smoothed out with face cream and a good night's sleep have become permanent furrows, and the silver in her hair is overtaking the gold. But all in all, she's in decent shape. She forces a double chin, wondering what to do with the rest of the night. Deciding to try sleeping, she snuggles in next to Caroline.

"There you are," Caroline murmurs and wedges into her. Frank holds her lover tenderly, glad at least for the comfort of the familiar body. As she so often does, Caroline falls asleep easily. Frank lies awake. The day comes back to her and she recalls the warmth of Marguerite's palm on her chest. Searching for Caroline's hand, she raises it gently, places it between her breasts, and covers it with her own. Only then does she sleep.

In the morning Caroline is true to her word, willing to take up where they left off, but Frank wakes antsy and irritable. "Let's get breakfast," she suggests, getting dressed before Caroline can argue.

They eat at a Mexican hole in the wall down the street. The waiter knows them well and refills their cups without asking.

"Do you have anything planned today?" Frank wonders.

"Mercifully, no. My calls are covered and I have the whole day off. What about you?"

Frank shakes her head. "Nothing in particular. Want to get that movie in?"

"Sure. And I need to pick up a birthday present for one of the nurses. I meant to get it last weekend when I was at your place, but completely forgot."

"What's up there?"

"A gift certificate from Alexandria."

Always on duty, Frank keeps an eye on the street outside the window. She sips her coffee, asking, "What's that?"

"The bookstore? By Cham's?"

Frank knows the Korean restaurant but doesn't remember a bookstore nearby. "As long as you're in the neighborhood, why don't you spend the night?"

"On a Sunday?"

The waiter lays steaming plates in front of them. As he leaves, Frank says, "Finish what we started last night."

Forking a bite of omelet, Caroline teases, "I didn't think you were interested."

"A girl can change her mind, can't she?"

She winks at Caroline and tucks into her enchilada, admitting, "I didn't sleep so well. Sorry I was cranky this morning."

"Why didn't you sleep?"

Though open-minded and tolerant, Caroline is surprisingly orthodox regarding spiritual matters, and Frank is having enough trouble processing Marguerite's information without adding Caroline's skepticism. She withholds mentioning last night's dreams of wildfires and twilit mountains.

"I don't know. Just stuff. Work."

"Are you still thinking about turning your papers in?"

"Every day."

"Then why don't you just do it?"

Frank stretches a string of cheese from plate to fork. "It's not that easy."

"Well, if you're not happy . . ."

"It's not that I'm not happy. I'm not unhappy either. But it always comes back to what would I do if I wasn't working?"

"What do you want to do?"

"That's the thing." Frank picks up her mug and gazes out the window. "I don't know. I've never bothered to make life outside work."

Caroline dabs her mouth with a napkin. "Then wait until you do know."

"You sound like Mary."

"That's a compliment. Have you talked to her lately?"

Frank wonders if that's Caroline's backhanded way of asking if she's been working with her sponsor. "Yesterday."

"How is she?"

"Good. Feisty."

"Did you run any of this by her?"

Frank answers with a nod and gets Caroline talking about movies. Cleaning her plate with a tortilla, she pretends interest but is trying to figure what the hell is wrong with her; it's a fresh Sunday morning, she hasn't been called out yet, she has a full meal in her belly and a lovely woman in front of her, yet she feels like she's missing something, something important, and she has no clue what it might be.

After breakfast they stop at Caroline's to pack an overnight bag. Frank calls Lewis, finds out the coroner has the body, and that nothing else was found in the area.

"So, I reckon," Lewis tells her, "I'm stuck with a body colder 'an a crackhead's heart."

"Got an estimate how old?"

"Nah. Coroner say they might get to it by tomorrow. He figured at least twenty years, probably more."

"Alright. You get any sleep?"

"Some."

Frank nods, familiar with the feeling. "See you in the morning."

"Ten-four, LT."

Caroline smiles brightly. "Ready?"

Frank slides the phone into her pocket and cups Caroline's face. "You're beautiful, you know that?"

"Stop," Caroline says but accepts Frank's kiss.

"Come on." Frank tugs her toward the bedroom. "The present can wait."

"The present is all we have," Caroline quips. "And no, it cannot. With our luck, one of us will get called out."

She pulls Frank toward the door but Frank stands her ground. "All the more reason to seize the moment. *Carpe diem* and all that."

"All the more reason to get that present while we can. And if you'd taken me up on my offer this morning . . ."

Frank gathers Caroline close. "How about a recap of what I missed?"

"A recap?" Caroline murmurs against her lips. "Or a preview of coming attractions?"

"Oh, I like that better."

They neck until Caroline pushes away. "Come on, lover girl. Save some for later."

Frank grins and follows, but already her desire is slipping away.

Chapter 7

Caroline finds parking on Shopper's Lane and as they stroll down the sidewalk she swings Frank's hand. Frank smiles at her, appreciating that Caroline is very out. Caroline drops her hand to open the door into the bookstore. Prayer flags drape the entrance and inside they are assailed by tinkling spa music and the singular smell of mingled incenses.

"How come I've never seen this place before?"

Turning to answer, Caroline runs into a large, blowsy woman in scuffed cowboy boots and frayed bell-bottoms. "I'm so sorry."

The woman laughs. "No worries."

She is taller than Frank and wears a collection of scarves over a tie-dyed blouse. When she pushes sun-streaked hair from an unmade-up face, her arm rattles with silver bangles.

"We're offering free tarot readings today. Would you like one?"

Frank is about to speak when Caroline answers for them. "No, thanks."

"Some other time, then."

The woman starts to turn away, but Frank asks, "They're free?"

She looks back with a broad smile. "They are."

"I'd like one."

"Then follow me."

Frank starts toward her, but Caroline tugs her sleeve whispering, "I thought you hated this kind of stuff."

"I don't hate it. And it's free. Why not try it?"

Showing them into a small room off the main floor, the woman introduces herself, and asks if they'd like the reading "together or separate?"

Frank answers, "Together."

Caroline says, "Separate."

The woman chuckles. She motions Frank to a chair. "How about we start with you and go from there?"

Frank sits, with a grin for Caroline. Her lover frowns and gives a short shake of her head. The woman must see, because she leans toward Caroline and promises, "I won't bite." She gives Frank a worn tarot deck, instructing her to shuffle as long as she likes. The cards are bigger than gaming cards and Frank mixes them awkwardly, dropping a half dozen on the table.

"No worries," the woman says. "Just put them back in."

Frank does and after a few more shuffles lays the pack on the table. The woman nods. "Pick ten."

Frank picks up the deck and cuts it a couple times. She is surprised how drawn she is to certain cards and quickly stacks her choices into a pile. The woman takes the cards and flips them upright into a spread.

"That," she says, forefinger circling the first three cards, "is very interesting. You dropped these ones. It's not unusual for the right cards to jump out at you. This first one, the Elder of Fire, tells me you are intimate with death and its many faces. It feels like you work in a death-related field, that death has always been very clinical, very objective to you."

Frank thinks it's a lucky guess and wonders if she still smells from her last visit to the morgue.

"But that's passed. Now it seems like you're about to explore the transformational aspects of death, to work with it on a whole new level, a much deeper level, focusing on the spirit of death, maybe the idea of transformation from one form to another. Your background with the clinical aspect of death has created a solid platform for this new work. A launch pad for a much deeper, more intimate journey. You're well prepared for this journey even though it's new terrain for you."

The hairs lift on the back of Frank's neck as the woman moves on to the second card.

"The challenge will be in letting go of old notions and preconceived ideas, rules and regulations, tangible facts. Like I said, this is new

30

terrain for you, much of it unknown, and the more you cling to old ideas and habits, the harder the going will be. You have to put logical thinking aside and trust where the road leads. In trusting that you don't know, the way will become clear."

Caroline touches Frank's arm. "Are you alright?"

The fortune-teller looks up. "You're very pale. Should I stop?"

Frank shakes her head. "Go on."

"Alright. Number three is the Lovers." The fortune-teller frowns. "It's reversed, yet I'm picking up a lot of love around you. I think a pairing, like a conventional coupling, isn't for you right now. It will hinder the journey you're facing and hold you back. Again, it's not to say there isn't love in your life, there's a lot. I just don't see marriage or settling down with a permanent partner.

She taps the card. "The upcoming journey is the focus of your life, not romantic relationships."

Caroline smiles with an "oh well" shrug.

The woman smiles at her. "You two are close."

She states it as a fact and moves on to the next card.

"You've spent most of your life looking for approval in a very male-dominated field, but that's behind you now. You have learned a lot and succeeded, but it's time to move beyond traditional or conventionally accepted fields. You'll take what you've learned and incorporate it on a much deeper, more fluid level. A much more integrated level."

"Card number five is your immediate future. It's telling me you will have many guides on your journey. You will never be alone."

She smiles reassuringly. "You'll find help from the least likeliest places. Natural sources. Places in nature. Animals, even. Also, this would be a good time to accept gifts from strangers. Your guides are going to work often through them. You have a very powerful support system. In fact, you have many guides around you right now."

"Around me?" Frank can't help glancing about.

"Uh-huh," the woman murmurs, concentrating on The Emperor. "Don't forget your biggest hurdles will be reason and logic, trying to do things the old, established way. They were crucial for past successes, but now they're only going to slow you down and maybe even stall

31

you out. You have to abandon your head and learn to listen here." The woman touches her chest. "With your heart."

"Okay, that's enough." Frank stands so fast she knocks her chair over. Caroline and the woman are speechless.

"Sorry," Frank says righting her chair. "I'm done."

She stalks through the store. Caroline is fast behind her and when they are outside in the bright, clear light she asks, "What was that all about?"

Frank paces a tight circle. "Go get your present. I'll wait here."

"What happened?"

"Nothing. Go get your present."

"Are you sure?"

"Yeah. Go on."

"Okay. I'll be right back."

Frank wishes she had a cigarette, which she figures is better than wishing she had a drink. The door to the store opens and Frank looks up, hoping it's Caroline. But the tarot lady walks toward her.

"Are you okay?"

"I'm fine."

"Is there anything you'd like to talk about? I didn't mean to upset you."

"I know. It's just what you said is an awful lot like what somebody else told me. It's kind of disconcerting, hearing it back to back like that."

The woman smiles. "Well, then, it must be true. It was a very powerful spread, very optimistic, if that's what you were worried about." She holds out a paper bag. "I'd like you to have this. I wrote the spread down for you. You can look the cards up on your own, or if you want I'd be happy to go over them with you. My number's in there."

Frank peeks in the bag.

"It's a Rider-Waite deck. We were using the Gaia deck, but this is one of the easier decks to read."

"Thanks, I don't think so." Frank tries to return the gift, but the woman backs toward the store with her palms in front of her.

"Keep them. Throw them away. Do with them what you will."

Caroline comes through the door and holds it for her.

Frank catches the look between them. She lifts the bag. "Did you tell her to give me this?"

"Not at all. She asked if you had a deck and I told her I sincerely doubted it. She said your first one should be a gift. And didn't she just say this would be a good time to accept gifts from strangers?"

Frank sighs and turns to watch the cars snaking down the boulevard. She flinches when Caroline puts a hand on her arm.

"What got you so upset in there?"

"Want to split a shake?"

Caroline narrows her eyes. "Chocolate or strawberry?"

"Your call."

They get seated at Hamburger Hamlet and after ordering a milkshake—strawberry—Frank tells Caroline about her encounter with Marguerite. As she suspected, Caroline greets the account with cool skepticism.

"So you have these *talents*—" her voice italicizes the word "—but you don't have any idea what they are."

"Correct."

"And some new path, but you have no idea what that is either."

"Look. This is why I didn't tell you yesterday. It's hard enough for me to wrap my mind around this without the added layer of sarcasm."

"Sorry." Caroline giggles. "But you have to admit it sounds pretty far-fetched."

Frank lifts her hands. "I'll be the first to admit it."

Caroline sips at the shake and pushes it toward Frank. She shakes her head.

"Are you rattled by this?"

"Wouldn't you be?"

Caroline hefts a delicate shoulder. "You have to believe in it to be rattled. Do you?"

Frank traces her finger through the water that has dripped down the milkshake glass. "I don't know. I don't want to, but . . ."

Caroline covers her hand. "But what?"

"It's a lot of coincidences. And Marguerite, strange as she may be, she's never lied to me. I trust her even when I don't want to." She

33

squeezes Caroline's hand. "And you have to concede that tarot lady pegged me."

Caroline sits back with a laugh. "Did she ever! She might even make a believer out of me." She adds seriously, "Do you think she's right about us?"

Frank evades the question by asking Caroline what she thinks.

"Who knows? We have today. That's enough, isn't it?"

Caroline's casual response is a relief and Frank smiles. "Only if you pass that milkshake."

Chapter 8

Tatum yells, "Phone, Frank!"

It's Lewis. She is going to be late for the morning meeting. "That's the third time this week, Cheryl. What's up?"

There is silence on the line. Frank can't legally ask what she wants to.

"I'll be there soon's I can, LT. Sorry."

"A'ight."

Frank gathers the squad. Except for Lewis, all her cops are on time with fresh faces and not one hangover. A pang hits her for the old days; Jill's "on time" had been ten minutes late, Briggs would have been struggling not to barf up last night's booze, Bobby would have been haggard and sleepy from walking the twins around at two in the morning, and she'd have had to scold Darcy about trimming his mustache and his hair. She can't help but marvel how plain damn vanilla this new breed of detective is. Braxton updates his grocery store shooting and she stuffs a sigh; even their cases are dull.

Lewis barges in and pulls up a chair. Her hands shake when she opens her laptop and she is a god-awful shade of gray.

Tatum is talking about his latest domestic. The suspect is the father of the dead woman's two kids. He beat her to death with a remote control and when it broke he went low-tech with his belt. He fled, leaving the kids—nine months and two years—unattended. A neighbor finally called the police when she got tired of hearing the kids crying.

"He's in the wind. The girl's mother says he has family in Guatemala City, so I guess that's where he's at."

Frank nods; it's not uncommon for Latin suspects to skip across the border. They all wait politely for Lewis.

35

"Sorry to be late," she grumbles. "Got autopsy notes from that body over to Western."

Frank realizes things are so slow Lewis can say the body on Western and everyone knows what she is talking about, unlike the old days when they'd have had three or four open cases on Western. As it should be, Frank thinks, tuning back into her cop.

"Adult male," she reads. "White dude."

Frank asks, "How do they know that?"

Lewis grins and lifts a palm. "Hold on. Between thirty-five and forty-five, but a forensic anthropologist's gonna have to look at the bones to determine how long they been in the ground. ME says he thinks they're at least twenty, thirty but not more than fifty years old. Says he might have been a laborer, arm bones all rough where the muscles attach. Plus he had leather gloves on. Cause of death likely a skull fracture."

Lewis touches her right temple, demonstrating. "Just over his ear. One blow." She snaps her computer shut. "But the good news is he had on a wedding ring. Initials MD dash DS, and the date, 5/20/42." Brandishing a notebook, her color improving, she singsongs, "Detective Lewis done a little detecting through public records last night and come up with a Mary Dusi and Domenic Saladino, Caucasian, married in Soledad on May 20, 1942."

Appearing unimpressed, Frank says, "Tell me more about the skull wound."

Lewis slumps with a pout. "Look like he got hit with something blunt, but with an edge. Like maybe a two-by-four."

"What else you got from public records?"

"Like I up all night working?" she whines. "She-et."

Frank finally cracks a smile. "Alright. Good job."

Accompanied by predictable moans, she gives a rundown of the new overtime memo from upstairs and the request for sick leave donations for a uniform at Harbor with leukemia.

"Take home," Tatum bitches, "is we ain't gonna help you, but we expect you to take care of each other. Thanks, City Council."

Frank stands. "Lewis." She points to her office.

The big cop follows her in.

"Close the door."

Frank sits, motioning Lewis to do the same. "Something you need to tell me?"

Lewis makes a face, scratches the back of her neck.

"Figured you could do it, I could too," she says with half a smile. "I'm pregnant."

Instead of swearing, Frank offers congratulations.

"Yeah. I'm happy 'bout it. Be better if I wasn't so damn sick."

"It'll pass," Frank says. She'd been lucky with only the briefest morning sickness.

"Yeah. Anyways. I kinda wanna keep it on the down-low 'til I'm a little farther along."

"Understood. It stays here."

"'Preciate it. Sorry 'bout being late."

"Don't worry about it."

Frank tips her head toward the door and after Lewis carries her bulk from the room she blows out the curse she's been holding in. She rests her hand on the retirement forms. A phone rings in the squad room. A minute later, Braxton sticks his head in to say they have a potential witness in his shooting.

"Need help?"

"No, just wanted to let you know we're gonna roll."

She waves him out and glances at the clock. She considers rolling with Braxton, then decides that will be little more exciting than the 0800 conference. She wanders out to the squad room, idly pours a cup of coffee, and peers over Lewis' shoulder while she's tapping notes into her computer.

Lewis stops. "Aren't you supposed to be in a DART meeting?"

"Oh, sorry," Frank says. "I thought you were one of my cops. I didn't realize you were my personal secretary."

"Damn, LT. What side a bed you got off on?"

"How 'bout I work your case and you go to the meeting?"

"Hell, no," Lewis grins.

"You just wait," Frank grouses. "That'll be you sittin' in meetings someday, all day, while I'm retired in Maui sipping on Mai Tais."

"Thought you didn't drink no more."

"I might take it up as special retirement hobby."

"You goin' to that meetin' or you gonna stand here foolin' wit' me all day?"

"I'm going, I'm going." She slips into the conference room without much notice. Mourning that less crime on the streets means less chance to skip meetings, she suffers the rest of the day in a variety of windowless rooms discussing stats and action plans. In the last meeting of the day, she picks up her legal pad and pretends to take notes while sketching a cabin with mountains behind it. She's drawing a crescent moon when she feels the wind. It whips through the chaparral, shrieking and pounding through the pass. It sets upon her like an angry master on useless hounds and, like beaten curs, she and her horse cringe beneath the blows.

"Frank?"

"What?" She glances around the sterile room, the bland faces mildly expectant.

The DART chairman is staring impatiently. "Do you have any?"

"Uh, sorry. Any what?" She searches for even a draft but the air is motionless.

"Recommendations," he says, sounding each syllable.

Returned to the discussion, she redeems herself with a number of wild-ass ideas that no one else has thought of. After the meeting, Frank stays in the conference room. She unfolds her sketch of the mountain and waits to feel the wind again. But the air doesn't move. She balls up the sketch and tosses it in the trash.

More water, she rationalizes, but intuitively knows that water, less coffee, more food won't help, because these are visions. Her dubious talents are manifesting just as Marguerite predicted, and just as Marguerite said, there's a measure of ease in accepting the fact.

She taps her pen on the table, thinking it's like getting sober. It was terrifying to admit she was a drunk and even more terrifying to think of life without a bottle. But she took the first baby steps of the journey and along the way there were always people to help her, guides who knew the unfamiliar path she was on.

It's an idea Frank can work with and she goes upstairs. The homicide room is empty except for Lewis typing furiously. Frank looks at the clock. Only five-fifteen and the new breed has all left for gyms and family. "What are you still doing here?"

"Just trying to make up for the morning."

"Sister Shaft," Frank snorts. "You're the last person that needs to be making up time around here. That was good work last night."

Lewis grins. "Got more."

She hands Frank a couple of sheets from the printer. "Family's up to Soledad. Looks like he got at least one sister and a daughter still alive."

"Looks like we need to make a trip up-coast."

Her cop makes a face, and the color she has regained during the day fades.

"Relax. I got this one. Pintar's on call this weekend. I'll run up Friday, maybe spend the night, knock on some doors."

Visibly relieved but still game, Lewis, asks, "You sure you don't want me to go?"

Frank shakes her head, glancing over the printout.

Lewis is a supervising detective. Because she has the most seniority in the squad, the best developed street contacts, and the most organizational skills, Frank lets her work cases solo. She skips every other primary rotation and when she gets a case, she rolls with the partner of the primary next up on rotation. If the secondary can't roll, Frank will fill in. It's unorthodox, but Frank has good bones for her cops; she knows Lewis can handle the load and will ask for help if she needs it. Beside, Lewis is so demanding she prefers working alone, claiming she doesn't need any "raggedy-asses" slowing her down. Figuring Tatum is about as raggedy-ass as they come, and not trusting him to work alone, she tells Lewis, "I'm taking Tatum off this. I'mma partner you."

"For rilla?"

"For rilla, Killah."

They grin and bump knuckles.

"Man, I owe you. Thought a drivin' all that way right now like to kill me."

"I hear ya."

She pats Lewis' shoulder. "Go home. Get some rest. Those bones are older than you are. They ain't going nowhere."

"Yeah." Lewis reaches around for her jacket. "I think I'mma take you up on that."

Frank starts for her office, then stops.

"Oh, and Lewis?"

"Yeah?"

"No work tonight, you hear? That's an order."

The cop snaps out a sharp salute.

"Ten-four, Lieutenant."

Frank settles with her feet on the desk, glad to be alone. She reads through Lewis' notes, then types a couple of words into her computer. Peering at the monitor, she places a call.

"Soledad Police Department."

Frank asks to speak to a detective.

"I think Sergeant Gomez is still around. Hold on."

While she waits, Frank fiddles with her retirement forms.

"Gomez how can I help you?" a woman answers as if the sentence is all one word.

After a brief case explanation, Frank asks the sergeant, "Do you know a—" she searches for the daughter's name in Lewis' notes, "—Diana Saladino?"

"Diana Saladino," Gomez repeats slowly.

In the ensuing pause, Frank hears clicking.

"I know her. What do you want with her?"

"Just some questions. Routine follow-up."

The sergeant chuckles. "Well, good luck getting to her. She lives out on the Mazetti Ranch, up Wildcat Canyon. It's all dirt road to the main house, behind two locked gates. We had to go out there a couple years ago in the middle of a storm. Got stuck twice. Pain in the ass. Second time we got stuck, we ended up walking the rest of the way. I don't think Sal even lives at the main house. She's back in the hills somewhere."

"Sal?"

"Sorry. That's what everybody calls her. Didn't know who you were talking about for a sec when you said 'Diana.'"

"How can I get in touch with her?"

"Well, I'm pretty sure she's at Celadores—that's just west of

40

here—every Saturday, at the store. That's all there is in Celadores, the store."

"How will I recognize her?"

"Oh, that's easy enough."

She hears the clicking on the keyboard stop.

"But if you're coming up this weekend, I'll take you there myself. I haven't been out that way in a while. Be good to check it out."

"Sounds like a deal. Meet you at the station, what time?"

"Tell you what. Sal's got business 'til about noon or so. But if you meet me at the station at eleven, I'll buy you lunch."

"Let me buy and you're on."

"Sounds good. See you Saturday. Can't miss us. Get off on the frontage road, turn right on Main, and we're a block down on the corner."

Frank drops the phone into its dock and her feet go back onto the desk. She nods. It'll be good to get the hell out of Dodge.

Chapter 9

The week passes quietly. The squad doesn't close any cases, but neither does it get any new ones. Friday morning, before the sun is up, she heads north with a full tank of gas, a cup of coffee, and two jelly doughnuts on the passenger seat.

Not only is Pintar more competent than the last captain, she's more willing to take turns on-call, and Frank hits the freeway with unaccustomed abandon. She's pleased to have three days to go to bed early, get up late, and not be called out on a midnight shooting spree. Better yet, she thinks, sipping her coffee, is going someplace where no one knows her or expects anything of her. For at least forty-eight hours she is free to reinvent herself. The prospect is daunting as well as thrilling and while she's certain to be the same old Frank she always is, it's nice to have the option.

Traffic thins as she merges onto I-5, and she sets the cruise control to eighty. Frank eyes the second doughnut but decides to save it. East, over the desert, dawn oranges the sky. Cool ocean air riffs through the car as the LA jazz station fades. She turns the radio off, happy to have nothing in her head but wind and an endless horizon.

Most of the traffic she meets is southbound and Frank rolls into Soledad just shy of eleven. Gomez meets her in the police station lobby right on time. The cop is short and wide, more or less Frank's age, and takes her hand with the grip of an arm wrestler.

Checking a wince, Frank flips her ID open.

Gomez waives it. "I know who you are. I Googled you while we talked."

Frank offers her charming grin. "Could use you on my squad."

"Fat chance. Born and raised in the Salinas Valley and I already have my plot picked out at the Soledad Cemetery."

She walks Frank to an old Crown Vic that looks like it has been in service since the first time Jerry Brown was governor. She drives them to a gas station at the end of town which houses a Mexican restaurant, and a young man greets Gomez as they come in. Pouring water, he slides Frank a menu and asks Gomez if she'll have the usual. "Yep."

"What's the usual?"

"Huevos rancheros, over easy."

Frank flips her cup up for coffee and hands back the menu. "I'll have the same."

The boy nods, walking off as he shouts their order into the tiny kitchen. The women talk shop a bit, but when their food comes, Gomez says, "Tell me why you're interested in Sal."

"I think a body we've got might be her father. ID'd him off the date and initials on his wedding band, the rest from vital records."

"Shoot, how sweet is that? A case falling into your lap like that?"

"Good thing, too. The lead detective on it just told me she's pregnant. I'm gonna need all the help I can get."

"Yeah, I wondered what would make a Lieutenant come all the way up here."

Frank lifts a shoulder. "It's not a big deal. Thought I'd come up, check things out, maybe head home via Carmel, Big Sur. Act like a tourist."

"It's a pretty drive, if you like that kind of thing."

"You don't?"

Gomez thrusts her chin toward the window. Beyond it, on the other side of the highway, dark mountains tower over the flat, dusty valley. "Santa Lucias keep the ocean on that side, where it belongs. You can keep your fog and your coast."

Wiping her plate with a tortilla, Frank says, "Wanna tell me what you know about Diana Saladino?"

Pushing her clean plate away, Gomez cups her coffee and leans on her elbows. "She's a character. But you should talk to my boss. I think he went to school with Sal and her sister. They were twins. I'm not sure if he was in the same grade, but he'd know more about them than I do."

"Is he available?"

"On a weekend?" Gomez laughs. "Not unless you have a subpoena."

"She have kids?"

"That's who you should talk to. Mike Thompson. Sal's ex. I don't think they lasted more than a couple years, but they're still friends, far as I know. They have a daughter down in your neck of the woods. I forget her name."

"You said Sal's a character. How so?"

Gazing out the window, Gomez tilts her head to the mountains again. "Do you know your Steinbeck?"

"'Fraid I don't."

"Where are you from?"

"New York, originally."

"That explains it. You can't grow up in Cali without getting him crammed down your throat. I hated it when I was a kid, but I've come to appreciate him now that I'm older. And a little wiser," she adds with a crooked-tooth grin. "He wrote a lot of good history about the area. Not facts so much, but a feel for the place. Like those mountains." Gomez points out the window at the muscled range. "Steinbeck called them dark and unfriendly, and if you spend enough time here you begin to understand why."

Checking that she has Frank's attention, Gomez continues, "The Saladinos were old Monterey County. The grandparents were part of the Swiss–Italian wave that came to the states in the mid-1800s. I guess the economy was bad there, so when they heard about all the gold in California it was natural to leave. Not many of them made it in mining, so they turned to what they knew, which was dairy farming. Which was perfect for this area. They just picked up where they'd left off in Europe. Actually, did a whole lot better for themselves. Land was cheap and plentiful—if you can imagine that." The cop shakes her head. "They were hard workers, those Swiss, and used to tough conditions. Before you knew it, they'd built a huge dairy industry up and down the coast. A lot of the old names like Saladino are legacies

44

from those dynasties. I think the Saladinos were originally from Monterey or somewhere on the coast, and it was one of Sal's great-grandfathers that settled here. He started a ranch, and it was a big one, but when he died his oldest son sold it to pay off a gambling debt. Now it's the Mazettis'."

"So why's Sal still there?"

The waiter comes over holding the coffee pot like a question. Gomez checks her watch. "We better get going."

Frank lays money on the bill and they slide out of the booth. Gomez picks up a toothpick at the register, offers Frank one.

"No, thanks."

Cleaning her teeth, Gomez explains, "When they lost the ranch, one of the boys stayed on as foreman. I think there were three boys, and I think it was the youngest ended up killing the oldest. Shot him in the dirt, right in front of Pasquale's Bar. Beef about the ranch, I guess. Anyway, Sal's grandfather, Domenic's father, was the one that stayed on, so Domenic grew up out there. Married a local gal and raised the girls out on the ranch. I understand he was a terrible drunk and one day he just disappeared. Guess we know why, now, huh?"

Frank nods. "Hard to come back from the dead." A sudden frisson passes through Frank, and she wonders if it really is.

They drive down the highway and take the next exit, west, toward the mountains. Frank studies them through the windshield, surprised at their heavily forested flanks. "What kinda trees are those?"

Gomez flaps a hand. "Scrub oak. Blue oak. Live oak. Bunch of different pines. Then when you get into the canyons you get madrone and redwoods, Doug fir. There's things in there people probably don't even know are in there. Hell, Bigfoot's probably in there."

Hunching over the wheel, she adds, "They say the Santa Lucia range is one of the wildest places on earth, and I believe it. Those mountains are their own country. It's all cliff and gorge in there. And fire and fog and wind. The Santa Lucias aren't tamable. They're not meant for man."

Frank leans forward, as if to get closer to the mountains. Her eyes lift to the ridges nipping at the sky. "You still haven't told me why this Saladino's such a character."

The cop pulls the toothpick from her mouth. She flicks it out the window and rests her elbow on the sill. "It's just different here, that's all. There's a lot of history. A lot of old blood. And like I said, you should probably talk to Sal's ex. Or my boss. They know more about Sal than I do."

"You seem to know plenty."

"About the history." Gomez shrugs. "The other stuff . . ."

"What other stuff?"

"You'll see."

Gomez slows as they come into a curve in the county road. She tells Frank, "This is where Sal's sister flipped her truck back in the 60s, early 70s."

The curve rounds a soft hill. On the left it falls off into a broad arroyo. Gomez stops and points to a small wooden cross on the face of the hill. Frank squints. She makes out "CASS SALADINO" in clean, square letters. Red roses rise behind the cross.

As if reading her mind, Gomez says, "In winter there'll be a wreath on it and in spring iris and daffodils come up next to it."

"Who tends it?"

"That'd be Sal."

Gomez takes her foot off the brake.

"They were twins?"

"Um-huh."

"Must have been rough."

"I reckon."

"Any chance of getting the accident report?"

"Nope. This is CHP jurisdiction and they throw all their reports out after a couple years."

A truck speeds around the next corner, slowing when the driver sees the patrol car. Gomez lifts a finger off the wheel in a country wave.

"Asshole," she grumbles, as the truck passes.

"Who is it?"

"Pete Mazetti. He drives like his balls are on fire."

"Mazetti as in the Mazetti Ranch?"

"The one and only."

"He must know the road pretty well."

"He does, but folks driving through to Carmel don't. In summer this is Blood Alley."

"I'll stick to domestics and drive-bys."

Gomez agrees, "I'd pay to never see another head-on."

The talk turns back to work. Frank lets it, aware that Gomez has again evaded explanation of Saladino. She settles for finding out herself but hopes Saladino's eccentricities are limited to something as innocuous as a peg leg or bad case of Tourette's.

They twist along the two-lane, parallel to the mountains. Nodding toward the high ridge, Frank asks, "You ever been up there?"

Gomez looks where Frank does. She shakes her head. "I'm happy down here."

"You scared of 'em?" Frank teases.

Gomez scowls and crouches over the wheel. "You hear stories about them."

"What kind of stories?"

"Old-timers say there's spirits up there. That the mountains are alive. I believe it. I mean, just look at 'em."

Frank does. Despite the noonday sun, the vertical flanks of the mountain appear almost black, as if the trees have grabbed and gobbled the light. Suddenly Gomez takes a curve and they are pointed straight into the heart of the mountains. Frank cannot look away. The more she stares, the more she feels the mountains are staring back.

Chapter 10

Southwest of Salinas, in a canyon tucked beneath the watchful gaze of the Santa Lucia range, is the tiny town of Celadores. All that's left of the original stagecoach stop is a general store selling beer, tobacco, and sundry non-perishables. The town is rarely mentioned on maps. But for the few families remaining in the surrounding *ranchos*, Celadores is no longer a destination. Except on Saturday mornings. Then, in the slanting light from the friendly hills to the east, dusty cars and trucks drive up quietly to the silver-boarded store. The drivers park randomly on the side of the road or in the sprawling shadow of an oak old enough to have shaded the conquistadors. One by one, metal doors squeal open. Usually a woman gets out, an older woman, and usually she is a Mexican woman from one of the nearby farming towns. Sometimes they come from Salinas or as far south as King City, but more often than not the women are local. Sometimes their men drop them off and drive quickly away, other times they get out and stretch, resigned to waiting until the women have concluded their mysterious business.

On this Saturday it is late in the day and the light spills from the west. There is only one car left in front of the store, resting nose-in to the oak like a weary beast of burden. Slowly, so as not to raise dust, Gomez pulls the squad car off the road. She checks her watch and glances at the empty bench in front of the tilted store. "Looks like she's about done."

"She run the store?"

"No, Sal does her business in back."

"What kind of business?"

"Well—" Gomez drums her fingers on the side-view "—that's the interesting part."

It's taken the cop this long to come around to why Saladino's such a character, so Frank stays quiet. The sun warms her lap and bees feed in a patch of mustard near the car. A breeze wafts the smell of dried grass and hot dust through the windows. Frank watches it nuzzle the bowed oak leaves.

"What do you know about alternative medicine?"

"Not much. I know some of it works."

Gail had used acupuncture to help alleviate the pain of the cancer coursing through her body. Frank didn't know if the practice worked because of actual healing properties or because her lover's belief was enough to give it a placebo effect. In the end, Frank didn't care; it had eased Gail's pain and that was all that mattered.

"Have you ever had anyone—" Gomez makes quote marks in the air "—lay their hands on you?"

"Nope."

"Well, that's what Sal does. She's like a *curandera*." Gomez grins at her. "You know what that is, City Cop?"

"Hell, Country Cop, I work in South-Central. I probably know more *curanderas* than you have in your whole county. Have you ever used her?"

"No sir, not me, but a lot of people do. They swear by her."

Frank shrugs. "I've heard stranger things."

Gomez gives her a squinting look while a woman who looks like a raisin left in the field too long limps from the store. "Let's go." Gomez pushes her door, but Frank is suddenly reluctant to leave the patrol car. "That was probably her last customer," Gomez explains.

Frank gets out but stands next to the car. "You're not gonna lock up?"

The cop looks around. "What for? Come on." She hitches her gun belt, waiting for Frank to move.

"How do you know she's here?"

"It's Saturday. She's always here on Saturday."

"Where's her car?"

"Probably around back. What's with the Twenty Questions? You should be talking to her, not me. Let's go." She starts for the store but stops again when she sees Frank isn't following. "What the hell? Are we doing this or not?"

Frank glances at the store. The old boards shine whitely in the afternoon sun. She raises a hand to the glare, certain the store is a Rubicon and that if she crosses over she won't be able to step back.

Gomez glowers with hands on her ample hips. "Are you big city cops always this flaky?"

"Give me a sec."

"What's the matter?"

"Nothing."

"Jesus, Mary, and her husband Joe."

The car under the oak starts with a loud cough and Frank jumps. A young man slowly backs the old Buick from under the tree. Across the one-lane road a yellow field baseboards a dark wall of mountain. Frank's eyes are drawn to the crooked, black ridge. She knows there is a saddle up there, a notch in the mountain that affords a 180-degree view of the western slope of the Santa Lucias, a view that falls from the stunted, ever-thirsting chaparral at the top of the slope down to somber redwood canyons cut perpendicular to the purple sea.

"City, if you don't want to talk, I'm going home."

Gomez starts toward the car and Frank struggles to think clearly. From the sound of it, she can't just drive out to Saladino's place and knock on the door whenever she feels like it. If she's going to talk to Saladino, it's got to be now or never. "Alright," she says, with more determination than she feels.

Gomez wags her head but leads Frank up the sagging steps. The boards creak under their weight. A rusty screen door answers them. Gomez holds it open for Frank.

Only two western windows light the store. Frank pushes the Ray-Bans onto her head, temporarily blinded by the abrupt change from light to dark. On a wooden counter the length of the room, a fan stirs pungent ghosts of old beer and pickle barrels but does nothing to cool the air. Frank is careful not to touch the counter thick with decades, maybe even centuries, of human grime and grease.

Gomez nods at a pasty girl waiting on a woman who hovers in the gloom like an apparition. "Hey, Sal. How are ya?"

Frank steps around Gomez for a better look at the woman. Eyes

50

that seem to hold the entire summer sky stare back, appearing disembodied in a face as dusky as the light.

"I'm fine, Angie, thank you."

As Frank's vision adjusts, the rest of Diana Saladino becomes corporeal—the ethereal body only a man's bleached shirt worn over faded jeans; the halo around her skull just silver hair gathered loosely in a braid. The sky-blue gaze rivets Frank.

"This is Lieutenant Franco. LAPD."

Frank dips her head in a brief nod. "Miss Saladino."

Sal mirrors the gesture. No one speaks. Sal won't take her eyes off Frank, and Frank won't look away first.

"I need to ask you some questions. Could we go outside?"

"Questions about what?"

"It's stuffy in here," Gomez says. "Let's go out."

She herds the women to the door. Sal's boots echo off the dusty floor. She stops at the bottom of the stairs and squints into the sun. Frank lowers her sunglasses, pleased to have a slight advantage. But Sal turns and the mountains rise behind her like protective brothers. Frank makes the mistake of glancing at them.

A faint trail winds snakelike from the dusty foothills up through cool, dark canyons to a pass on the ridge, where wind fresh from the ocean sings in a stunted pine. Plank-winged birds soar beneath the bald ridge. A horse tied nearby jangles its bridle.

Gomez coughs. Frank blinks. Sal and the cop are staring at her. Frank darts a look over Sal's shoulder, not surprised that the trail is gone.

Gomez prods, "You said you had some questions for Sal?"

"Uh, yeah. Your father. Is he Domenic Saladino?"

Sal nods.

"When was the last time you saw him?"

"1968."

"And where was that?"

"At home."

"Which was where?"

She dips her head to the mountains. "Here. The ranch."

"And the circumstances?"

51

"Circumstances? It was our home. The normal circumstances."

"Morning, night, afternoon?"

Sal re-crosses her arms, shifts her weight.

"It was morning. At breakfast he said he was going down to LA, to work with his uncle. He went down there when things were slow."

"What kind of work?"

"Construction. The uncle owned his own business."

"What was the name of the business?"

"Saladino Construction."

"Do you remember the date he left?"

The woman thinks briefly. "December 16."

Frank thinks her answer's too quick. Innocent people questioned about dates or events rarely have accurate recall, but liars practice their stories over and over—usually with enough minutiae to hang themselves. "You're pretty sure about that."

"It's a hard date to forget. My mother died two days later."

Frank nods, remembering something like that from Lewis' notes. "Was she ill?"

"She had a stroke. A blood clot."

"And your father didn't come home after that?"

"No. Officer, what exactly is this about?"

Next of kin are unpredictable. It's good to get information from them before notification, but Frank feels she has gotten enough. For now. "It's 'Lieutenant.' We think we've found your father's remains. Positive ID is pending his dental records."

Saladino finally looks away. Frank wants to touch her, to see if the blue denim is solid or if her finger will pass right through it, if the brown skin is warm flesh or artfully crafted mud. Even in the white light, Saladino seems unreal, a golem crafted from bedrock and wind and silver-running streams.

"Where did you find him?"

"Near Culver City."

"Where in Culver City?"

"At a body shop on Western Avenue. They were doing some work and dug up what we believe are his remains."

"How do you know it's him?"

Frank notes that Sal seems more curious than upset. "Like I said, we can't be certain until we get the dental records from the VA, but he had some identification on him."

"What kind of identification?"

"I'd rather not say. Some details haven't been released yet."

"I see." She glances at the ground as if it offers encouragement, then back to Frank. "You said he was buried?"

"Yes."

"At a body shop." Arriving at the obvious conclusion, she states, "You're saying he was murdered."

"That's what it looks like."

"I see."

Frank wonders what she sees. After this much time it's understandable that Sal's not upset about her father's death, but it's odd she's not concerned he was murdered.

"Is that all? Can I go now?"

"Is that all? Your father was murdered, Miss Saladino."

"I understand that. But to me he's been dead a long time."

"Okay, but I still need to ask more questions."

"My dogs are penned. I don't like to keep them waiting."

"It won't take long. If I could—"

"Am I under arrest?"

"No."

"I'm going home. If you want me, that's where I'll be." Sal thuds up the steps into the store. The screen slams behind her.

Frank appeals to Gomez. "Well?"

"Well, Jesus, Mary, and her husband Jo. I was off at two, you know."

An engine growls and Sal drives from behind the store in a rusted pickup. Sun and dust have faded it the color of Sal's eyes, the same pale blue of the summer sky.

Waving the dust away, Gomez wags her head sorrowfully. "Come on, City. Let's go. May as well get this over with. You go up there on your own, you're liable to get lost and I'd have to go in and find you anyway."

Frank hesitates. "I don't want to put you out."

53

"If you dilly-dally another damn minute, I might change my mind. You coming or not?"

Frank listens to the fading pickup and wonders where it will lead. She nods at Gomez. "Let's go."

Chapter 11

A couple hundred yards from the store, the paved road ends behind a locked gate. Sal has left it open and Gomez drives through.

"Want to close it?" she asks Frank with more command than question.

Already Sal's dust is settling and her pickup is out of sight. Frank bolts the gate and before she can shut the squad car's door Gomez accelerates after the vanished pickup. Lifting a rooster tail of dust, she says, "Better roll your window up unless you still want to be eating this at dinnertime."

Frank does but already fine grit covers the dashboard. "How far do we have to go?"

Gomez laughs. "Sit back, City. We're just getting started."

The road climbs steadily between emerald fields of alfalfa and vineyard. The vines are broad and gnarled. Frank comments that they look old.

"They are. Aliottis planted them long before anyone had heard of California wine. They used to make some of the best in the county, but now they sell all their grapes to some winery down south. I forget which one. Going to do any wine tasting while you're here?"

"I don't think so."

"Well, you should. We've got some of the best wineries in the world."

The green crops give way to yellow grassland dotted with cattle and broad oaks. Stealthy gray fingers of chaparral reach down from the mountains. Gomez pauses at an unmarked crossroads.

"I thought you knew where you were going?"

"If you hadn't dragged your feet getting in the car, I wouldn't have lost her."

Frank points. "That's her dust up there."

Gomez turns left, taking a right at another junction, then left again.

"You're right, Country. I probably would have gotten lost."

Gomez grins.

"Hope you're charging for this."

"Are you kidding? I don't even get overtime on my regular shift."

She stops at a gate and Frank hops out. But for the rumble of the V-8 engine, the landscape is quiet. An open lock hangs through a hole in the latch. Frank removes it and slides the bolt back. The gate swings without a sound. Gomez drives through and Frank closes it. Getting back in she remarks, "It's spooky out here."

"How do you figure?"

"It's so quiet. Even the gate didn't make noise."

Rounding a bend with a huge oak on the shoulder, Frank is certain she's been here before, which is impossible, but the feeling persists. They pass the oak and Frank searches the mountain behind it. About a third of the way up a sheer granite cliff, she sees the oval shadow she expected. She sits back abruptly. "Are there a lot of caves around here?"

Gomez shrugs. "You'd have to ask Sal that."

"Does she live by a creek?"

"I don't know. I've only been to the main house. Why?"

Frank shakes her head. She would bet even money that Sal lives near a creek, a shaded creek where fish wait out the heat of the day in cool pools under gnarled tree roots. She shivers and rubs her arms. The visions seem more frequent here, but at least they're not as intimidating as the ones she had with Mother Love. If anything, they are almost peaceful.

Frank wants to ask how much longer, but as they top a hill Gomez says, "That's the main house."

Frank doesn't know much about architecture but the dormered house looks old—Victorian, she thinks. Orchards range to one side, on the other sprawl weathered outbuildings and a corral. The faded pickup is parked at the barn.

"We have to get out here and go the rest of the way on quad."

56

"Seriously?"

Gomez parks near the truck and points toward a far line of trees. "Yeah, I think she lives back there somewhere."

"And you're okay with that? Leaving your car?"

"Why not? I want to see where she lives."

Frank gets out. She searches warily for snakes as Sal drives up in a four-seater ATV. "Get in," she tells the cops.

Gomez takes the back while Frank lifts a brow at the ripped front bench and rusted metal frame. The women stare at her. Against her better judgment, Frank gingerly climbs on.

Nodding at the plastic bags beside Gomez, Sal asks, "Could you hold onto those?"

"Sure thing," Gomez answers, laying a plump arm over them.

Frank gropes for a seatbelt as the machine bucks and lurches. She gives up looking and holds tight to the frame. The quad crunches over late summer grass and Frank worries it will catch fire, then decides if Sal isn't concerned, she shouldn't be either.

They drive across a yellow valley guarded west and north by the broody Santa Lucias. Ahead of them a line of trees emerges from the toe of the mountains and meanders east. That will be the creek, Frank thinks, and the cabin is on the other side.

The quad hits a bump and they all lift from their seats. Frank clings to the frame, glancing at Sal driving like grim death. She thinks it was a bad decision to come out here, though she doubts Sal will try anything funny with two cops in tow. Besides, Gomez seems unconcerned. Plus she has to admit the whole place has her intrigued.

Yet as they approach the crooked line of trees, she feels the uneasiness she felt before entering the store. The quad grinds closer, and Frank is sure that the trees and the certain creek flowing beneath them delineate another point of no return. For a panicky second she thinks to tell Sal to turn around, to take her back to the main house and the comfort of the waiting squad car.

But the trees are upon them. The wide sunny fields bow to the sudden shade of conjoined oak and sycamore. The quad jerks to a stop. It wobbles as Sal and Gomez step from it. Frank is dimly aware of them gathering

57

the plastic bags. Gomez says something, but Frank stares straight ahead, at a bridge over a creek.

She watches Sal walk onto it, boots knocking the wood. The bridge is wide enough for the quad, maybe even a truck, and Frank wonders why Sal hasn't driven over. Dogs howl from behind the curtain of trees. A bird cries above Frank's head, a shivery call, like a loon's.

Gomez stops just before stepping onto the bridge. She looks back at Frank. "I'm about to put you on a leash and drag you after me. You coming or you gonna sit there all day?"

Frank is happy with the idea of spending the rest of the afternoon on the quad. Like the patrol car, its rubber and metal are all that stand between her and whatever lies on the other side of the bridge. She wants to go but doesn't. She tries to remember if Marguerite or the tarot lady had said anything about a ranch, but what she remembers most clearly is that logic and reason wouldn't help her where she was going.

"City! What the hell?"

Frank loosens her grip and steps off carefully, like the ground might open and suck her down. She starts toward the bridge. A carpet of leaves muffle her tread. All she hears is her heart pounding. And the gurgle of the creek. She shoves the glasses up and walks onto the bridge. Halfway across, she stops to look over the side.

The water flows clear and bubbly over mossy cobbles. The creek is not deep, only a foot or so, but sunless pools swirl along the bank under arched tree roots and she knows come evening that gold-flecked fish will rise from them to snatch at hatch flies too close to the water. Frank almost laughs. She was born and raised in New York, and her whole adult life has been spent in the tar and cinderblock heart of LA. What the hell can she possibly know about fish?

Gomez and Sal are across the bridge and out of sight. Frank is alone with the chortling water. Unable to tell if it laughs with her or at her, she hurries to catch up. Just as she is about to step off onto the other bank she stops, foot frozen in mid-stride. A dog blocks the path through the trees. It's not big as dogs go, but it's black and it's a dog. Frank instinctively covers the arm scarred by a pit bull during the Mother Love case. The beast lowers its head level with its shoulders. She remembers from somewhere that's what bulls do just before they charge.

Sal treads back down the path and stops. She takes in the standoff. "Bone," she calls, but the dog doesn't move. "Bone, come!"

Reluctantly the dog gives way and trots to Sal, but keeps looking over its shoulder. Frank lets out the breath she's been holding and follows from a reasonable distance. The trees open onto a sun-filled clearing. The pressure in Frank's chest eases and she takes a deep breath of sky and sun. Gomez stands in a dirt yard next to a cabin and pets a leaping golden retriever. To Frank's surprise, Sal is offering coffee.

"I'd love some," Gomez says. She looks from the retriever to Frank.

"Sure," Frank adds, her voice swallowed by hill and tree and sky.

Gomez settles at a stone fire pit, humoring the yellow dog. The black one, Bone, sits next to Gomez but stares at Frank like she's dinner. Frank stays where she is, taking in her surroundings.

The cabin looks like something a child would draw—peaked roof meeting a stone chimney bracketed by symmetrical windows. West of the cabin, an old barn sags inside a corral and yellow hills roll away to the foot of the mountains. The top of the dirt yard is delineated by a ragtag assortment of coops and sheds, and a cliff behind them pocked with boulders and tough scrub. The creek and its marching green phalanx curve up from behind Frank to encircle the yard in a motherly arm.

Sal comes from the cabin, carrying two mugs. She hands one to Gomez, then turns to Frank. Frank points at the black dog.

"He won't bother you," she says. Just the same, she calls him. Bone abandons his post to stand by her side. A little white mutt that has been sticking to Sal's heel like a piece of toilet paper jumps and licks at Bone's muzzle. "He's friendly," Sal assures. "Just not effusive like Cicero—" she nods at the golden "—or Kook, here."

The little dog wheels at his name, but Bone maintains his vigil. Frank approaches doubtfully, taking the mug Sal holds out.

"Sugar or cream?"

Both cops shake their heads.

There is only one chair, an old Adirondack worn smooth and gray. Frank perches on its edge. Sal returns to the cabin with the scrap of fur at her heels. Gomez stretches a hand to Bone. The dog licks her gently.

"You're good with them."

Gomez laughs. "Most times I like animals better than people. I've got three of my own. Little ones, though. You?"

"Nope."

"Old Sal, she's a regular Cesar Milan and horse-whisperer thrown into one. She does most of the vet work on the Mazetti stock."

"She's a vet?"

Reappearing with her own mug, Sal settles on the wide lip of the fire ring. The dogs settle with her, though Bone still keeps an amber eye on Frank.

"I told her you take care of the Mazetti animals."

Sal flips a hand. "Simple things that don't need a vet."

Frank puts down her coffee and takes a small pad from her pocket. "Can you tell me about the days leading up to your father's disappearance?"

"I'm afraid there's not much to tell."

Frank swallows a sigh, resigned now to teasing every little detail from Sal. "You said he did construction work in LA. What kind of work did he do here?"

"He was the ranch foreman."

"Did he leave on good terms?"

Sal nods.

"I understand he drank a bit."

"He did."

"How was he then?"

Sal sucks at her cup. "He could be mean."

"How so?" Frank coaxes.

"My father was sweet when he was sober. But when he drank, everything that bothered him came to the surface."

"What bothered him?"

Sal shrugs. "His chronic complaint, and my mother's too, was that by all rights the ranch was his, that Ben Mazetti stole it from his grandfather. That the Mazettis were all thieves. His standard rants."

"Is that it? Just the Mazettis that bothered him?"

"Mostly."

"How did the Mazettis react to that?"

60

"Ben was great. He put up with a lot from my father. It was harder for John, his son. But they put up with him. I think they felt sorry for us."

"Why?"

"I think they sympathized that we'd lost the ranch, especially Ben. He knew how much my father loved it here. And besides, he could practically run the ranch single-handed."

"Your father had siblings?"

"Three. My aunt Ellie's the only one still alive."

"Was your father the only one that stayed on?"

"Yes."

"What about the other siblings?"

"Ellie married and stayed in town. My uncle Donald was never interested in the ranch. He moved to San Francisco when he was young. Uncle Carl stayed on until my father married."

"Where'd he end up?'

"In town."

"Was it his idea to leave or your father's?"

"My father's."

"How'd Carl take that?"

Gazing toward the creek, Sal admits, "Not well. He got into insuring farm equipment and never came back. At least, not to the cabin."

"How'd he and your father get along after that?"

"They were civil."

"Did the Mazettis have any say in who lived here or who didn't?"

"Of course. It's their ranch."

"Did they back either brother?"

"I'm sure Carl was only here by Ben's grace. He loved this place, too, but he wasn't half the hand my father was."

"What about your grandfather, where was he during all this?"

"He'd bought a place in town after Ellie was born. It was too cramped here for everyone. So when the kids were younger, they all moved to town. He'd stay here during the week, but then later as he started turning more and more of the work over to my father, he stayed in town or down at the bunkhouse."

Frank shifts in the slatted chair and Bone lifts his head to her.

Keeping an eye on him, she asks, "How'd your mom feel about living out here?"

"She loved it. She was raised on a ranch, too. Not as big as this one. Every morning she'd leave crumbs at the base of that oak." She points to a sprawling tree behind Frank. "'For our hosts,' she'd say."

Gomez exclaims, "My grandmother does the same thing! She leaves little scraps of food out at night for the *duendes*, so they won't steal her children. When I asked her why she still does it even though her children are all grown, she said, '*Mijita*! Imagine what the *duendes* do after all these years if I *didn't*!'"

Sal smiles for the first time and Frank thinks that despite her mileage, Diana Saladino is still a good-looking gal. She looks down at her notes. "You said your mother died two days after your father left. What happened to her?"

"She had a stroke. An embolism."

"Pretty young, wasn't she?"

Checking the dregs of her cup, Sal agrees.

"And your father didn't come home for the funeral?"

"No. We couldn't find him. My sister and I drove down to LA to look for him. We went to his uncle's shop, and he said as far as he knew, my father was probably still at the job site. He gave us the address and we went there, but it was dark. Everybody had gone home."

"Where was the job site?"

"I don't remember. My sister was driving. We weren't familiar with the city."

"Was it north LA? South?"

"Honestly, I don't remember much, other than it was cloudy. I was afraid it was going to rain and our tires were bald. I remember fretting about that the whole trip."

"How long did you stay there?"

"We came home the next day. We didn't know where else to look."

"You didn't wait for him to come to work next morning?"

"We were exhausted and our mother still had to be buried. Uncle Lou knew what was going on. He'd tell him what had happened."

"Did the uncle ever see him again?"

"Not that I know of."

Gomez taps her watch. "I need to get going."

Sal stands and the dogs jump up. Cicero runs ahead to the bridge, but Bone and the little white thing follow Sal as if velcroed to her. Frank trails behind. Before going into the trees, she stops to look back.

The cabin's shadow lies long across the yard. Soon it will reach all the way across to the trees. Frank imagines the night, can see Sal in the lone chair, by an orange fire, the sky pierced with stars. There's the snap of burning wood, the canticle of stream and bough, and from a ridge high in the watchful mountains a coyote howls to an impassive moon, the night's prey cooling between its paws.

"Dammit, City."

Frank flinches. Gomez and the black dog wait, staring. The quad is idling. She steals a last glance at the cabin and jogs to the bridge.

Chapter 12

Frank pays for another night at the hotel in Soledad. In her room she calls a number Gomez has given her. Larry Siler, the Chief of Police, reluctantly agrees to meet her on Sunday. She is at his front door first thing in the morning. It isn't as pleasant as lunch with Gomez, but Siler at least offers coffee.

"If it's no trouble," she answers, taking a seat on his patio.

Siler clumps off, cowboy boots loud on the tile. Admiring the early sun on the Santa Lucias, she imagines Sal in her yard and how the morning light might look coming in behind the trees, dappling the yard.

"Here you go." Siler hands her a mug.

"Thanks for seeing me on your Sunday. I appreciate it."

Siler grunts. "So you found Old Man Saladino."

"Looks that way. We'll know more when we get the dental records. Did you know him?"

Appearing to relax into his chair, he explains, "Everyone knew Old Man Saladino. 'Course he wasn't that old. Younger than I am now," he says reflectively. "He was the town drunk. Nicest guy you'd ever hope to meet when he was sober, but drunk, he was a regular pain in the ass. Always running his mouth, bragging, picking fights. About once a month the cops would lock him up."

"You went to school with his girls?"

"Uh-huh." He picks his cup off the table and sips. "Cass and I were in the same grade. She was a wild one. Took after her old man. Always up for a party, ditching class, skinny-dipping if the river was high, hopping the train." He smiles as if watching a faraway pleasure.

"You go out with her?"

Siler wags his head. "Just once. Cass had her pick of us. I couldn't get near her."

"But you wanted to."

"Hell, yeah," he booms. "She was a looker. Smart. Funny. But just like her old man—a sweetheart when she wasn't drinking, but trouble when she was." He pinches his thumb and forefinger together. "She was always just a gnat's breath shy of getting into serious trouble. It wasn't any surprise when she ran off the road."

"Gomez showed me where it happened. Was she drunk?"

"Drunk, stoned, higher than a kite."

"That was how long after the dad disappeared?"

"I don't know. Couldn't have been too long. Maybe a year or so. She was just a kid. Not even twenty yet."

"Must've been tough on Sal. Losing her whole family like that in such a short time."

"You'd think so. You'd never know, though. She was always a strange one. Sober as a judge and as quiet as Cass was loud. She's got some steel, though, staying up there all these years."

"Wasn't she married?"

He flicks a hand. "That didn't last. She and Mike Thompson got hitched a little after Cass died. More a reaction to that, I suspect, than anything she felt for him. Poor bastard."

"Why?"

"He was crazy about Sal. They'd dated since junior high. Mike thought she was always gonna be the one for him."

"What do you know about her father disappearing?"

"Just that he took off and never came back."

"I hear she and Cass drove down to LA looking for him."

Siler agrees with a nod.

"What do you know about that?"

"Just that they didn't find him. As I recall, they weren't gone long."

"Why do you say they didn't find him?"

He frowns. "What are you saying?"

"I'm saying we don't know what happened down there, what the girls found or didn't."

"You think they had something to do with him disappearing?"

65

"I don't know. It's possible."

Siler snorts. "Anything's possible. But likely? I doubt it."

"It's an open investigation. I have to look at everyone."

"I understand, but I don't think that dog hunts."

"Maybe," she placates. "Just dotting my i's."

Siler spreads a broad hand on the tabletop. "Who else do you plan on talking to?"

"Who else do you think I should talk to?"

"Tell me who's on your list and we'll see who's missing."

Frank smiles, curious why the Chief is holding his cards so close. "Besides his daughter, what relatives does Saladino have left?"

Siler tugs on his multiple chins. "You'd have to check with Sal about that, but I know for sure his sister Ellen is still alive. He's got one brother long dead and another that left town when I was just a kid. That's about it as far as I know." The Chief chuckles. "You've sure got a cold one."

"Tell me about it. Did he have any buddies, any friends he was close to?"

"Let's see." His fingers return to the folds under his jaw. "George Perales used to bail him out most weekends. Sometimes John'd come into town if they needed him back at the ranch." Siler chuckles, "That is, if he wasn't in jail right next to him. He could cut it up just as good as Saladino. Many's the night they wound up in a cell together."

"What for?"

"Drunk in public, fighting. They loved a good brawl, those two."

"About what?"

"Hell, I don't know. Whatever it is drunks fight about."

Frank is busy writing. "And who's Perales?

"He was one of the Mazettis' hands. Good one, too, from what I heard. Used to fill in when Saladino wasn't there."

"Still alive?"

Siler rearranges his bulk to the other side of the chair. "I think so. Down in Greenfield. Living with one of his kids, I want to say."

"Anyone else?"

"I can't say as he had too many friends. Acquaintances, sure, probably knew everyone in town. But a man that drinks like he did doesn't keep friends."

"Did Cass ever get into any trouble? Anything more serious than hijinks?

"Nah. They were good girls. Cass was just a little wild, is all."

"I understand they were pretty gifted."

"You mean that woo-woo stuff?"

Frank nods. "What do you know about that?"

Siler laughs and his faraway look returns. "They had it alright. Cass could tell you things to make you blush. You didn't want to get on her bad side, that was for sure."

"Why not?"

"She could see things, hold your hand and tell you things you knew but sure didn't want anybody else to know."

"She do that to you?"

"No, but I saw her do it to plenty other kids."

"Was she mean about it?"

"What are you driving at? I already told you, you're barking up the wrong tree with those girls."

"You seem pretty sure about that."

Siler glares at her.

"Do you see Sal often?"

"Rarely."

"What do you know about the work Saladino did down in LA?"

"Nothing."

She's lost him, but his defense of the sisters is intriguing. Frank folds her notepad, makes a show of putting it in her pocket. She rises and reaches for Siler's hand. "I appreciate your time. You're right that I've got a cold one. Just beating the bushes as best I can."

He nods and gives her a shake, sees her to the door. Frank starts her car and gets the air conditioning going. She could track down Sal's ex, but the morning has faded and she still faces a long drive home. She starts to put the old Honda in drive, but the mountains grab her attention. Hot air from the valley shimmies before them, but the mountains remain cool and aloof, untouched by the concerns of men on the valley floor. The more Frank watches them, the more she feels they watch back. She hears clacking and reaches to turn her radio down. But the noise gets louder. Sweat stings her eyes and she is dancing with a crowd of women and girls, barefoot in a tamped dirt circle. They step and clap sticks together in perfect unison, moving and sounding as one great being.

She jumps when her cell phone rings. "Caroline," she breathes.

"Hi. How's it going?"

The spell broken, Frank starts the car and steers toward the highway, unsure if she's relieved or disappointed. "It's going. I'm heading home."

"Where are you?"

"Just leaving Soledad."

"Was it productive?"

Frank glances at the mountains. "It was interesting. But I'm not finished here." She cruises Main Street to the on-ramp, explaining, "I'll probably have to come back up next weekend." She feels curiously guilty telling Caroline this, like she's cheating on her.

"I thought this was Lewis' case?"

"It is, but turns out my Number One Lady Detective is pregnant."

"Hm. Does she need an obstetrician?"

Frank smiles. "I'll ask, tell her I know the best."

"Speaking of Number One Lady Detectives, when do I get to see you again? I miss you."

"How 'bout tomorrow? Dinner and a date?"

"Sounds like a deal. My place?"

"Yep. I missed you, too."

Frank knows her lover will like hearing that, and though it's not exactly true she finds herself looking forward to their date. But tonight she just wants to hit the six o'clock meeting in Pasadena and get a good night's sleep in her own bed.

It's a fine plan, and though Frank gets home in time for the meeting, she doesn't get the good sleep. Instead she tosses and turns, waking fitfully from dreams that hover at the edge of memory's reach. The alarm rings before dawn and she lies a moment grasping at dream threads, but all she can recall is a vague feeling of flying in darkness. By the time she rolls into the station, she has forgotten even that.

Chapter 13

"Whatcha got?" Lewis asks, rubbing her hands together.

"Interesting stuff."

Frank drags a chair over to her desk and straddles it. "Saladino's daughter was pretty cool when I told her. Didn't seem upset or surprised. Didn't ask much other than where we'd found him. Tried to brush me off. Had to follow her back to her place. Cabin in B. F. Egypt. Fortunately the cop with me, Gomez, was nice enough to take me. Probably never would have made it in my old chitty."

She flips open her notes.

"Evidently Saladino wasn't the most popular guy. Sounds like he was nice enough sober but a prick when he drank. Lot of people didn't like him. Lot of 'em with a fair reason to hurt him."

"To kill him?"

"Maybe. Who knows? We've seen people kill for less." She scrolls through her notes, filling Lewis in on Saladino's temper, his fists, Cass' wild side. "Back story's kinda interesting, too. Great-grandparents used to own the ranch. Saladino's grandfather lost it in a poker game and it became the Mazetti Ranch. Saladino's old man stayed on as a hand, became a foreman. Lived in the cabin. As he got older, Domenic and a brother took his place and the old man moved into town."

She deciphers her handwriting. "When Domenic got married, the brother that had been living with him at the cabin moved into town, got into insurance, and never went back to the ranch." Frank looks up. "Found out from Gomez that the brothers didn't speak unless Saladino was drunk, then he'd pound on his brother's door at two a.m. and stand there calling him names until the cops came. Seems he spent a lot of weekends in the local pokey. Which brings us back to the

Mazettis. They'd bail him out because they needed him back at the ranch, but it seems like there's been bad blood between the two families going way back."

"Then why'd they let the grandfather stay on?"

"I don't know. Gotta get to the bottom of that." She is already eager to go back, and the mountains rear tall and green-black in her mind. She thinks of the dusty valley towns and sees the Salinas River flowing brown and muddy past banks hand-plowed with sweet peas and celery. Boots echo on wood and a porch swing creaks. A hummingbird beats the air, holding its beak steady inside a trumpet flower. Cows graze belly deep in new grass and across the river the Gabilan Mountains shine greenly.

"What else you got?"

Frank swallows. She squints at the paper in her hand. "Uh, the Mazettis. John Mazetti. Quite a drinker. He and Saladino used to get into it."

"Where'd you find this all out?"

"Apparently most of it's local legend, but the Chief of Police verified it. He's a Soledad native, went to school with Saladino's girls. Was awfully protective of them. Kept insisting I was on the wrong track looking into them."

"Well," Lewis points out, "whoever killed Saladino whacked him hard enough to crack his skull. Takes a lotta energy, lotta adrenaline to kill someone like that. Not saying a female couldn't do it, but..." she spreads her hands wide. "ME couldn't see any defense wounds, no broken hand bones, arm bones. And ain't no other wounds, which makes me think he was taken by surprise. So probably not the girls, but maybe not a stranger either—if some Joe-blow come up an gonna jack you, he gonna point a gun at you or a knife, he gonna threaten you. You gonna be prepared to defend yourself. And some old Joe-blow decide he gonna rob a laborer, he ain't gonna hit him so hard as to kill him. He don't want to kill nobody, just want some money. Let's say he did kill Saladino by accident, he sure as hell ain't gonna stick around and bury him."

"And he was found under the framing, so whoever buried him must have known they were going to be pouring concrete sooner or later."

Lewis speculates, "A construction dude. Saladino's a dick. They get in a fight. Dude whomps him too hard. Oh shit. Looks around. Quick, bury him here."

Frank argues, "You just said no defensive wounds."

"They have words. Saladino thinks they're done arguing. Dude's still pissed. Picks up a two-by-four and whacks him."

"Hard enough to kill him?"

Lewis turns palms up in a supplicating gesture. "Hey, man, adrenaline's a funny thing. Ain't no telling what a man do when he all hopped up."

"What were they arguing over?"

"Who knows? Sound like it could be anything with Saladino, always runnin' his mouth. Money? Way the guy was workin'? A woman? Maybe Saladino stole the dude's boo."

"He sounds like an ass, but no one's accused him of philandering. Yet."

"Phi-*lan*-dering," Lewis repeats with a grin. "That's a good word. Maybe they just arguin' over how to do the job. It's late, right? End of the day? Dude been doin' it one way, then Saladino breeze into town and say now we doin' it this way. You know we seen people killed dead for lesser 'an that."

"Truth. And we're seeing a pattern with Saladino's drinking, his mouth. You keep working names. Try and find the uncle, his wife, any relatives. Maybe someone down here who worked with Saladino. I'll keep talking to the daughter, see if I can't shake something loose. Maybe go back up next weekend, see what her ex has to say. And Saladino's sister. If I can get Pintar to cover for me."

"I bet she'll cover. I think she misses being on the street. It's almost like she enjoys rolling on a scene in the middle of the night." Half-heartedly Lewis adds, "Sure you don't want me to go?"

"Naw, I got it." Frank knows that once or twice last weekend she'd have gladly traded places with Lewis, but now she can't remember why. "We got any kinda money trail? Any financial on this guy?"

"Nothin' to speak of. Why?"

"Come on, girl. The three motives for murder."

Lewis ticks off, "Money, pride, and pussy."

71

"That's about it." Frank stands and arches her back. "Sooner or later, what they all boil down to. Keep on it, sister. I'mma check on a couple names from up there, see where they go."

"A'ight, LT."

"Hey," Frank turns. "How ya feelin'?"

"I was on time this mornin', wasn't I?"

"You were. That's good. Hang in there."

"Like I got a choice?"

"There's always a choice, Lewis."

Before reviews and bureaucracy sideline Frank for the day, she makes a quick call to Gomez and asks which of Saladino's in-laws on his wife's side might still be alive.

"Hell's bells," the cop says. "Mary Dusi. Let me think on that. I know her sister died a couple years back. Off the top of my head, there's Carly Simonetti. She'd be Mary's niece. And Carly's brother Jeff, her nephew. He's still out to the Dusi place. They lease it for grapes. Their father was . . . oh, I can't think of his name, but he was one of Mary's brothers. I know she had a bunch of 'em, but I don't know what happened to 'em all. I'm sure the kids would know. Might want to start there."

"Good deal." Frank takes the names she's jotted down and gives Lewis the paper. "Check these out. Get me addresses and phone numbers."

Seeing Braxton sign out, she asks where he's going.

"Knock on some doors about my shooting."

Frank nods. It's been ages since she rode with him. And she really doesn't want to sit through back-to-back meetings. Copying his estimated return time next to her name, she tells Braxton she's going to roll with him.

He looks surprised but says, "That'd be great."

Trim and of average height, Braxton has such completely un-remarkable features that Frank's still not sure if she could pick him out of a lineup, but the kid's instincts are good and he's willing to learn. Until Figueroa, his career was behind a desk, but he has always wanted a detective shield and is eager to work the street, even if that street's in South Central.

They pass the corner on Slauson where a DL Blood was gunned down by a Raymond last week. Frank notes the shrine that has sprouted at the base of the building. "See that hood weed? Keep an eye on it. The DLs claim east of the 110, but it varies on the west. They beef hard with the Raymonds, so if that shrine starts getting bigger they might be escalating for payback."

Braxton nods.

She tells him, "Turn left."

He does but asks why.

"There's an old gal lives right . . . here. Pull over."

He slides against the curb next to a carefully manicured lawn. The houses on the block are small but lovingly tended.

"Years back, before the priest scandals came out, her daughter killed the bishop at the United Church of All in Jesus. Claimed he'd been molesting her since she was eight and she'd had enough. Beat him to death with a candlestick." Frank shakes her head. "It was a mess. She confessed right off, never denied it. Said she'd do it all over again. They sent her off to juvy, then she got life in Chowchilla."

They get out of the car. Frank stretches and Braxton asks, "Why are we here?"

"That bishop was one of my first cases. I'd heard things about him on the beat, rumors, that kind of thing. Never gave 'em much credence until I knocked on Betty Lacey's door," she nods at the house they're approaching, "and saw her daughter sitting on the couch, still covered in blood. 'I did it,' she says right off. 'I killed Bishop Patrick.' Her mama was heart-broke. Killed me to have to take her daughter in. I made it a point from then on to take care of Betty. Keep an eye on her, check in now and then, see how she's doing. And Betty, good God-fearing Christian that she still is, believes it's her duty to keep an eye on the 'hood."

A tiny, white-haired bird of a woman swings the door open before Frank can knock. "Officer Frank!"

"Miss Lacey."

The woman takes both Frank's hands and holds them warmly. "How *are* you?" she asks.

"I'm well. And you look fit as ever."

Miss Lacey lets go to clasp her hands in prayer. "Thanks to the Lord. Come inside, come inside."

She herds them into an immaculate living room sparingly decorated with paintings of Christ in his various adventures. Frank introduces Braxton, and after a bit of small talk gets to the point.

Miss Lacey has heard about the man killed at the Pik-Wik. She tells the cops all she knows about the shooting but contributes nothing new. Dismayed she can't be of more help, she promises to ask around. As a respected community volunteer and member of her congregation, Miss Lacey's reach is far and wide; Frank leaves empty-handed but well pleased that Miss Lacey is on the case.

"You watch," she tells Braxton as they walk to the car. "A week or ten days, we'll get a call. She'll have something."

Braxton's back on Slauson when Frank says, "Whoa. Hold up."

He steps on the brake and the driver behind them lays on his horn. Frank points to a used furniture store. Faded yellow paint peeks through in spots not covered with graffiti.

"Read that wall. What do you see?"

The car behind roars up alongside and the driver, a shaved Hispanic with a droopy mustache and tatted head, starts yelling obscenities.

"Seriously?" Braxton mutters. "He doesn't recognize an unmarked?"

Frank leans across Braxton, smiles brightly, and flashes her badge. "Is there a problem?"

The driver swears in Spanish and speeds away. Braxton bends over the wheel to study the graffiti. "Gosh, there's a lot."

Instead of asking if his last rotation was in Mayberry RFD, she punches his hazard lights. "Concentrate on what hasn't been crossed out, what's new."

"Let's see. Looks like 1 Bloods, Rollin' 30s." Muttering other clicks, he makes out a Florencia 13 tag.

"Okay. Stop. You got black gangs and a Latino gang that haven't been x'd out yet. Now look at what has."

Another driver honks and he says, "I should really park."

She points at an overlay of local 18th Street clicks, all crossed out with One Blood and F13 tags. "Look at the tagger on those."

"Hey, it's the same guy."

"Yeah. And see the two lines and three dots under his name? You know what that means?"

"Thirteen. Mexican Mafia."

"That's right. La eMe. Same guy's in both gangs. Could be an alliance. You don't get a lot of interracial mergers, and it wouldn't be a big deal if the Florence weren't so heavy into dealing for the eMe. See all those 59 HCGs tagged over with 1 Bloods? This is Hoover Criminal territory. We get 1 Blood in a beef with HCG, backed by F13 against 18th Street, and we're gonna be lookin' at enough overtime to retire early."

"Slick," he murmurs admiringly.

"Stick around long enough, it becomes easier than reading the back of a cereal box. Quit holdin' up traffic."

A block later they slide past a tag on the side of a house.

"What's that say?"

Braxton slows. "That's easy. East Side Eight Tray crossing out a Rollin 60s. The tagger's name is KrayZ."

"Who they feud with?'

"Who don't the 83rd feud with?"

"See?" Frank grins. "You're gettin' it."

Chapter 14

When they get back to the office, she sees Lewis has left early but there is a neatly typed list of contacts on Frank's chair. She picks up the paper and dials the number for Carly Simonetti. A machine answers. Frank doesn't leave a message. She dials the second number, then Googles North Salinas High Class 1968.

She strikes out on the phone call, but scores with her search. Dialing the given contact number, she wonders how she did her job before the Internet.

Nancy Snelling is the website author and one of those people who lives more happily in the past than the present. She is delighted to talk about the Saladino girls, verifying that Mike and Sal were an item throughout high school, and that Cass went steady with Pete Mazetti at least through their senior year.

"You're sure about that?"

"Of course. I heard Pete proposed before they were even out of school. He wanted to marry Cass before anyone else could steal her away. Those two. They were nuts for those girls. You should talk to them. They followed the girls down to Los Angeles the night their mother died."

"Pete and Mike did?"

"Oh, yes. They heard about Mrs. Saladino and went to the hospital to find the girls, but they'd taken off already. The boys went after them."

"And how do you know this?"

"Everybody knew. Pete took his father's truck and was grounded for a week. The whole school was buzzing about it. The girls didn't come back to school and the principal—that would have been Principal Clark back then—was thinking of suspending them. The only reason he didn't was because of the extenuating circumstances. That the girls' mother had died. They chalked it up to that and let them come back."

"When did Mike and Pete get back from LA?"

"Oh, right away. They only cut the one day, and Principal Clark let their parents deal with them."

"What did they say about their trip?"

"Nothing specific that I remember. As I recall, they were pretty hangdog about the whole thing."

"How so?"

"Well, the girls took it hard, being parent-less and all, and I think their beaux took it hard, too. Everyone was upset, not knowing what was going to happen to poor Sal and Cass."

"And what did happen?"

"Like I said, they were allowed to come back to school. They were both just a few months shy of eighteen. They'd have been legal adults before the paperwork could have gone through to make them wards of the state, so the Mazettis let them stay on at the ranch and they graduated with their class."

"Did you ever see the father around after he disappeared?"

"No, never. No one ever saw him again. Poor fellow. What a tragedy."

"It is." Frank plays to the woman's sentimentality. "The least I can do is try to figure out who murdered him."

"Oh, my. Oh dear. I had no idea. Whe—"

Frank preempts a spate of prurient questions. "I understand the girls had plenty of suitors, besides Mike and Pete."

"Oh, yes. They were quite the pair. Beautiful girls, both of them. Like peas in a pod on the outside, but inside they were night and day. Sal was always very quiet and thoughtful. Introspective, I guess you'd call it, but Cass—my Lord—she was a hell-raiser, if you'll forgive my saying so."

"What kind of hell? If you'll forgive my asking."

"Drinking, partying, carrying on with boys. Cass had any number dangling on a string at one time."

Frank asks for names and Snelling reels off a half-dozen. When she asks about Saladino's relatives and friends, Snelling confirms the contacts Gomez gave her and adds three more.

"How well do you remember Domenic Saladino?"

"Very well, unfortunately. I hate to speak ill of the dead, but Mr. Saladino was the town drunk, in jail more weekends than not."

"That must have been embarrassing for the girls."

"Oh, it must have been mortifying. I think Sal suffered for it, but you wouldn't know it by looking at Cass."

"What about girlfriends? Who'd Cass and Sal hang around with?"

"Cass didn't have many girlfriends. Girls that hog all the boys tend not to be too popular with other girls. Then there was poor Sal." Snelling's voice lowers. "She and Leslie Ferrer were best friends, inseparable, always huddled in a corner of the library, noses crammed in a book. The kids made fun of them, and called them names."

Frank has guessed but asks, "Like what?"

"Oh, you know how awful kids can be. Because they were together all the time, well, you know, there were rumors."

"That they were lesbians?"

"Well, yes."

Snelling sounds uncomfortable and Frank pushes: "Were they?"

"Oh, who knows? Probably not. Leslie went on to marry Mike Davies and Sal married Mike Thompson. Funny they both married Mikes."

"Does Sal ever come to reunions?"

"No. She explained to me once that high school wasn't the best time for her. I can understand that."

"Why's that?"

"Well, as if it wasn't bad enough that their father was the town drunk, both of the Saladino girls were a little, well, *odd*."

Frank has been wondering if Snelling would get around to that. "In what way?"

Snelling struggles to explain. "Now, don't think I'm crazy, because everybody knew this about the girls. They had what you might call a gift. Well, what some people would call a gift. Me, I'm not so sure. It was the funniest thing, but you could give the girls something, say a ring or a book, and they could tell you where it had been. Rattle off a whole history of the darned thing. It was uncanny, but frankly, I found it creepy. It smacked of bad religion."

Letting the comment pass, Frank asks about Sal's purported healing abilities.

"Oh, I know people swear by it, but if you ask me it's all quackery."

"But you said the girls could see things, that they had—"

Snelling cuts her short. "I really don't know anything about it. I never trucked with any of that."

Glancing at the wall clock, Frank disengages gracefully from the conversation and hangs up. She slings her suit jacket over her shoulder and palms the light switch. For a moment she stands in the dark. She thinks about Sal and what she might be doing, maybe standing in the yard with dogs all around and the shadow arm of the mountains curling around the cabin.

Then Frank is leaning against the wall. From high above, she circles over the darkening mountains and an ocean made red by the sinking sun. She swirls in a silence complete but for the wind. Below, coppery fires dot the dusky canyons.

Frank comes to against the wall. She leans against its unyielding solidity, trying to reason out the visions, but Marguerite and the fortune-teller both warned that reason and logic wouldn't be any help. She pulls her phone out and hits a speed dial.

From his breathless answer and the splashing in the background, she knows Darcy is giving Destiny her bath. "Bad time?"

"No, I'll put you on speaker. What's up?"

"Don't do that. Rather Dez not hear."

"Hear what?"

"I don't know, man. Just some funny shit going on." She tells him about Marguerite and the tarot lady, all the visions. When she stops talking, she hears the splashing has stopped. His end of the line is quiet. "You there?"

"Yeah, I'm here."

"What do you think?"

He takes a long time to answer. "What did Marguerite say about them?"

79

"I haven't told her yet. But she said that whatever was going on with me was gonna manifest soon, so I'm thinking this is part of it."

"Sure sounds like it could be."

"That's it? 'Sounds like it could be'?"

"What do you want from me?"

A deep breath produces the honest answer. "Look. You warned me about Mother Love and I laughed at you. I'm not laughing now. I just want to know what you think this is. And I'd really like for one of you psychic types to tell me that whatever it is, it isn't gonna be as bad as it was with Mother Love."

"I'm not picking up anything bad. I think I'd know if you were going through that again."

"Even from two thousand miles away?"

"Distance doesn't matter. You should read about entanglement theory."

"What the hell's that?"

"It's a quantum physics theory that one object can affect another despite a lack of proximity. Einstein called it 'spooky action at a distance.'"

"Is that what you're saying this is?"

"All I'm saying is, it doesn't matter how far away I am from you. If there was something bad going on, I'm pretty sure I'd feel it, like I did last time."

Frank shudders. The last time, she was strung up by her heels about to become a Mother Love sacrifice—and would have been if he hadn't responded to nagging visions of her dangling in The Mother's old abattoir.

"So do you feel *anything*?"

There's a long pause. Destiny babbles faintly. "I know you're stressing about this, but all I'm really picking up is a . . . a kind of quiet, a sense of peacefulness."

She confesses her boredom of late, admitting, "At least the visions are interesting."

Darcy chuckles. "Then don't worry about them."

"Easy for you to say. You been seeing shit since you were little. This is terra incognita for me."

"Weren't the Mother Love visions more about you than her?"

"Mostly, yeah."

"So maybe what you're seeing now is, too. If this is an ongoing thing with you, like Marguerite says, throughout lifetimes, then you will have been someone different in each lifetime. More than just the soldier you saw with Mother Love." He pauses. "You with me so far?"

"If I suspend a rational disbelief in reincarnation." She winces, remembering all the advice about thinking with her heart instead of her head. "Go on," she says reluctantly.

"I'm just saying don't be so goddamned judgmental. I don't know what these are and you don't either. Just let 'em be."

"Trust them?"

"Absolutely. They're there for a reason, Frank. Something's trying to get through your thick skull."

"No doubt one of my many guides."

"Maybe so. In which case you should be more grateful and less afraid."

"Do you know what a pain in the ass you are?"

"Yeah. That's why I can't ever get my women to stay."

"You said it, man. Look." Frank rubs at her brows. "Promise you'll let me know if . . . if you feel anything weird."

Dropping his voice, he tells her, "Even this far away, I promise I won't let anything bad happen to you."

It's an impossible covenant, but Frank is touched nonetheless.

"Thanks, man." She clears her throat. "Not letting your daughter drown, are ya?"

"Nah, she's playing with her Little Mermaid."

"She still wearing that bone necklace?"

"Not in the tub, but yeah. Speaking of which, any luck on that body you dug up?"

She tells him about her trip to Soledad and the branches on the Saladino case. She realizes Caroline's probably waiting for her but is reluctant to hang up. The splashing has resumed, and she can hear Destiny talking to Ariel. Frank smiles. Darcy is a good man, a good father, and she has never regretted bearing him their child. The hormones kicked in after Destiny was born and it was hard giving her daughter

81

up after the short maternity leave. She wonders momentarily if she made a mistake letting them go, but knows in her heart she was never meant to be a mother or a man's wife.

She asks questions until Darcy has to get Destiny ready for bed. She keeps the phone to her ear until she is told to please hang up and try again. She slips the cell in her pocket just as a text from Caroline comes in. *Running late should be there soon xxoo*

10-4, she writes back.

Darcy hasn't explained what's going on with her, but she is more relaxed as she drives to the condo. She picks dinner up at Trader Joe's and while waiting for Caroline she opens Google Earth on her desktop. She arrows west of Soledad, finds what she thinks is Wildcat Canyon Road, and follows it to the end. She squints at the highest resolution she can get, thinking the terrain looks like the canyon that ends at Celadores. A thin dirt road continues past the gray block that is probably the store, but she loses it in the maze of hills and canyons.

"Hi!"

Frank jerks the arrow up to the close button. The screen fades just as Caroline puts her arms around Frank's neck.

"What are you looking at?"

"Nothing." She swivels in Caroline's very expensive deck chair and kisses her. "Just fooling around."

Caroline straddles her lap. "It looked like a map. You going somewhere?"

"Nah, just trying to get the lay of the land in Soledad." Unwilling to share her dark mountains, Frank says, "Tell me about your day."

"It was okay. The usual." She nods at the monitor. "Do you have to go back up there?"

"Yeah, I'm not finished."

"I thought this was Lewis' case?"

"It's ours. I told you. I'm helping her."

"Right, but why are you the one that has to keep going up there?"

Frank hasn't a simple answer. She shrugs and wriggles out from under Caroline. "It's not a big deal. I don't mind."

Caroline doesn't answer but becomes appreciably cooler. Frank guides her to the kitchen. "Come on. I bought you a Chinese chicken salad." Spooning their dinner onto plates, she explains, "It's hard for Lewis right now. She's got almost a full caseload on top of her morning sickness. You know how it is. Besides, none of us can just run up there in the middle of the week, and I started the questioning, so I may as well see it through."

Caroline's unconvinced, but she asks, "Are you getting anywhere with it?"

"Little by little. At first it was just the two girls that followed their father to LA after the mother died. Now it turns out their boyfriends went looking for them. Seems they were worried about them, but you don't randomly try to find someone that's two hours ahead of you in a city the size of LA. They had to have known where the girls were going, but the daughter claims she didn't know where her father might be until she got down there."

"Maybe they called the boys and told them where they were going."

"Impossible. The boys were already on the road—no cell phones back then."

"Oh, yeah."

Now that Caroline has thawed a little, Frank can't help tease, "And now I'm really curious to go back because a woman the daughter went to school with intimated that the daughter was a lesbian."

Caroline frowns. "How's that relevant?"

"It's not at all." Frank grins. "I'm just trying to make you jealous."

"How old is this woman?"

"Early sixties. Not bad lookin' if you like a weathered, lived-in kinda look."

Caroline spears a snow pea. "Knock yourself out."

"That's it? 'Knock yourself out'?"

"That's it."

"Aw, come on. Not gonna put up a fight for me?"

"Nope."

"Damn." Frank wraps her fork full of noodles. "That's cold."

"No, it's not. I can guarantee she's got nothing on me."

"Oh, yeah?" Frank laughs and leans across the table to kiss her. "Prove it."

"Here? At the dinner table?"

Such a Caroline response, Frank thinks. She goads her, patting the table. "Right here. Right now."

To Frank's surprise, Caroline drops her fork and does exactly that.

Chapter 15

The squad catches a hit-and-run on a twelve-year-old girl. The driver turns out to be an octogenarian they find quivering in his daughter's house. The next day officers get a call about a suspicious smell and find a Hispanic male dead in his apartment. He was apparently despondent that his wife left him and took their infant son. They'll know more pending the coroner's report, but even without a note, it appears to be a slam-dunk suicide.

Later in the week there's a holdup at the Silver Dollar on Manchester. The clerk in the liquor store is braver than smart and decides to fight back. Her valor earns her a quiet ride in the back of an ambulance. Braxton and Lewis have a lead that the shooter is one of two wannabe bangers trying to make their bones and be noticed. The clerk had a three-year-old son and was pregnant. It won't be long before the shooters are ratted out.

Thursday afternoon, Frank is in her captain's office explaining that the rash of homicides is likely an anomaly. Pintar is going to cover for her again this weekend, and Frank reassures her there is nothing to worry about. Pintar is smart, pretty, and ambitious. Because she could easily have a crush on her young boss, Frank keeps their relationship as professional as possible.

"How soon can you wrap these trips up?"

It's the kind of dumb question her old captain would have asked, and Frank gives Pintar a pained face.

"Come on, you know I can't answer that. Every time I talk to someone, I get a new lead. I don't have anything hard yet, but I'm getting a lot of interesting stories. Some corroborate, some don't. Just gotta keep knocking."

Pintar's head bobs. Frank watches the auburn curls dance over a pair of enticing collarbones. She considers how it might be if she were twenty years younger. And Pintar wasn't her boss. And not straight. And—

Pintar waves a timesheet. "I see you didn't charge time for the weekend. I appreciate the time you're putting into this."

"It's not a big deal." Frank stands. "I'm just glad I can leave the squad in good hands when I go. You don't know what a relief that is."

The captain grins, acknowledging what an ass her predecessor was.

"I can't handle a case as well as you do, but I like to think I'm a step up from Foubarelle."

"A step?" Frank says at the door. "How about a couple flights?"

She tells the squad Lewis is in charge and to call if they need anything, then takes the stairs two at a time down to the parking lot. The 1-10 is right next to the station and she sees the north-bound lane is stalled. Listening to traffic reports, she finagles side streets to the 1-70, where traffic is heavy but at least moving.

In the old days she'd have a cold one between her legs and the rest of the six-pack close at hand on the passenger seat. Now she settles in behind a sedan and pulls a binder onto her lap. She steers with her knee, one eye on the road, the other devoted to the murder book Lewis has copied for her. She tries to concentrate on names, dates, and relations, but her focus keeps wandering north. She is booked into the motel in Soledad so she can get an early start in the morning. If all goes well, she will talk to Sal's ex, the aunt on her father's side, and Mary Saladino's niece and nephew. The evening is open and she has Saturday morning for additional knock-and-talks, but what Frank is really looking forward to is dropping in on Sal at the store.

Still steering with her knee, Frank veers and honks as a truck cuts into her lane. An inch before creaming her, the driver corrects. Deciding there will be no surprise visits if she can't get to Celadores alive, Frank closes the binder and returns a hand to the wheel. Traffic lightens as the evening wears on. Once she clears Santa Barbara, Frank pushes the accelerator to eighty, eighty-five. She speeds not for the pleasure of it but from an indefinable urgency.

It is dark when she drives through San Luis Obispo. North of the sleepy coastal city, tall hills blot the stars. Climbing a pass north of town her heart beats faster. She is at the tail end of the Santa Lucia Range. She has never read this in a book or seen it on a map, yet like a beast homing to its den Frank knows exactly where she is. The familiarity thrills even as it unnerves. Racing blind, with only stars and mountains for company, she thinks how excited she is to be heading home.

Frank wonders what kind of Freudian slip it is to call the mountains home, but presses harder on the gas. By the time she speeds through King City, she is almost giddy. She tries to convince herself it's just the excitement of leaving LA and working a case that's not a routine banger or drug-related homicide. The lie doesn't work.

When she reaches the motel, Frank pulls into a parking spot facing west. She cuts the engine and hugs the steering wheel. Out past the highway, beyond flatlands tamed, drawn, and quartered, rise the mountains, dense and lightless, their bulk so black as to render the night pale. There is no moon. Only stars hang over the mountains. She listens to a cricket sing its summer song. Blocks away, a dog barks and there is the constant, lonesome rush of the highway. A wordless song lifts in Frank's throat. She swallows it and rests her head on the wheel. When she looks up, the stars have shifted.

A polite young man checks her in at the motel. Frank strips and falls into bed, but she is not tired. She lies with her hands under her head, reading the ceiling by the light leaking in at the curtains. Throwing the covers off, she opens the window and stands naked in the tender air, holding a palm to the mountains. The dark mass is inscrutable. She lowers her hand and returns to bed. The breeze brings the mountains to her and she sleeps.

When the alarm goes off, Frank is surprised she slept through the night, hard sleep being a rarity in the comfort of her own bed, let alone this strange one. Over eggs and bacon next door, she prioritizes her to-do list. Sal's aunt will be her first visit.

The address takes her to a neat, comfortable home on the east side of town. A frail, blue-haired woman eventually answers the doorbell. She invites Frank in, explaining as they settle amid immaculate furnishings that Sal has told her about the investigation. Frank answers

87

a few of the aunt's questions, then asks what she knows about her brother's disappearance. After the same story everyone else has given her, Frank moves on to the day Mary Saladino died.

The woman shakes her perfectly coiffed head, saying, "That was a terrible day. Just terrible. Of course, everyone said it was an accident. Mary herself said she'd fallen, but I knew. I just knew."

The old woman is still shaking her head and Frank asks, "What did you know?"

"Lieutenant, I loved my brother, but it was no secret that Dom had a horrible temper when he drank and it wasn't uncommon for him to take it out on poor Mary."

"How would he do that?"

"Why, with his fists, of course. About every six weeks or so, fairly regularly, the poor dear would appear in town with a fresh bump or bruise. Of course, she always laughed it off, saying how clumsy she was and that she'd fallen. For a while we believed her. Mary liked a bit of a nip herself, but then the bruises became regular, and of course the girls talked."

"What did they say?"

"Nothing direct, but it was intimated. I don't think either one of them ever wanted to go against their parents. But I know it frightened them."

"How do you know that?"

"Lisette—my daughter—she told me once that the girls hid in the barn whenever they fought. I was horrified and made a point to talk to Dom about it. He was upset, very contrite. He never meant to get angry. It just happened. And in all fairness, when Mary was in her cups she had a tendency to egg him on."

"About?"

"Oh, Mary came from money, the Dusi Ranch. She wasn't spoiled exactly, she'd work as hard as any hand, but I think she expected more from life. Dom always had it in his head that someday he'd get our land back, and while Mary didn't put the thought there she certainly encouraged it." She makes a helpless gesture with her hands. "But the years went by and Dom was never more than the Mazettis' foreman. He wasn't any closer to owning the ranch than he'd ever been. It was an unrealistic goal, of course, but still it was a bitter pill for them to swallow."

"So which Mazetti was running the ranch when your brother worked it?"

She thinks back. "Ben ran it when we lived there, but he took a bad spill some years after the war. That was when John took over most of the fieldwork. I know Ben still took care of the business side of things for many years."

"So your brother probably interacted most with John?"

"Yes, that's right."

"How was their relationship?"

"I suppose *strained* would be the best way to describe it."

"And the cause of the strain?"

"Mostly Dom wanting the ranch back and having his own ideas about what should be done on it."

"Mostly?"

The aunt drops her gaze and rubs at a gnarled knuckle as if she can make it round and young again.

"What else caused the strain?"

Clasping her hands, the old lady meets Frank's gaze. "Just that."

Frank nods, willing to let what is unspoken remain so. For now.

There is more confirmation of dates and times, after which Frank thanks the woman and heads north. The highway cuts through agricultural towns bordered by square fields of broccoli and cauliflower. Over it all, the mountains stand watch. Frank purposely ignores them. She finds the pallet plant right next to the highway and asks for Mike Thompson. The front office pages him and a tall man with a fringe of sandy hair enters expectantly. Frank flashes her ID.

"Lieutenant Franco, LAPD. I'd like to talk to you about Domenic Saladino."

"Oh, yeah. I'd heard you were asking about him. We can talk in my office."

Following him, she asks, "How'd you hear that?"

"My wife told me. Here, let me grab a chair." He lifts a molded plastic one from the reception area and closes his door. Motioning Frank to take it, he rolls his own from behind the desk and sits next to her.

89

"Where'd she hear it from?

"Oh, shoot." He frowns and runs a hand over his bald spot. "I don't remember. It's a small town, could have been anybody."

Not wanting him on the defensive, she nods with a smile. "Guess I'm just used to being in LA, where nobody knows anyone. Can't get used to how friendly everyone is here."

"We try," he says with a smile. "How can I help?"

"I know you're busy and I don't want to take too much of your time, but you can start by telling me how you heard that Mary Saladino died."

"That was a long time ago."

He has been leaning forward eagerly, but now Thompson sits straight and buffs his head again. He is fairly trim, but his All-American good looks have crumpled, as they tend to do in men past a certain point, and he is stranded, looking his age.

"I remember I was in school, on the way to class. Pete—Pete Mazetti—grabbed me in the hall and told me she was dead and that the girls were driving to LA to look for their dad. And that Cass was drunk. I was scared—we were both scared—that she was gonna get in an accident. Cass was a daredevil, and the more she drank, the crazier she got. Pete had his old man's truck, so we took out after them. We didn't have any idea where we were going, but we knew they had to be on the 101 somewhere. We were going to try to catch up to them." He shakes his head. "It was just dumb luck we didn't kill ourselves."

"Did you catch up to them?"

"Nah, we never did. We got into the city and drove around. Pete remembered that Mr. Saladino worked in Culver City somewhere, for his uncle, so we looked him up in the phone book. Found a Saladino Construction and called, but there was no answer."

"What time was that?"

"Shoot, I don't know. It was dark. Maybe six, seven? We drove around a couple hours looking, then figured we'd better go home. We looked for the truck on the way back—hoping we wouldn't see it smashed on the side of the road—and we didn't. That was a relief. But we still had to face our parents." Thompson flashes a grin and she sees

90

the handsome boy he once was. "We just lit out, didn't tell anyone where we were going."

"When did you see the girls next?"

"Uh, let's see, that'd have to be either the next day, or the day after. Pete told me they were home and I went up to the cabin after school."

"Were you and Sal dating?"

"Yeah, we were going steady."

"You must have known her pretty well."

He agrees.

"What did she tell you about the trip?"

"Not much. That they drove around looking, like we did."

"Did she say where they looked?"

"I think they were around Culver City, like we were. Surprised we didn't run into each other. I think they went out to a job site he'd been working on, but he was gone."

"Did you know where he stayed when he was down there?"

"Pete knew he bunked with his family. We got a bunch of dimes from a 7-11 and called every Saladino in the phone book. Half the people didn't know him and the rest, no one had seen him."

"What time did you get home?"

"Shoot. I don't remember. It was late, I know that. I only got a couple hours sleep, then my mother made me go to school."

Frank smiles. "Could have been worse, huh? What happened to Pete?"

"Oh, he was lucky. His mom just yelled at him and said it was a good thing his father wasn't home."

"That'd be John Mazetti?"

"That's right."

"Do you remember where he was?"

"I think in Stockton, or someplace. I think he was at a cattle auction. He went a couple times a year. That's why we got away with taking the ranch truck. His old man wouldn't have let him if he'd been home."

"So John Mazetti was out of town the same time Domenic Saladino was out of town?"

"Yeah, that's right."

She asks him about Dom beating his wife, and Thompson reluctantly confirms what the aunt said. Following the aunt's thread, she asks how Saladino got along with John Mazetti.

Like the aunt, Thompson turns vague. "Okay, I guess."

"I heard there was a little tension between them? Any idea what that might have been about?"

"Hey, you know, that's a question best saved for Sal. I—I really couldn't speak to how they got along."

You could, Frank is thinking, *but you won't.*

She asks about Sal's friends, and Thompson tells her, "You know, Sal's fifth-generation Soledad. I'd say most of the town is acquainted with her in passing, and through rumor, but I couldn't really say she has any friends."

"Why is that?"

He shrugs without rancor. "That's Sal. She's married to the mountains. They're all she's ever needed."

It's an odd summation, but Frank thinks she understands it. After wrapping it up with Thompson, she calls Carly Simonetti from the parking lot. There's no answer. Considering what to do next, she leans against the car and basks in the golden light. From the slant and color of the sun, she realizes that summer has passed into autumn without her knowing. She finds herself staring at the mountains. They are stark and motionless, yet very much alive. Under their coat of furze and evergreen, the mountains keep the secrets of owl and mouse and deer, of striking snake and pouncing fox. There is a trail there she knows. It climbs from the yellow foothills to a notch in the ridge, where a breeze fresh from the ocean stirs the needles of a single, struggling pine. Below the ridge, dark-winged birds ride the air.

A truck applies its air brakes. The hiss makes her jump. She glances around and ducks into her car unnoticed. She squeezes her forehead as if to press in Darcy's notion that the visions might be helpful. She drives back to Soledad, not sure what to do when she gets there. It's lunchtime, but she's not particularly hungry. She puts Simonetti's address into her GPS. It leads to a ranchette north of town. A pack of unseen dogs bark as she pulls up. She debates getting out and finally does. No one answers her knock except the dogs.

Back in the car, she writes notes. That Saladino beat his wife opens a whole new area of motive, and she starts a list of potential suspects. Sal's name heads the column. It's also noteworthy that both Thompson and the aunt shied from describing Saladino's relationship with John Mazetti. It's even more interesting that he was out of town when Saladino died. Or, at least, was buried. They can't prove when he died, but it's reasonable to work with the assumption that if Saladino didn't show up for work the next day, he died sometime the night before.

The dogs are still barking maniacally. She recalls Bone's steady gaze and wonders what Sal does when she's not in Celadores. Frank starts to look toward the mountains, then catches herself. Thinking maybe if she keeps busy enough the visions won't come, she decides to drop by the police station.

Gomez is chatting with another cop and breaks off to greet, "Hey, City! You're back."

"Can't stay away."

"What's up? And no, I can't run you up to Sal's this weekend."

Frank grins. "Wouldn't ask you to. You've already gone above and beyond the call of duty."

"Are you here for follow-up?"

"Yep."

"Any luck?"

"Some. How come you didn't tell me Domenic Saladino beat his wife?"

Gomez lifts a shoulder. "Don't know that I knew that. Besides, domestics aren't exactly uncommon around here."

"Not uncommon anywhere," Frank agrees.

"Any luck with the niece?"

"Not yet."

When Frank adds she will try Simonetti again after dinner, Gomez invites her to come home and eat with her family.

"No, thanks. Appreciate it, though."

"Aw, come on. You don't want to eat out. I think my husband's making spaghetti for dinner. It's nothing fancy, but it's good, and there's plenty extra."

Fibbing that she has more doors to knock on, Frank wiggles out of the offer. She likes Gomez, but Frank's social skills are rough at best. Being a regular member of Alcoholics Anonymous has rounded some of their sharper edges, but she's a habitual loner and her favorite company is her own. She grabs a Big Mac and waits at the ranchette for Simonetti's return.

Frank is lucky; she catches Carly Simonetti coming home to feed her dogs before heading to the rodeo. Simonetti reluctantly agrees to give her a few minutes, standing in the driveway. Frank starts with what the niece remembers about Mary's death.

"I was pretty young, but I remember my grandmother coming home from the hospital. She was pretty shook up. And then on top of that my cousin Cass went ballistic and accused Dom of killing Mary and then took off for LA to find him. And all my uncles were furious, saying they were going to kill him. It was a real mess, I remember that."

"Your uncles said they were going to kill Dom Saladino?"

Simonetti rolls her eyes. "They didn't do a damn thing. It was all just liquor talk."

"Did any of them go down to LA?"

"I don't know. I don't think so."

"And Cass accused her father of killing her mother?"

"Yes. Everyone knew he hit Mary. She told the doctors she fell on the edge of the table, but it was obvious he'd gone to town on her."

"What exactly did Cass say when she accused him?"

"I don't know, I wasn't there. But I remember my grandmother saying that Cass kept screaming, 'He killed her!', and then she ran out to look for him. That's really all I remember."

Simonetti glances pointedly at her watch, but Frank is writing furiously.

"Did you ever see Saladino again?"

"Nope."

"Did either of your cousins ever say what happened when they went down to LA?"

"No, they didn't find him. The whole trip was a waste of time."

"Did anyone else go looking for him?"

"Not that I know of. Oh wait. Mike—Sal's ex-husband—he followed them down there. He and Pete Mazetti. I think he was Aunt Cass's boyfriend then."

"Then? He didn't stay her boyfriend?"

Simonetti laughs. "Heavens no. She'd show up for birthdays and dinners with a new man on her arm every time. My aunt was quite the playgirl."

"So I've heard."

"Look, I've really got to get going. My daughter's showing her pigs. Can we finish this later?"

Frank thanks her and lets her go. She takes back roads to the hotel, enjoying the cooling air. Glancing at the mountains hoarding dusk, she wags a finger in what she surmises is the direction of Sal's cabin.

"Lucy," she says with a Latin accent, "You got some 'splainin' to do."

Chapter 16

Five women sit clustered on a bench in front of the store. Only one appears under the age of fifty. Each clutches a plastic bag in her lap. Empty-handed, Frank takes a seat at the end of the bench. Other than a brief nod, none of the women acknowledge her. Each sits silently in her thoughts.

Frank hears footsteps inside the store. Seconds later a woman pushes through the screen door. As she does, the woman at the opposite end of the bench rises and walks around behind the store. The remaining women scoot as one to fill her space. When Frank doesn't move, an old gal with a face like a walnut pats the space between them, motioning her to slide over. It's silly, but Frank complies. After shifting along the worn plank a few times, she begins to understand the gravitas of the ritual.

Sun beats upon the bench, yet the women sit as uncomplaining as mules. When a woman walks out of the store, the red-shawled woman at the head of the bench stands. She crosses herself and walks behind the store. Only one other has come after Frank. There is plenty of space on the bench, yet the old gal with the walnut face slides to the end. Frank moves too, and the woman beside her. The three of them watch a pickup lug itself up the road. The truck stops in front of the store; its engine ticks in the summer silence. A Latino male in boots and a cowboy hat gets out from behind the wheel. Three kids tumble after him. A woman lowers herself from the passenger side. The children trail the man up the wide wooden steps into the store. They glance shyly as they pass. The woman works her way to the bench with an awkward limp. Frank recognizes her from her first visit. She bobs her head at the women next to Frank. Each responds with a muted

"Buenos dias." The woman sits heavily. Right next to the woman beside Frank. The kids run out of the store, but quietly. Each holds a popsicle. They lick them reverently in the shade of the oak and stare at the women.

All heads turn as the red-shawled woman exits the store. The old gal on Frank's left stands. Saining her breast, she trudges a worn path to the back of the store. Frank takes her place at the head of the bench, the woman next to her pulled along as if by an invisible cord.

A bead of sweat starts from under Frank's hair. It rolls to her temple, gathers speed, and falls from her jaw. A lazy breeze cools the wake on Frank's cheek. She closes her eyes to the golden sun. A fly hovers at her ear. She waves it off, wondering idly why she has chosen to wait rather than badging her way back to Sal. The men talk quietly in the shade. Her ear catches the word "lluvia," then, "Claro . . . esta noche."

She cracks an eye open. The sky is blue but hazy. Her lid falls like a window shade. Maybe the men are right; maybe it will rain. Time oozes by. Frank may have dozed, she isn't sure, but the clumping of the walnut-faced woman on the steps signals it is her turn. The woman is empty-handed and Frank realizes they have each carried their bags round back but left the store without them. She rises reluctantly. She won't cross herself and brings no offering. Frank almost sheepishly turns for the car. Then chides herself; she's investigating a murder for Christ's sake, not dabbling in superstitions or trying to buy Diana Saladino's goodwill.

She follows the path around the fence into a grove of pepper trees. The fence is made of silvered six-foot planks she can't see over or between. She walks slowly in the sweet shade, pausing at a latched gate. There she is struck again by an impulse to cross her chest or bend a knee. The breeze has picked up. Chimes sigh behind the gate. The fence wavers and she presses her head into the soft grain. She waits for a vision, but there is only the wind, passing through her as if she is hollow. Frank pushes the gate.

The courtyard is hard dirt, swept clean but for a few skittering leaves. A mossy fountain circled by rusty chairs burbles in the center. Thick-trunked roses cover the fence with vivid red and yellow blooms.

A shed cowled in grapevines leans drunkenly against the back of the store. Frank walks toward it. Her mouth has gone dry and her heart beats much faster than it should. Her hand wants to rise to her breast, but she keeps it firmly in her pocket. A beaded curtain with a faded image of Our Lady of Guadalupe dangles in front of the shed. Sucking in a breath, Frank gathers it aside.

"Hi there."

Without waiting for an invitation, she drops into a metal chair. It rocks crookedly and she squares it with a grin while Sal recovers.

"I'm working, Lieutenant."

"I know. I'm here for a reading. Or whatever it is you do."

Sal sits up, momentarily straightening a chronic slump. "What's bothering you?"

"You're the one with the magic hands. Why don't you tell me?"

Sal sighs. "Is there really something you'd like help with or are you just testing me?"

"A little of both."

Their wills arm-wrestle over the table. Sal's bends first. She closes her eyes and shifts in a chair as rickety as Frank's. The cloth-covered table between them is an old door laid on stacked cinder blocks. Tin retablos and burning candles flank a Lady of Guadalupe on an altar behind Sal. Another cloth hides the shelves beneath, where the bags from the ladies peep out. Bare party lights circle the corrugated plastic ceiling, its opacity long dulled by weather and persistent leaves. The air is dense with candle wax and the spices from the women's offerings.

But suddenly the room disappears and she crouches by a fire in a dim, smoky space. Rain beats on thatch. Drops get through and splat on the ground, but she is warm and dry. Her stomach growls. A woman speaks from the shadows and hands her a leathered strip. She chews on the fishy meat, counting the different colors in the fire.

"May I?"

Frank looks down. Sal's hand hovers over her scarred arm and she instinctively jerks it to her lap.

"Do you want to tell me what happened there or am I supposed to guess?"

Frank takes a deep breath. She puts her arm back on the table. "Guess."

For a moment Sal looks as if she'll refuse, but with a small shake of her head she repositions her palm above the scars. Her eyes close. Frank feels pressure from her hand, even though it's held a good seven, eight inches above her arm. She's tempted to pull it back again and fights the urge to squirm. Sal's eyes pop open, such a startling blue, and for an instant Frank is the one taken by surprise.

"Physically this has healed very well, but there's still a great deal of unresolved energy here." The sky-colored eyes lift to Frank's. "Do you know what a *susto* is?"

"A scare, a fright."

Sal nods. "That's the literal translation. In healing it means a trauma. Say a woman is raped. The flesh will mend, her tears and bruises will heal, but she'll retain the trauma of the attack. She has a psychic and physical memory of the assault. That's a *susto*, and it has to be healed if the woman is ever to be well again. You have a great *susto* here."

She lowers her hand, and again Frank hides her arm in her lap.

"It looks like bite wounds, yes?"

"Yeah."

Sal nods. "I get the image of a reddish dog, chunky like a pit bull, on a chain. And lots of blood."

Frank unconsciously cradles the arm mauled by a roan pit bull. The dog had crawled through a gap in a chain-link fence and though tied to a tree had enough slack to lunge for Frank's arm. It hadn't let go until her cops beat it off with a two-by-four. She doesn't know if it's the vivid memory or Sal's accuracy that makes her queasy. She grasps at the rationalization that Sal knows pit bulls are common in ghettos, and with so many scars of course she was traumatized. That the dog was red is just a lucky guess. "Enough about my arm. How's the rest of me?"

Sal stands and tells Frank to. She cups a hand in front of Frank's torso. "There's a lot of heat here. Around your liver. Do you have hepatitis?"

"Nope."

99

Sal lowers her hand a couple of inches. Frank feels its heat through her clothes. "Do you drink?"

"Everyone drinks."

"Alcohol," Sal says patiently. "Do you drink a lot of alcohol?"

Frank stares into the brilliant eyes. "Used to."

Sal nods. "It feels like you did a lot of damage to your liver, but that it's healing. Drink water, lots of clean water, probably for the rest of your life. And if you're serious about taking care of yourself instead of just playing with me, I can give you some dandelion to help." She continues her scan, explaining, "This is a very physical energy."

"As opposed to?"

"As opposed to a spiritual wound, like your arm. Those send out the most energy. I could feel your arm across the table. Physical wounds send out the least. I don't usually feel them until I'm about this close." She repositions her hand about a foot from Frank's waist. "Emotional wounds—" she raises her hand to Frank's chest and steps back "—are about this close. Do you have a cold, or bronchitis?"

"No."

"Have you ever had pneumonia?"

"No."

"It feels like there's liquid here."

Her hand is a good two feet away, yet crazily, Frank still feels it. Sal frowns. "Your lungs are congested."

"I'm fine," Frank assures. "Just passed my annual physical with flying colors."

Sal shakes her head. "This is an emotional wound. Not something a physician would pick up. It feels like blood here."

Frank flashes on her first lover. Maggie took a shotgun blast to the chest during a liquor store robbery and bled to death on a pile of candy bars. Frank grips the back of the chair.

"I need to talk to you about your father."

"It's been a long morning. My dogs are penned. You know where I'll be."

Frank is about to argue. She could threaten Sal with hampering an investigation, obstruction of justice, any of half a dozen charges, yet hears herself say, "I'll wait. What do I owe you?"

100

Sal shrugs. "I don't have a set fee. My patients pay however they can."

Frank drops two twenties on the table.

Tucking the bills into her jeans, Sal asks, "Did any of what I said make sense?"

Again their wills lock, but this time Frank caves. She nods. "I'll be in my car."

She steps through the swinging curtain into the normalcy of sun and sky and blood-red roses. The fountain gurgles. A jay swoops to it from a pepper tree and hops along the rim, a cool eye cocked to Frank. Overhead, in the brilliant blue, a vulture circles. Frank stalks through the dimly lit store, signaling to the last woman on the bench that she is through.

Chapter 17

The bench is in shade and all the women gone by the time Sal's pickup rumbles from behind the store. Frank rights her seatback and follows. The Honda drops onto the bumpy dirt road, and Frank wonders if her old car will make it all the way.

When Sal stops to open the first gate, she saunters back to Frank. She says, "You're never going to make it in that."

"Can I hitch a ride?"

Sal studies Frank blankly. "Park over there."

She points to a turnout on the side of the road. Frank locks up, hoping the car won't be vandalized by the time she gets back. She hops in, automatically reaching for the seat belt.

"They're busted," Sal says, shifting into second. Frank sees she doesn't wear one, either.

"I'm a cop. I could arrest you for that," she jokes.

Sal ignores her.

Frank cranks the window down and sticks her elbow out into the rising dust, happy to be on the move. She tries to concentrate on the cattle that graze the stubbled range and ruminate in clumps under the oaks, but inevitably her gaze is drawn to the mountains. She sees the trail again, the dusty brush on either side. There is silence but for the steady fall of hooves and monotonous drone of a fly. She rocks to a horse's drowsy rhythm.

Frank is thrown against the dashboard. Sal leans across her, pointing out the window. "Bears."

Frank sees a shambling hump on the far side of the fields, followed by two smaller humps. The women crane their necks to watch the animals lope across the meadow.

"Do you see a lot of them?"

"Not often. Plenty of signs, though. They prefer the high country, but it's not unusual for them to come down this time of year."

"What do they eat?" Frank asks nervously.

"Anything they can. Berries, insects, leaves. Sometimes they'll kill a calf or older cow."

"People?"

This elicits the first smile Frank has seen on Sal. "Only if you piss them off." The cubs dip out of sight and she puts the truck in drive.

Frank grins. "That was great. I've never seen a bear."

"Not even in captivity?"

Frank thinks back to an outing at the Bronx Zoo. There's a picture in her head of her father holding her hand and her mother sitting on a bench. He is pointing to a giraffe munching leaves. She feels like he is trying to get her to feed the giraffe and she wants no part of it. "Nope. I don't think so."

Silence settles in the truck like the dust. They come to the next gate, and Sal explains that the first gate is kept locked to keep people out. The rest are for cattle and unlocked, so when she stops Frank hops out to open and close them. Each time she is struck by the immensity of the silence.

As they near the ranch, the mountains rise taller. Pointing at a toothy ridge, Frank asks, "You ever been up there?"

Sal glances where Frank points. "Sure."

"What's it like?"

The ranch materializes over the top of the hill. Sal drives to the corral and parks. "Come on." She jumps out. "I'll show you."

Frank has opened her door, but when she sees two horses watching from the corral, she says, "Oh, no."

Sal disappears into the black hole of the barn and Frank wonders at her inordinate involvement with women fond of horses; Gail had adored the beasts, and here she is, interviewing a woman who lives on a working cattle ranch. She shakes her head as Sal emerges from the barn with two halters.

"I don't do horses."

"You do if you want to talk to me."

103

Frank checks a curse. It's one thing talking to Sal on her own turf, quite another doing it from the back of a half-ton quadruped. She thinks again about pulling rank, yet eases from the cab and slips into the corral. The horses turn and stare as one.

"I don't know how to ride," she says, hating the whine in her voice.

"Don't worry. Anyone can ride Buttons."

Sal holds out a halter. Frank starts as if she's been offered a rattlesnake. Sal shakes it. The trail rides at Griffith's Park, purely at Gail's insistence, are a fond memory compared to what Frank is afraid Sal has in mind.

"Shit."

Frank grabs the halter. The horses prick their ears and study Sal's approach.

"Come here, Dune," she says sweetly.

"Doom?"

"Dune," Sal corrects. "That's a good boy."

The horse nickers as she drapes a rope around its neck, slides the halter on, and buckles it in one smooth motion. Then she turns to Buttons and puts a rope around the mare's neck.

"Your turn."

"Uh-uh." Frank tries to give the halter back, but Sal refuses it.

"Come on. I'll help you." Scratching under Buttons' mane, Sal patiently, insistently coaches Frank through the task of grooming and saddling her ride.

"The bridles are tricky," Sal says. "I'll do them, but watch."

Sweating, trembling a little, Frank is relieved to step away from the horses. But the relief is short-lived. Sal deftly slips the bit into Buttons' mouth and hands Frank the reins.

"Up you go."

"When do I get to ask some questions?"

"As soon as you get on."

Frank watches the mare bob her head. "Why's she doing that?"

"She's just adjusting herself to the reins. Don't worry. Just trust her."

Frank scowls. She's been hearing that a lot lately.

"Do you need help?"

"No," Frank snaps.

Inserting a sneakered foot into the stirrup, she drags herself up into the saddle. It's an ugly mount, but she's on. Then Sal lights onto Dune as effortlessly as a butterfly onto a flower. She wheels the horse around and bends to the gate, riding it open. Buttons follows without prompting and Sal orders, "Make her stop."

Frank pulls the reins. Buttons takes a step or two forward, but Frank pulls again. The horse stops. She whinnies for Dune and he answers. Frank eases her grip, expecting Buttons to follow sedately, but the old horse takes off at a trot. Frank has to grab the pommel to keep from falling. She remembers Gail telling her to stand in the stirrups to get her balance. Just as she does, Buttons catches up to Dune. The horse jerks to a stop and Frank almost flies over her head.

Sal graciously allows, "She's not the smoothest ride."

"She just tried to throw me."

"Buttons hasn't thrown anyone in twenty years. Probably couldn't even if she wanted to. If it's any comfort, all my grandchildren learned to ride on Buttons."

"How many do you have?"

"Three."

Frank repeats what Gomez told her, that Sal had a daughter down south.

"That's right. Cassie's in LA."

"You named her after your sister?"

Sal nods.

Frank adjusts to Buttons' wide-bodied stride. The rhythm is awkward but not uncomfortable. "Where are we going?"

"Just to the cabin."

"Why didn't we take the quad?"

"Pete's got it."

A cool wind brushes past and Frank glances at the sky. "Jesus. Where'd that come from?" She's been so busy staying in the saddle she hadn't noticed the clouds surging from the north.

"It's early for rain, but I saw a couple tarantulas last week."

"Tarantulas?" Frank involuntarily scans the ground. "What have they got to do with rain?"

"It usually rains a couple weeks after you see the first tarantulas of the year."

"Great."

Frank looks up from the trail long enough to admire Sal's loose-boned fit in the saddle, and when Buttons snorts and bobs her head, Sal leans easily to tug at her forelock, teasing, "Old barn-sour girl."

Buttons gives a louder snort and Dune answers. The horses quicken their pace toward the line of trees guarding the creek. Buttons starts to trot, but Frank reins her to a walk, more leery of the trees than getting thrown. The scabrous sycamores bend and sway, dancing to the most ancient of songs. The wind, the clouds and trees, the grasses bowing at the storm's approach, all seem uncannily alive, and Frank's breath halts between wonder and fear.

Buttons whinnies, tamps a hoof and pulls against her rein. Frank finds Sal twisted in the saddle, watching her. For a second, she is unsure who is interviewing whom. She loosens her grip on the reins and squeezes Buttons with her knees. The mare trots to catch up, slowing only after her nose is in Dune's tail. The horses cross single file over the dark-running creek, hoof steps muted under the keening wind. Frank follows Sal into the corral, where she slides gracefully to the ground, but Frank stays mounted.

"You can get off now."

"I know." Frank holds out the reins. "Can you hold her?"

Sal takes the offered straps, but still Frank sits. She doesn't trust her legs to hold her once she falls. A cold drop of rain anoints her face, then another. She pulls her feet from the stirrups and swings a leg over Buttons' rump. The saddle grabs her shirt on the way down and she lands as awkwardly as she feared she would. She steadies herself against the horse, grateful for Buttons' unflinching patience. Rain splats her arms and hair, the exposed skin where her shirt rode up.

She tugs her shirt down, takes back the reins, and copying Sal, pulls the saddle off. But she doesn't grab the pad beneath and it falls at Buttons' feet. The mare jumps and Frank does too. Heart racing, she grabs the pad as the rain begins in earnest. The horses move willingly into the barn, where Sal hands her a curry comb. Water pours from the roof. It splats loudly on the ground as if shocked it's become mud. The wind shrieks at cracks in the barn. Speech is impossible without shouting, so the women work quietly. When the horses gleam, Sal climbs to the loft and throws down flakes of hay. Frank looks around, making note of a shotgun hanging in a case by the door.

"Well?" Sal shouts, eyeing the watery curtain. "Ready?"

Clutching her plastic bags, Sal dashes from the barn with Frank only a step behind. They sprint to the cabin and Sal throws the door open. "I'll be right back," she says, dropping the bags.

Frank watches her run to a pen and free the dogs. They race to the cabin with much jumping, barking and tail wagging. Sal bursts in and the dogs shake water everywhere. Without a trace of self-consciousness, Sal peels off her shirt and tosses it in the sink. Disappearing through the only other door in the room, she calls, "I'll get you some clothes."

Frank starts to protest but sees she is dripping all over the floor. Bone wags his stump and gives her hand a lick. She wipes the kiss off on her leg but cautiously pats his head.

"Good boy. You wouldn't bite old Frank, would you?"

The stump wiggles in reply. Cicero noses between them, begging his share of attention. Frank scratches his flank like Gomez did. That appeases him and she looks around. The cabin is primitive, comprised of a rough kitchen along one wall and a massive stone hearth catty-corner. Where there aren't windows, the walls with the doors are crammed floor to ceiling with books.

Sal comes through the inner door in dry jeans and a sweater. She hands Frank a mismatched sweat suit. "You're a little bigger than I am, but they should fit."

"Do you have a bathroom?"

"Through the door, to the right."

Frank steps over a tall threshold into a skinny hall facing two doors. One is open, supplying a feeble gray light to the hall. She steps into the bathroom, feeling for a switch. Her head grazes a chain. She yanks and a bulb comes on. The bathroom is rough, clearly added after the rest of the cabin was built, but Frank is relieved to see a toilet, and surprisingly enough, a deep, claw-footed tub. She drapes her wet clothes on the porcelain edge and takes advantage of the john, trying to imagine the chore it must have been getting the tub to the cabin. She squeezes into the sweats. The legs come to her shins and the top is snug. She returns to Sal, who feeds sticks into a growing fire.

"Are you hungry?" Sal asks without turning

"I am, actually. I'm famished."

"Let's see what the ladies gave us." Sal swipes her hands against her legs and peers into the plastic bags on the table. "Tortillas. Corn and flour." Pulling out ziplock bags, she opens them and sniffs. "Ah. Marta's menudo. Oh, and look at this." She unwraps a foil bundle. "Chiles rellenos."

Sal puts the food on the stove and adds an old-fashioned percolator. Frank's chill recedes before the fire. Rain slashes the windows. The scent of chili and warm oil wafts from the stove and Frank's stomach responds loudly. She studies books packed into shelves. They appear to be mostly nonfiction organized by subject. There are thousands of titles, but the subjects seem limited to hard science, philosophy and religion. The light is poor and Frank squints. A whole shelf is devoted to tarot books.

"Could you throw another log on?"

"Huh?" Frank jumps. "Oh. Sure."

She places a log in the fire and stands at the head-high mantle. It is bare but for dusty candles, an oil lamp, and an open box of shells. She takes due note of a shotgun mounted on the chimney and the rifle above it—both oiled and gleaming. She glances at a pair of old wing chairs flanking the hearth, the matching couch with its soft, cracked leather. Library books are stacked on an end table. Frank bends to the book splayed open on top of them.

"*War and Peace.* That's some heavy reading."

"Hm."

"Any good?"

"Actually, yes."

Frank shrugs. "I guess I just want to be distracted. Give me a mindless mystery any day."

Sal turns from the stove. "Do you solve them before you're finished?"

Frank grins. "Always."

Reminded why she is here, she asks, "How'd you get to school when you were a kid?"

"Our father drove us to the store and we'd catch the bus from there. When we got older we drove ourselves."

"I bet you started driving young out here."

"As soon as we could see over the dashboard."

Sal sets steaming bowls on the table and pours coffee without asking. "Black, right?"

"Yeah." The coffee is good. She holds it between her hands a moment, enjoying its smell mingling with the spicy menudo.

"Did you ever live in town?"

"For a while." Sal digs into her soup. "When I was married."

Frank nods. "To Mike Thompson. What happened there, if you don't mind my asking?"

"It wasn't Mike's fault. It just didn't work. He couldn't live here and I couldn't leave. I should have known better. He's a wonderful man. We're good friends. He made all those shelves." She gestures around the room.

"How long were you married?"

"Five years. Almost six."

"And you raised your daughter here?"

"No." Sal looks into her bowl. "I wanted to, but it wouldn't have been fair. I had my sister, so I was never lonely, but Cassie would have had nobody."

"So Mike raised her?"

Sal nods. "I had her on weekends until she turned into a teenager and refused to come up anymore."

"How come?"

"She hated it. Said I was boring."

Frank spoons the soup. It is hot and rich and good.

Sal asks, "How about you? Any children?"

It isn't professional to entertain personal questions during an investigation, but if Frank had been conducting the Saladino case professionally she wouldn't have gotten a reading from Sal, gone horseback riding with her, or be eating her dinner. Or wearing her clothes, Frank reminds herself, almost dripping menudo on the sweatshirt. Having so far abandoned protocol, she continues. "A daughter." Working their bond, she adds, "Her father raises her."

Sal rolls a tortilla and dips it in her bowl. "How old is she?"

"Three."

Catching the startled blue glance, Frank grins. "It's a long story."

They eat to the symphony of the rain. Frank knows there are questions she must ask but is loath to disrupt the companionable silence. When they finish, Sal piles their dishes in the sink and pours more coffee. She takes her cup to the couch and Kook curls on her lap. Frank settles into a wing chair. Bone and Cicero sprawl contentedly by the fire. It snaps and darts in cheerful contrast to the rain outside.

Frank looks to the darkening windows. It's almost dusk and she's barely asked Sal a damned thing. She puts her empty cup down and stands. "I should be heading back. Can we can talk tomorrow?"

"If you can find your way back here by yourself."

Frank considers her old car and nods. "I can get to the ranch. How do I get to the cabin?"

Over the rim of her cup, Sal says, "You could walk, or saddle up Buttons. Just leave her in the corral tonight when you're done. Make sure you brush her down."

"Wait a minute. You expect me to ride back alone?"

"Sure. Buttons could get to the ranch blindfolded."

Frank makes an incredulous snort. "I'm not going out in that alone."

"I'm not going out in that at all." As if to underscore Sal's point, the rain hurls itself at the windows.

"You're the one that dragged me out here."

"I didn't drag you anywhere. You came of your own volition."

"Yeah, but I didn't *get* here of my own volition. I had a little help. And I'm gonna need that to get home."

Sal flaps a dismissive hand. "You'll be fine. The keys are in the truck. Just leave it inside the gate."

Frank reaches back to squeeze her neck. "I don't believe this."

Sal sips her coffee. "I'll be glad to take you in the morning, but I'm not going out tonight."

"I can't stay. It's just not done." Frank is already on the verge of compromising the case. Spending the night with a potential suspect would destroy it.

"There's the door. I'll saddle Buttons if you want."

Frank can't imagine staying but has more trouble imagining a

110

horseback ride in the dark, in the rain, and alone. Not to mention the muddy drive downhill to Celadores. "Look." She tries again in her most reasonable voice. "It would be completely against protocol for me to spend the night here. There's no way I could ride out alone, and even if I did, I'm not sure I could figure out how to get back to the main gate."

"I told you—Buttons knows the way. You'll just have to be firm with her. She won't want to leave Dune. And I'll give you directions to the gate. There's just a couple places where the road's steep and you don't have much shoulder, so you have to be careful you don't let the truck slide. The four-wheel drive doesn't work, but you should be alright in first gear."

"Oh, yeah, sure. I can barely ride in the clear light of day and now I'm supposed to go out in a storm and ride in the dark, then drive down a muddy hill without four-wheel drive?"

Sal nods. "Or I could put you up in the other room and take you back in the morning. Your choice."

"Doesn't seem like much of a choice."

Frank has to admit she can't blame Sal for not wanting to go out in the storm. She doesn't want to either, just to spend the night in a damp hotel room poring over questions she should have asked hours ago. Still, it's an egregious violation. Wind squalls against the blackening windows and Bone lifts his head to give her a searching look. Staring at the fire, trying to figure her next move, she recalls the touch of Marguerite's palm between her breasts.

"Okay." She settles into the wing chair. "But if you won't give me a ride, you have to answer questions."

Chapter 18

"I hear your father hit your mother."

"Where'd you hear that?"

"Couple places. True?"

Sal reaches for a pouch on the end table and holds it in her lap. Instinctively assessing the size and shape of the pouch, Frank decides its contents are harmless. Just because she's agreed to wait out the storm with Sal, it doesn't mean she trusts her.

"Sometimes."

"Often?"

Sal shrugs. "Whenever he got drunk and thought the world was too much against him."

"What would you and Cass do when that happened?"

"We'd wait in the barn until he lost steam. A few times when we were younger, we ran down to the house to get John."

"Mazetti? What did he do?"

"He stopped him."

"Did they fight?"

"Sometimes, but it was never a match. My father was always pretty drunk and John could knock him out with an easy punch. That usually settled it until the next time."

"What if John wasn't there? What did you do then?"

Sal tugs the strings on the pouch. She fingers out a pack of rolling papers. "Pete came up a couple times. We'd try to stop him, though. He was brave but not much older than us. We didn't want him to get hurt, so that was when we decided we'd hide in the barn until it was safe to come back in."

"That's a shitty way to grow up."

Sal lifts a dismissive shoulder. "I suppose there are worse ways. And it didn't happen all the time."

"Still, it must have been scary when it did." Frank surprises herself by volunteering, "I had it the other way around." She twirls a finger around her ear. "My mom was loopy. Every now and then she'd go after my father, start swinging at him with a knife or a baseball bat. One time she took a saw to his arm while he was sleeping. We never knew what was going to set her off."

Sal bobs her head in agreement.

"I also heard that your parents fought the night before your mom died. Is that true?"

"Yes."

"Tell me about the fight."

Seeming to remember the papers in her hand, Sal takes one and folds it. Frank watches her make a crease and pinch tobacco into the fold. "It started like they always did. He came home drunk and belligerent. She started nagging about how much he'd spent at the bars, and when I saw where it was headed I went to the barn."

"Where was Cass?"

"In town. With Pete, I think."

"Did you see any of the fight, or hear it?"

"No."

"What was it like when you came back into the cabin?"

"It was quiet. My mother had gone to bed. He was passed out on the couch with his boots on. It always amazed me how he could sleep with his boots on."

"When was the next time you saw your mother?"

"At breakfast that morning. Her eye was swollen. She said she had a terrible headache and went back to bed. That's when my father told us he was going down to L.A."

"And then what happened?"

"What do you mean?"

"Your mother goes back to bed. Your father announces he's leaving. What happened next?"

"I guess we went to school, just like a regular day. We took the truck. Then Corette came and got us out of school. Told us—"

113

"Corette was John's wife?"

Sal nods. "Evidently mother got herself down to the ranch and told Corette she felt like her head was exploding. Corette took one look and drove her into town. Apparently the aneurism had already happened and her brain was filling with blood. She was unconscious by the time Corette got her to the hospital." Sal licks the glued paper and tamps the ends.

"I understand Cass was pretty upset."

"She was."

"She accused your father of killing her. Did anyone ever think about pressing charges against him?"

Sal shakes her head. "Mother told the doctor she fell and no one actually saw him hit her."

"But you heard them fighting."

"I did."

"And you saw she was hurt after the argument."

"Yes, but it wouldn't have mattered. Things were different back then. Domestic violence was the norm, not the exception. How a man raised his family was his own business."

In an attempt to verify what Carly Simonetti has told her about Mary Saladino's brothers, Frank baits, "So no one was upset about this except Cass?"

"I never said no one was upset. I just said there wasn't anything we could do about it."

"How did the rest of the family react?"

Sal admits, "My uncles wanted to kill him."

"They said that?"

"Uh-huh."

"And what did they do about it?"

"Nothing."

"Are you sure? Did any of them take a trip after the accident? Disappear for a while?"

"Not that I recall. It was a pretty crazy time."

"How'd your uncles get along with him before your mom died?"

"They tolerated him. No one liked him except my Uncle Rod, and that was only because my father would buy him drinks. When he wasn't fighting with him."

"What did they fight about?"

"They drank in the same bars, and every couple months they'd have a go at it. My father would call him a loser and make fun of him. Uncle Rod was manic depressive and drank on top of it. He couldn't ever keep a job. So if they weren't fighting about that, they'd fight over what a loser my father was, being John Mazetti's slave. I think sometimes my uncle would pick a fight just to keep the heat off my mother."

"And where's his family?"

"He never had one. I don't think he ever had a steady girl. Too unstable."

Sal offers the cigarette she's been holding. Frank takes it without thinking. They smoke and listen to the rain hammering the windows. Sal puts another log on the fire and settles with Kook beside her.

"Tell me about your sister."

"What about her?"

"I hear she was a wild one. True?"

Sal nods, petting Kook.

"Cass was always the daredevil. She always wanted to ride farther, stay out later, climb higher. When she got older and started drinking, she was absolutely fearless. She'd do anything, no matter how ridiculous or dangerous."

"Like what?"

"Break into people's homes. Steal beer from the gas station. Play chicken. Moon the police. Anything. She'd take on any dare."

"Play chicken, like with cars?"

Sal nods. "She loved to drag race down Main Street or the frontage road."

"Was she good at it?"

"The best. I told you, she was wild when she drank. She'd rather die than lose a bet."

Frank gets up to pitch her cigarette into the fire and squats beside it. When she rises, Sal's gaze is full and expectant upon her, as if she waits for something from Frank. Again Frank wonders just who is doing the interviewing.

"Why didn't you tell me Mike and Pete followed you to LA?"

"I didn't think of it. It's not a secret."

Frank tries, "What happened when they found you?"

"They didn't. We didn't even know they were there."

"When did you know they'd followed you?"

"I couldn't say. Maybe the next day."

"When was your mother's funeral?"

"That Sunday."

"And they were home for that?'

"Yes."

"What about John Mazetti? Was he at the funeral?"

She nods. "He drove us into town that day."

"Where was he when your mother died?"

"I don't know. I don't remember. But I know he wasn't here because Corette hated driving, so she wouldn't have taken my mother to the hospital if John had been around to do it."

"What was her relationship like with your mother?"

Sal tenses, barely but perceptibly. "It was fine." Not bothering to hide a yawn, she asks, "Do you mind if we take this up again in the morning? It's been a long day."

Her abrupt change of subject is intriguing, but Frank decides to follow it later. "Sure," she agrees.

Sal shows her to the second room off the hallway. "There are clean sheets in the bureau. I'll get you something to sleep in."

"The sweats are fine."

"You sure?"

"Yeah."

Sal leaves and Frank opens a tall, faded cupboard. Amid boxes and folded clothes, she finds linens and turns to the bed. It bows in the middle, and she starts to regret her decision.

Sal returns with a glass of water. She sets it on the nightstand and helps Frank with the sheets. "There's a blanket in the bureau if you need it."

She moves for the door and Frank asks, "Mind if I look through your books?"

"Not at all."

After Sal calls the dogs and closes the door to the other bedroom, Frank returns to the living room. It's lit only by the dying fire. The rain has eased and glides smoothly over the windows. Frank stands near the books but makes no attempt to read titles. The cabin is serene. She stands listening to rain tap on glass and to the fire gnawing at its wood—until the room tilts and the whirling begins. Putting out a hand to steady herself, she spills books onto the floor. Frank hears the high, thin keening of women. Her last thought before she flies over twilit mountains is that she knows what the women are crying for.

Chapter 19

Frank is on the floor. Sal sits cross-legged beside her, backlit from the kitchen; she is dark and unreadable. Frank rises to an elbow. Bone touches his tongue gently to her cheek. Sal nudges him away, but he continues to hover. "What happened?" she asks.

Frank remembers circling over mountains and a wine-red sea, the wailing of a woman. And more. Winter stars and a solitary fire. "I get these . . . dizzy spells." Even though she's the one lying on the floor, Frank feels a little smug that Sal didn't picked up on the visions back at the store. She gets to her knees. Sal tries to help, but Frank shakes her off.

"How do you feel?"

"I'm okay."

"I'm going to make you some tea."

"No," Frank says more forcefully than she means to. "I'm fine."

Sal ignores her and runs water into the kettle. Frank eases onto the couch and Bone stands beside her. When he drops his chin on her knee, she pets him, wondering if passing out might become a regular part of the visions.

"Here." Sal hands her a steaming mug.

It smells like wet forest floor and Frank wrinkles her nose. "What is it?"

"Just herbs. They'll help you sleep."

But Frank doesn't want to sleep. She is suddenly irritated by Sal's obstinacy and dogs and reeking tea, the rain and reeling visions, but mostly Frank is pissed at herself. She never should have gotten into Sal's truck. It was an irrational, impulsive decision and now she is stuck with it. She just wants to be home in her own bed, and barring that, at least the cool, reasonable comfort of her hotel room. She might not be able to stop the visions, but at least there she won't be passing out in front of strangers and making a fool of herself.

"Look," she tries to reason. "This is ridiculous. I'm a homicide detective. You know that, right?"

"I'm aware," Sal replies cautiously.

"Are you also aware I could arrest you for hindering an investigation?"

"I'm not sure how I'm hindering, but if you say so I suppose it may be true."

"*May* be? It *is*! I could handcuff you and take you off this mountain right now."

Sal shrugs. "I'm not stopping you."

Frank shakes her head and paces in front of the fireplace. The more circles she makes, the more she knows she doesn't want to leave the cabin or its dark surround of mountain. She should, that would be the right thing to do, the rational thing. Bone pads to her and stares with questioning amber eyes. She touches his head and as his stump comes alive, she remembers the fortune-teller advising her to take gifts, especially from strangers. Sal has shared her home, dinner, clothes, and even her damn dog.

"Look, I'm sorry. I shouldn't have come. I should have detained you at the store and made you talk to me there."

"Why didn't you?"

Frank opens her mouth to answer but has no words. She retrieves her mug, sips the cooling liquid. It smells worse than it tastes and in a show of goodwill she drinks more.

"If it's that important, I'll drive you back."

"No. It's okay."

"You're sure?"

"Yeah."

Sal lifts Kook off her lap and stands. "Finish that," she says with a nod to the mug. "It should help. If you need anything, just call. I'm a light sleeper." She steps over the threshold into the hall.

"Sal?"

She turns and Frank hoists her mug. "Thanks."

119

Sal's smile is faint. "You're welcome. Sleep well."

Frank drains the mug and rinses it in the sink. She turns off the lamp and feels her way to the bedroom. She closes the door gently, loosens the curtains and spreads them to the darkness beyond. Aware of being in the home of a possible murder suspect, she noiselessly slides a small desk in front of the door. It will give easily if Sal pushes on the door, but Frank sets a lamp on the edge that will topple and wake her if it's disturbed. The precaution is driven more by habit than concern. She stretches on the mattress, testing if it's as uncomfortable as it looks but falls asleep before she can reach a verdict.

At some point she wakes. The light by the bed is on and she still wears Sal's clothes. Desk and lamp guard the door. Frank switches the light off and rises to the window. A hunched moon gallops over the spine of the mountains. Clouds course alongside and the wind howls like hounds to the hunt. Frank rests her cheek on the old, soft wood of the frame. Only as the moon begins its ride down the far side of the mountains does she return to bed.

Blue sky shows her she has slept later than intended. Surprised she doesn't ache from the old mattress, she quietly moves the desk back where it belongs. She steps into the hall and smells coffee. The cabin is empty. Frank pours a cup from the simmering percolator and stands at the front door. The yard is muddy but spilled in sunshine. She follows tracks to the barn.

Sal is laying wet saddle blankets over the corral. The two big dogs see Frank and come wagging their tails. The little one stays next to Sal, barking furiously. She nudges him with a muddy, bare foot and his bark becomes a weak growl. Frank bends a hand to the larger dogs, asking Sal why she didn't wake her.

"I stomped around and the dogs barked for breakfast, so I figured if you could sleep through all that you must have needed to." She ducks between the boards. "Are you hungry?"

"I am. Must be all this fresh air."

Chickens have been foraging in the leaves under the sycamores and when they see Sal they come running. Frank watches warily, waiting for carnage, but the dogs ignore the flapping birds. "Why don't they chase them?"

"They're not allowed to, though Bone wanted to herd them in the worst way."

"He's a good dog, isn't he?"

Sal holds the screen door to the cabin open for him and smiles. "The best."

Frank sits while Sal fries eggs. After she slides their breakfast onto tortillas and pours salsa over it, she carries the plates outside, asking Frank to bring the coffee. They sit on the fire pit and eat from their laps. The chickens come running again but respect the wide arc Sal swings with her foot. The dogs, allowed to crowd closer, crouch expectantly at their feet.

"This is really good," Frank mumbles. "Do your clients always feed you this well?"

"Let's just say between the chickens and my ladies I'll never starve."

After they've finished eating, Sal tosses each dog a scrap of tortilla, scrapes the crumbs for the chickens, and returns the plates to the cabin. Frank shifts into the old wooden chair. Fed and surprisingly well-rested, she closes her eyes and lets the sun play on her face.

"Don't move." Sal's voice carries calmly but loudly across the yard. "There's a rattlesnake under your chair."

Frank almost jerks her feet onto the chair, but intuitively realizes the snake's reflexes are probably faster than hers. She freezes, gripping the arms of the chair to keep from moving. The screen door creaks, shuts, then creaks again, and Frank hears the soft snick of a rifle bolt.

She realizes with frigid logic that Sal could easily shoot her. No one knows Frank is here. Her body and her car could be dumped somewhere in the mountains and it would be decades before anyone found her. If then.

Sal circles into her line of view. A .22 held high, loosely angled at the chair.

Frank swallows the rock in her throat. The backup Beretta she usually carries on days off is secured in the lock box of the Honda's trunk, right next to her service revolver. She doesn't know if she's more afraid of dying or pissed at not being armed.

"Don't move," Sal repeats quietly. She rests her cheek against the stock, sighting along the barrel. The gun dips. There is a sharp crack. Dirt and rocks sting Frank's ankles and she yanks her feet onto the seat. Something thumps under the chair and a whirring fills the air. Bone sets to furious barking. Frank feels the snake thrashing against the chair and wonders in a sick panic if it can jump into her lap. The snake writhes into view, rolling and twisting in a death knot. Its broad head flops at the spine, pierced by Sal's bullet. Yet the animal still moves. For a second, Frank thinks she is going to faint, but the idea of falling out of her chair onto a rattlesnake sobers her.

"Bone! That's enough."

The dog glances at Sal. His bark turns to a growl, but he keeps fierce attention on the roiling snake. Frank is mesmerized by the ceaseless looping and coiling. "How long's it going to do that?"

"They can go for hours, even after the head's chopped off."

"Shit."

Kook sniffs close to the buzzing snake and Sal calls him off.

"Can they still bite?"

"Absolutely."

"Jesus." Frank rubs the goose bumps on her arms. "That's just wrong."

"Keep an eye on the dogs," Sal tells her.

Sal ducks into one of the sheds and comes out with a shovel. She starts digging under the trees. Dead leaves slither and rustle and Frank wraps her arms even tighter around her knees. She watches the snake's twisted, torturous dying until Sal scoops it up and carries it into the trees. Frank hears the shovel blade strike ground once, then twice, and the rattling stops.

Frank drops her bunched shoulders and checks under the chair before lowering her feet. She stands woozily, making a wide circuit of the fire ring to see if the snake brought any friends. Sal finishes in the trees and walks up to Frank, presenting the rattle.

Frank lunges back. "What the fuck?"

"I thought you might want it."

She stares at the bloody nub in Sal's palm, gingerly prods one of the hollow segments. Pinching the rattle, she gives it a shake. "It sounds so harmless. Like something a baby would play with."

Frank lays the keratinous tail on the fire ring. Her hand is shaking and she tucks it into her pocket. Sal totes the rifle into the cabin and returns with the coffee pot. She pours without asking. Frank leaves her cup where it is, not sure she can hold it without spilling.

"Cigarette?" Sal asks, pulling the tobacco pouch from her pocket.

"Sure. I could use one."

Sal expertly rolls a cigarette and passes it to her.

"How often do those things show up in your yard?"

"Not often at all. I probably only kill one every four or five years. I don't like to, but if they're in the barn, or around the house, that's too close."

They smoke in the sparkle of the fresh-washed morning. The big dogs work off their energy tug-of-warring over a stick. Kook dances around them on his hind legs, looking for his chance to grab the prize and run off with it. Frank's hand steadies, and as she reaches for her coffee she catches Sal's eyes upon her. The cool blue gaze is oddly satisfied. Suddenly Frank understands why. "You touched me last night, when I was passed out."

Sal looks to the dogs, but not before Frank sees a flicker of acknowledgement. She drags on her cigarette and follows the violet exhalation. She thinks she should feel angry or violated, but mainly she is curious. They watch the dogs until Bone gives up to lick his paws in a pool of sunshine. Cicero contentedly splinters the prize while Kook worries a lazy orange cat just out of claw range.

"Well?"

Sal only shrugs. "I thought you had more questions."

Frank nods, unsure if she's disappointed or relieved. "What was your father's uncle's name?"

"Lee Saladino."

"Did Lee say why your father was working late?"

"I don't recall a reason. Just that he might still be at the site."

"And he gave you the address?"

"I think so. I can't remember a number, but I know we got there. It was the only construction site on that stretch of Western Avenue."

"You went straight there?"

"Yes."

"And what did you find when you got there?"

"Just a construction site. They'd done the framing for a building."

"Was the site paved or just dirt?"

Sal drops the cigarette butt and rubs it under her heel. Frank winces, but realizes Sal has been barefoot since she removed her boots last night. "You don't wear shoes much."

"I don't wear anything much."

Frank almost smiles. She remembers now, but at the time she was so startled to see Sal peeling off her shirt that she didn't notice how solidly brown she was. Sidetracked, Frank steers them both back on course. "Was the ground sealed at all or was it raw dirt?"

"I think it was dirt. What we saw at least."

"How much did you see?"

"Enough to know he wasn't there."

"Did you get out and look around or just drive up?"

"We looked around. We had a flashlight."

"So it was dark by the time you got there?"

"It was dusk. Cloudy. I don't know that it was night yet, but it was fairly dark."

"Dark enough to need a flashlight?"

"We shined it around, just to make sure."

"And there was nobody there?"

"No one."

"Were there any cars or trucks parked there?"

Sal thinks. "Maybe nearby, but not like they belonged on the site."

"What did you do after you looked around?"

"Cass was still upset, so we drove around some more. She stopped to get another bottle of bourbon."

"Where did you stop?"

"I don't know. Some liquor store."

"How long did you drive around?"

"I don't know. It seemed like forever, but it probably wasn't more than a couple hours."

"Did you make any other stops?"

"We called Lee again, from a pay phone. My aunt said he wasn't there. Neither was my father. She tried to get us to come over and eat and spend the night, but Cass wanted to keep looking."

"Did she say where Lee was?"

"I don't think we asked. I know he had a bar he liked to go to after work. He'd take my father sometimes, but not always. He didn't like it when he started trouble."

"Did you go to that bar?"

"No."

"Why not?"

"I don't know."

"Did you go to his aunt's house, where he was staying?"

"No."

"How come?"

"I just told you. He wasn't there."

"And you believed her."

"Why wouldn't we?"

"Didn't you assume he'd be back, sooner or later?"

"I don't remember. I doubt we were thinking very rationally."

They watch the chickens scrabbling in the dirt. One of the hens finds a particularly choice item and the rest give chase as she runs off with it.

"Do you miss your family?"

The question is unplanned, its intimacy embarrassing, and Frank wishes she could take it back.

"I miss their physical presence, but they're always near. They're always close."

"How do you know?"

Sal takes her time before asking, "Have you ever been near a high tension wire?"

"Yeah."

"And felt the electricity?"

"Uh-huh."

"It's like that. It's a . . . a humming-ness of them. A vibration."

"An energy?"

"Like that, yes."

"Can you tell them apart?"

125

"Definitely. My father's energy is light and warm, very steady. Cass's is wiggly like a puppy, and my mother's too, but more pulsing, less erratic than Cass."

"That doesn't scare you?"

"Not at all. I'd be scared if I didn't feel them."

"Do their energies change?"

"Not that I've ever noticed."

"Can you feel other people?"

"Sometimes."

"When?"

"Mostly when I concentrate, when I think about them."

"So you could feel me right now?"

Sal nods. Frank is again curious but doesn't press. "Tell me about Leslie Ferrer."

Sal arches a brow. "You really have been doing your homework."

Frank grins. "It hasn't been all horseback riding and tea leaves."

After meticulously rolling another cigarette, Sal offers it to Frank. "Thanks. Nancy Snelling says Leslie was your best friend."

"Nancy." Sal smirks. "What else did she say?"

"Was she?"

"She was."

"But not anymore?"

"No."

"How come?"

"Leslie and I were sad, mixed-up girls. She went on to become a sad, mixed-up woman."

"Do you ever see her?"

"I run into her in town sometimes, but we just exchange the normal pleasantries."

"Why were you a sad, mixed-up girl?"

"High school's hardly the easiest time for a child. Were you happy?"

"No. But I had my reasons. What were yours?"

Sal shakes her head and the silver braid swishes on her back. Frank has the idea that if the moon were a horse, its mane would be Sal's hair.

"I love my sister. I miss her every day. We were so alike, yet we were so different. I always wanted to be like Cass. I was always shy, but Cass could walk into a room and it was like the sun coming out after a storm. I was jealous of her friends, her popularity, all the attention she got. I wanted her to myself. I was lonely in school. So was Leslie. I don't even know that I liked her that much."

"Were you lovers?"

Sal laughs. "That would be Nancy again?"

"She said the kids teased you about it."

"Mercilessly. With a name like Leslie, naturally she became Lezzie. We both had boyfriends, but it didn't seem to matter. Mike would get so mad." She finishes rolling a second cigarette and seals it with a lick. Striking a match, she holds it for Frank. "Why weren't you happy in high school?"

Frank takes a deep drag of the sweet smoke. She's already broken more procedural regulations than she can count on one hand. She pictures the retirement papers on her desk. She really must turn them in when she gets back. "My dad died when I was pretty young, so it was just me and my mom. I told you about her. It was a rough time." Steering the conversation back to Sal, she asks, "Did your father ever hit you or Cass?"

"No. He tried once, when we were little. He grabbed Cass, and my mother swung a pan off the stove, a big cast-iron skillet. There were onions and bacon grease everywhere. It took us forever to clean it up. But she waved that pan and told my father if he ever touched one of her children again it would be the last thing he touched. He backed off and went outside. It was the only time I ever saw her fight back."

Bone is stretched near her foot and Frank realizes she has been stroking him.

"Would you like another cup of coffee?"

"God, no. I'm shaky enough as it is after that damn snake. I really should get going." But she makes no effort to move. The sun is warm and the breeze cool. The creek warbles and coos, and she wonders if it has risen with the rain. She sees it in the gut of the mountains, gushing over the edge of a great stone fall, past rock and boulder down a thin, dark canyon hemmed with fir and redwood that block the sun.

127

Sal stands and Frank is surprised to be in bright light. She swipes at her eyes and follows into the cabin. Squeezing into her damp jeans, she looks around the tiny bedroom, recalls standing at the window in the middle of the night watching the moon and clouds ride over the mountains. And then she is leaning against the wall and the room is dark but for starlight and the red, shadowy dance of a small fire. She hears a chant mumbled in a low, sexless voice, a rhythmic grinding of stone on stone. An animal stirs near, a black dog lifting its muzzle to the night.

Bone's wet nose pushes her hand. Frank shakes her head and the vision clears. "Jesus." Bone wags his stump. She pets his sleek head, then goes to find Sal. She is in the barn, and Frank notes happily that Buttons is already saddled. The old mare nickers as she approaches and Frank scratches under her mane, surprised how relaxed she is around the beast.

They ride out of the corral toward the trees. The dogs run ahead and clatter over the bridge. The horses follow single file.

Halfway across, Frank stops. She looks down, hoping to see the fish she knows are there. But she also knows they are hiding, practically motionless in the deeper pools at the edge of the stream, as perfectly flecked and brown as the water that holds them.

Buttons knocks an impatient hoof and tugs on the rein. Frank smiles and crosses to the other side.

Chapter 20

A short, thick man with a shaggy gray mustache steps from the barn as they ride into the corral. Braiding the ends of a rein, he watches them dismount.

"Pete, this is Lieutenant Franco, LAPD. Lieutenant, Pete Mazetti."

She shakes his hand. It is rough and callused, and Mazetti doesn't lessen his grip because she's a woman.

"Mind if I ask a couple questions?"

He shrugs.

"I understand you and Mike Thompson followed Cass and Sal down to LA the day Mary Saladino died."

"Yep."

"What can you tell me about the trip?"

"Didn't find 'em."

"Did you find Domenic Saladino?"

"Wasn't looking for him."

Frank smiles. "Is that a yes or a no?"

"No."

"Mind laying out the details of the trip for me?"

He looks up sourly from the bridle he's working. "What do you mean details?"

"When you left, what time you got there, what you did when you were there."

Pete weaves the ends of the strips into the body of the braid. "Left here right after the girls did, got there—"

"How soon after the girls did?"

"I don't know. Half-hour, forty-five minutes. We weren't exactly on their tail, but we weren't that far behind."

She prompts, "You drove straight down?"

"Yep."

"No stops in between?"

"Nope."

"What was your plan?"

"Didn't have one. Stopped when we got down there and stole a phone book out of a phone booth. Gonna arrest me for that?"

"Go on."

"Looked up Saladino Construction. Found it over in Culver City. Knocked on the door, but the lights were all off. They were gone for the day. Stopped at the next pay phone and called all the Saladinos in the book." He glances at Sal. "Went over to the uncle's where Dom was staying. The aunt said she hadn't seen him or the girls. Parked a while, hoping they'd turn up there. When they didn't, we drove around looking for 'em, but we didn't find 'em. Called the aunt one more time to see if she'd heard from anybody, then gave up and came on home. Figured the girls would surface back here sooner or later."

"You seem to remember that pretty well."

"I heard you was snooping around. Figured you'd get to me sooner or later."

"Why?"

"Why not?"

"What'd your folks think about you running off like that?"

He heaves broad shoulders. "Nothing."

"Lucky you. 'Course your daddy—John Mazetti, right?—he wasn't home that night, was he?"

Pete's eyes narrow, and dart to Sal before settling back on Frank. "Seems like you already know the answer to that."

"I do, but I can't remember exactly. Where was he?"

Pete stares hard at her. "Cattle auction."

"That's right. And where was that?"

"Merced."

"Merced, that's right." She nods amiably. "When did he leave?"

"The day Sal's momma went into the hospital."

"They have good cattle in Merced?"

"Some."

"He go there often?"

"He looked at cattle often."

"How long was he gone?"

"No more than a night or two."

"One or two?"

"Hell, I don't know. The girls' mom was dead. I wasn't exactly keeping track of my father."

"He come home with any cattle?"

"Nope."

"Can you prove he was there?"

Pete spits between her feet. "Can you prove he wasn't?"

He throws the bridle onto a rail and as they watch him stomp to the ranch house, Sal says, "That was quite the third degree."

"Hardly. I wasn't even warmed up."

They turn the horses loose and get in the truck, but before starting the engine, Sal tells Frank, "I guarantee you Mike and Pete had nothing to do with my father disappearing."

"How's that?"

"I know them. Pete might have been able to lie about it, but not Mike. He's a terrible liar. I could never tell him what I was getting Cassie for Christmas because he'd always give it away."

Sal drives while Frank admires the clean morning shadows and raindrops weighing the tips of bushes like Christmas ornaments.

"How soon did John Mazetti replace your father after he disappeared?"

"I don't know that he ever did. Pete was out of school that spring and he and the foreman—that would have been George Perales back then—picked up the slack. Pete got drafted that fall, and George ran things until he got back and took up where my father left off."

"Why'd Mazetti let you guys stay on without your father here?"

Sal hugs the wheel. Her tan doesn't hide the purple shadows under her eyes and Frank wonders how she slept last night. "Saladinos are good luck. The land needs us."

Frank frowns. "John Mazetti let you stay because he's superstitious?"

"Not superstitious, a wise businessman. Why take the risk? And besides, how would it look if he tossed two orphans out of their home?"

"You had family you could have stayed with."

"We did, but we didn't want to. I helped out as much as I could. I'm a fair ranch hand and I picked up the chores my mother used to do."

"Like what?"

"She helped Corette with the orchard and the gardens, the cooking."

"What was your relationship with her like?"

"With Corette?" Sal asks in surprise. "It was fine."

Frank is thinking there is more to why John let the girls stay, but Sal pulls up to the last gate and jumps out. Frank watches her bend to the lock. She doesn't want to get out of the truck, but Sal waits, holding the gate. Frank opens the door and drops down into mud. She kicks it off on a tire rim, but instead of crossing the road to her car, she joins Sal.

Leaning on the warming metal, she says, "I might have more questions."

"You know where to find me."

A squirrel scurries across the road and dives into a burrow. The dogs watch from the back of the truck, rigid with attention. Frank looks at the mountains. Scrubbed in the day's new light they hold a green, inviting promise.

"When I was passed out, what did you see?"

Sal studies her. "Your energy is amazingly strong, but it's confused."

Frank nods. "Like a storm that doesn't know which way to blow."

"Yes, exactly. How do you know that?"

"I've been told." Frank juts her chin toward the crooked ridge. "I thought you were going to take me up there."

Sal chuckles. "Would you have wanted to go in the rain?"

"No."

"Next time."

Frank looks at her. "How do you know there'll be a next time?"

"Won't there be?"

Frank doesn't answer, surprised how much she hopes Sal is right.

She lifts a hand and walks to the car. Sliding the key into the ignition, she prays the faithful Honda won't start. But of course it does. She drives through the gate, refusing to look back at Sal or the guard of mountains behind.

Chapter 21

Farther down the road she passes the store, then brakes, and turns around. The store is empty but for a new clerk, a grizzled man in a John Deere cap with a wad of chew in his cheek. She pays for a bottle of water, asking if he's ever at the store when Sal does her thing.

"Sure, all the time. Let her work on my arthritis if she's not too busy. She's a peach. Does it for free."

"Does it help?"

He chuckles. "Better 'an what the doctors gimme. You that cop they been talkin' about?"

"Reckon I am," she answers, adopting the geezer's drawl.

"Yeah, I heard you found old Dom Saladino, that right?"

"Yep. Did you know him?"

"Why sure I knew him, and his daddy, too. Worked with him plenty of times. Branding, gathering. He was a good hand, Dom was."

"That's what I heard. When he was sober."

"Well, now, nothin' wrong with a man takin' a drink now and then."

"No, I reckon not. You go to school with his girls?"

"Aw, I didn't get much schooling. Been working all my life."

He slaps the counter. "This here was my great-great-grand-daddy's store. Built in 1868. Wasn't nothing but a tent and barrels to start with."

"You don't say?"

"I do," he defends proudly, and as he talks Frank sees a sagging, soot-stained canvas, tied at the corners with frayed manila ropes. Barrels stocked beneath on one side. Dry goods, boots, pants, implements arranged on long planks. A cool wind puffs the roof high. Just outside burns a fire. A woman clutching a blanket squats beside it. Black, stringy hair hides her face. Beside her on the ground a baby chews its fists.

Frank is leaning against the counter. She interrupts the man. "Your grandmother. She was from here."

"Full-blood Esselen," he agrees. "How'd you know that?"

"Lucky guess," she lies. "You worked with Dom and John Mazetti?"

"Sure did. Brandin', castratin', roundups. Worked for the Mazettis every chance I got. They always paid good and on time. And put out a good spread to boot."

"How'd those two get along?"

He pulls at the bill of his cap. "Well, you know Dom's people used to own the Mazetti ranch, and I don't think that ever settled too well on him, taking orders from a man on what he felt was his land."

"Did they fight?"

"Oh, you know how it is when a man gets a few under his belt. Starts talking, don't you know, and one thing leads to another." He scratches under his cap. "You know how that is."

"They come to blows?"

"Couple times that I heard of. Never actually saw it, though. Heard old John had enough one time. Almost ran Dom off the ranch."

"Why didn't he? Seems like more trouble to keep him on."

"Well, you know," the man becomes evasive. "People have their reasons."

"Do you know what they were?"

He spits a brown jet into a Styrofoam cup on the counter. "Let's just say there's a lot of things happen up in them mountains that should stay up in them mountains."

"Like what?" She gives her most charming aw-shucks grin. "You're making me awfully curious."

Probing a bent finger under his cap, he says, "I reckon you'd hear it sooner or later anyway. I ain't crazy now. You can ask anyone been around these parts long enough, they'll tell you the same thing. It's haunted up there. The first Saladino that settled here, that woulda been Angelo Saladino, he married a full-blood Esselen, just like my great-great-grandma. There's always been Esselen blood on that land. When there's not, well, that's when the trouble starts."

"What sort of trouble?"

"Drought. Fire. Hoof-and-mouth. Last time the Saladinos left, a lightning storm killed Ben Mazetti's baby brother. Felled an oak tree right through the nursery into his crib." The old man shakes his head woefully. "Ain't nothin' good can come of a Saladino leaving the land. It's just a fact."

The morning is warm and the air in the store close, yet ice ripples over Frank's spine. Her arms welt with goose bumps.

"Good to know." She slaps the counter. "Thanks for your time."

"Hell," he looks around the empty store. "I got plenty of that."

Frank walks out into the welcome light. She sits in her car, nursing the bottle of water. All her visions seem somehow connected to the mountains, and she wonders if maybe the old guy's right. Maybe they are haunted.

She checks her watch. It's barely mid-morning. She should stop in Soledad and talk to more people. She sips the cool water. A light breeze sweeps through the oak in front of the store. She admires the crisp delineation of mountain against sky. On impulse she starts the car and heads for the highway, but turns left at the first crossroad, heading north instead of south.

The two-lane road winds up dry, hilly rangelands under the aegis of the mountains, gradually pinching down to a single lane in a densely shaded canyon. She misses the mountains' tall company. Soon homes, then suburbs and towns replace the big ranches. But when the road intersects the Pacific Coast Highway, the mountains reappear on her left.

She waits at the stoplight. Carmel is straight ahead. She's never been to the ritzy seaside town. She should stop for lunch and wander around. The light changes. Frank glances at the mountains rising steeply from the ocean. An SUV behind her honks. She turns left, away from the town. Malls and businesses give way to secluded, multimillion-dollar, ocean-view homes. After a couple of winding miles, those too fade away, until the only sign of civilization is the sinuous snake of blacktop.

The mountain side of the road is sheer granite, dotted with shrubs tough enough to withstand wind, salt, drought and the constant pull of gravity. On the ocean side, a narrow shoulder drops hundreds of feet to the breaking ocean. The water lunges at the foot of the mountains and she remembers Gomez' odd gratitude that the Santa Lucias keep the ocean where it belongs. Frank drives slowly.

Hours later, where the mountains flatten and become tame, she catches up to the storm that blew over the ranch. It waits in dirty gray piles over the rounded hills, and she decides to eat and stretch before driving into it.

Exiting at a seaside town, she follows signs to the harbor. She walks up and down the marina, enjoying the clanging rigging and slapping hulls. Gulls cry and wheel over the restaurants along the dock and the salt air whets her appetite. Stopping to grab her briefcase from the car, she ducks into the closest restaurant with a view. A veteran of solitary dining, she knows a single woman is usually shunted off by the kitchen, so Frank tells the host she needs a table by the water. The black-tied young man starts to explain they are all taken, but she points to one of three large, empty tables. Doubtful it is reserved in the off-season at five o'clock on a Sunday night, she says, "That one right there will be fine."

Frank walks past the host, who has no choice but to trot behind. He lays a menu down, clearly miffed, and says her server will be right with her. She opens her briefcase and catches him talking to a waitress, who glances at her. Frank smiles and waves her over.

The woman forces a cheery response and when she gets to the table Frank assures, "I know I'm taking one of your money tables, but I'll make it up to you. I'm in kind of a hurry, so could you get me a cup of coffee, fresh coffee, while I look at the menu?"

"Sure thing," the woman says and this time her smile is genuine.

Frank scans the menu, then opens her notepad and starts writing. She hasn't bought a laptop yet, preferring to let her imagination roam in the interplay between hand and pen and paper. The waitress returns with a pitcher of water and pours a glass, asking if Frank's decided. She orders steak and fries, then glances at the view. Fishing boats bob in a choppy, gray sea, but after all her fuss for a window table, Frank barely notices. Between dropping in on Sal and the unexpected sleep-over at the cabin, she is losing perspective on the Saladino case and is determined to make up for it. She dives into her notes, not looking up until the waitress brings her steak, but even then it's just to cut and stab her food.

She amends, adds, and comments between bites, intrigued that Sal isn't more interested in how her father died. In her experience, there are only two reasons people aren't interested in a homicide—they either don't care about the deceased or they already know how it happened. It's possible that after forty-odd years Sal just doesn't care anymore. It's equally possible she knows more than she's telling.

Frank pushes her plate away, empty but for a few fries. She looks out over the water to check the storm's progress. It has flattened the sea into a sheet of bronze brighter than the gun-metal sky. The boats anchored on the eerie calm hold their breath as if awaiting the storm's first blow. Behind the silent bay, bruised clouds purple the hills. A faltering sun squeezes through cracks in the clouds, slashing at the hills with brilliant streaks of umber and lighting the fishing boat windows.

The waitress asks how everything was, and Frank asks for the check and coffee to go. She slides her notes into the briefcase and glances at the harbor.

The fishing boats are gone. In their place are Chinese junks, bobbing under wrinkled sails and burning smudge pots. The sepia hills glow not with the broken sun but the thousand oil lamps of a crowded city. On the skinny wooden dock, horses and drays jostle for space amid the crates and shanties of peddlers and fishmongers hawking their goods over the cacophony of scavenging gulls.

"Here you go." The waitress sets down the bill and a Styrofoam cup. "Everything alright?"

Frank looks from the waitress back to the water. The junks are once again Whalers and SeaCrafts. Cars are parked on the concrete dock in front of taffy shops and sushi bars. The defeated sun has left the hills dark and barren.

"Yeah. Fine."

She follows the waitress to the register and leaves an impressive tip. Pushing through the door, she is relieved to see her car in the lot. A drop of rain smacks her face. Her hand trembles as she puts the key in the lock. She settles the case and coffee, then grips the steering wheel, glad of its solidity in what is fast becoming a slippery world.

Cell phone reception at the ranch and down the coast was spotty to nonexistent, so Frank left her phone in the car. She checks it now, seeing all the messages from the weekend have rolled in. The last is from Caroline. Frank calls, anxious to hear a familiar voice.

"Well, there you are. I thought you'd gotten lost in the mountains and eaten by lions."

Frank squeezes her eyes against the memory of the snake rolling, flashing its pale, vulnerable underbelly. "Not quite. Awful reception, though."

"Where are you?"

"Still up north. Morro Bay."

"Oh." In one short word, Caroline's disappointment is clear.

"How'd it go?" she asks gamely.

"I'm getting more questions than answers, but at least that's something. More's better than less."

"Sounds like you're not done up there."

"No," Frank reflects. "I think I've barely started."

"Damn. That means I'll never see you."

"Not necessarily." Franks squints at the lowering sky, the spats of rain hitting her windshield. "Got a storm up here, but I bet I can outrun it, and unless I hit traffic I should be home by eight or nine. Feel like company?"

"Sure. If you're up for it."

"Definitely, but I better go so I can concentrate on getting home to you."

"Okay. Drive safe. I'd rather see you later than in a coffin."

Frank frowns; another great visual. She finds the highway and locks the cruise control onto eighty. The storm chases her all the way but doesn't catch her.

Chapter 22

Frank lets herself into Caroline's plush condo and calls hello.

"I'm in the kitchen!"

She finds Caroline at the stove, stirring spaghetti sauce. Frank hugs her from behind and murmurs into her ear. Caroline turns into her, laughing low and rousing a tickle of desire. Frank makes small talk to keep Caroline warm against her, so that she can caress her lips along the willing neck, circle a light, teasing tip of tongue round the curve of an ear.

Caroline leans back, observing, "Aren't you the amorous one?"

"Hm." Her lips seek Caroline's throat for a last course, then Frank gently releases her. "How hungry are you?"

Arching a brow, Caroline answers, "I could eat something that's not necessarily on the menu."

"Me, too." Frank tugs her through the door. "I'm ravenous."

They undress each other in the bedroom's dark. Caroline's body rarely sees the sun and it glows beneath Frank's bronzed hands. She cups a breast, bending, and it is like taking the whole cool of the moon in her mouth. She recalls the moon galloping over the Santa Lucias.

"On the bed," she instructs Caroline. "Belly down."

Caroline complies in a languorous pose.

Frank kneels and strokes, reaching and fondling. She kisses her lover's pale mounts and plains, straddles an alabaster thigh as Caroline spreads to receive Frank's palm, writhing atop it, panting, grinding hard into the bed. Burning slick against Frank's upturned hand, they surge together, mare and rider become one, the climax of one spurring the other.

Frank slides onto the bed and leaves an arm draped around Caroline's silvery waist. Sharing a smile, Caroline murmurs, "That was wild. What got into you?"

"Just felt like riding bareback."

Caroline laughs into her pillow. Drowsy and content, they lie, each petting the other like a companionable dog. Twining Caroline's long hair round a finger, Frank tells her, "I'm starved."

"Go put the water on. I'll be right there."

Frank pads naked into the kitchen. She sets a pot of water to boil, snags a handful of nuts, and wanders back to the bedroom. Caroline is sound asleep. She studies her lover for a moment, then covers her lightly with the spread. She returns to the kitchen. Too hungry to wait, Frank rips a hunk from a baguette by the stove, dunks the bread into the sauce, and devours half the loaf in huge, bloody gobbets.

She is restless after eating, more energized than sated from the intense coupling, and she stares into the open freezer. There's caramel gelato, her favorite, but tonight it's not appealing. She turns off all the lights and feels her way to the bedroom. Caroline always sleeps with the drapes closed and Frank parts them to reveal a swath of sky. Clouds scull beneath a moon in repose. She wonders if the stars are shining over Celadores and the ranch, keeping the mountains company in their silent watch. Slipping in beside Caroline, Frank falls asleep in the shifting beam of moon and cloud.

Ten minutes before the alarm goes off, Frank is fully awake. She cancels the alarm so it doesn't wake Caroline and turns to the window, irked to find Caroline has gotten up in the night and closed the curtains. She dresses quickly, leaves a note, and lets herself out. The storm has passed without rain and the sun rises through a brown haze. If she wasn't driving, Frank would have closed her eyes to better picture dawn at the cabin, the clear light and fresh shadows, dogs and chickens at ease in the yard, Sal rolling a cigarette.

She gets to the station well before the rest of the squad. They trickle in while she copies her notes for Lewis.

Braxton asks, "How'd the trip go?"

"Okay. No signed confessions. How's everything here?"

She hadn't heard from Pintar, so is surprised when he says, "Caught a hanging off Normandie, by the fish market."

"No shit?"

Incredibly, Braxton blushes. "Yeah, I think it was Pintar's first double-clutch."

Frank can't hide her grin but autoerotic hangings are rare in the 'hood and she asks, "Sure that's what it was?"

He shows her the pictures of a tattooed young man tied off over a pile of skin mags with his junk hanging out. She looks closely at the knots. They're loose and easily slipped if he hadn't lost consciousness.

"Hope it was worth it."

"It was damn embarrassing all around. First the kid's sister finds him, sweet little thing, then she has to translate for the mother. Man," he wags his head, "I'll be happy if I never get another one of those. What a waste."

Frank claps him on the back as they settle in for the morning meeting. Frank gives the professional highlights of her trip, then afterwards drags a chair over to Lewis' desk.

"Whatcha got?" Lewis asks.

"Seems like every time I go up there I come back with more questions than answers. Turns out Saladino had a regular habit of beating his wife. She dies from a fall—" Frank makes quote marks in the air "—and no one thinks that's suspicious. Then Saladino disappears the day after this supposed fall."

"Yeah, but he couldn't a known she was gonna die."

"No, but when she does, there's a lot of upset people. The daughter, Cass, accused him of killing her and takes off after him in a hot rage, and Mary Saladino had three brothers that all threatened to kill him."

Lewis lifts her brows. "Oh yeah? Any of 'em still around?"

"Nah. All dead. But see what you can dig up on a—" Frank has to sift through her notes. "—Roderick Dusi. One of the brothers. He and Saladino used to get into regular fights." She closes her folder, continuing from memory. "Then, we got Saladino's boss. John Mazetti. He owned the ranch. Tension between him and Saladino about how to run the place. Seems Saladino wanted to get it back, thought he could someday. Mazetti's at a cattle auction when the wife dies—at least, that's the story. I want to track that down. See what you can find out about cattle auctions in Merced, where they'd have done that and if they have any kinda records going back that far. Mazetti's son says he didn't buy anything, but he might have had to register for one of the auctions or something."

Frank flips a page on her notepad, smoothes it down.

"Then we have the girls' boyfriends. Turned out they followed them to LA."

"No shit?"

"Yeah, didn't find 'em, though. Supposedly. I talked to both of 'em. The one, Sal's ex, he seems on the level, but the other one's a surly bastard. For what it's worth, Sal assured me they'd have had nothing to do with her dad's death. Which leaves the girls themselves." She lifts another page.

"You think one of 'em killed their pops?"

"Who knows? Cass is hysterical. They go to all the trouble to drive down there to look for him, but they don't even go to the uncle's house where he was staying. That's kinda weird. After the worksite, that'd be the second place I'd go. Just to see for myself. They go to all that trouble, then turn around and come home. Wouldn't you have hung out and waited for him to turn up, either at the house or at work the next morning?"

"I would've, yeah."

"But they didn't. Just tucked tail and came home. From what I'm hearing about Cass Saladino, that doesn't sound like something she'd have done."

"What'd the sister say about it?"

"Says they weren't thinking clearly."

Frank bends a finger for each of her next points. "She didn't tell me about the boys following them down, she didn't tell me her old man beat on her mom, and she didn't tell me they had a fight the night before she died. Why's she holding out?"

"She afraid to say too much 'cause she knows somethin'."

"That's what I'm thinking. Plus she's still arctic about all this. Didn't ask me one question about her old man. Not one."

Frank hasn't put it into notes about why the Saladinos were allowed to stay on the ranch, and she is glad Lewis doesn't think to ask.

"That it?"

"That ain't enough?"

Lewis grins, "Naw, I mean you done?"

"I'm done, Sister Shaft. What you got?"

The big cop sits back, neatly crossing her ankles up on the desk. "What's the first thing you'd do if somebody disappeared on you?"

Frank plays along. "Very first thing?"

Lewis says impatiently, "After twenty-four hours."

"File a missing persons."

"Zac'ly. I done a little sleuthing. Know when they finally get around to filing one on Saladino?"

Frank shakes her head. It's a good question. She's glad Lewis has thought of it, and thinks reassuringly of the retirement forms on her desk.

"Not until almost seven years later. Like nobody's in a rush to find this dude."

"That's a long time."

"Ain't it, though? They coulda at least been collectin' social security or something. Life insurance maybe. Like they don't want anybody to know he gone."

Writing a note to follow up on that with Sal, Frank warns, "He might have been getting paid under the table. Run a financial on this guy. See what you can find."

Lewis drops her feet and taps at her keyboard, asking, "You gonna go back up there?"

"Yeah. Have to."

"Damn. Sorry about that, LT."

"Nah, don't sweat it. It's not that bad."

But Lewis is engrossed in her notes. She grunts and keeps typing. Frank wanders to her office and double checks her calendar. Meetings all morning, then ironically enough she has to teach a sexual harassment class at the Police Academy. On a hunch she swiftly types a name into her computer and scrolls through the results. Jotting an address onto a pink pad, she tears off the paper and crams it in her pocket. With luck, she can follow up when school's out.

Chapter 23

Sal's daughter lives within an easy forty minutes of the academy. Frank cruises west through sluggish late afternoon traffic. Snoop vibrates through her speakers and she slaps time on the door. The lazy autumn light falls golden, even through the smog, and Frank is almost happy. Turning off Sunset, she twists up narrow, overgrown roads that are a firefighter's worst nightmare. She slows to read house numbers and wonders if Sal ever visits her daughter. Passing the address she wants, she backs up into a skinny driveway and climbs a small porch shrouded in fragrant, pale-blossomed vines. A woman cracks the door at her knock.

Frank holds her badge out but is speechless. For a vertiginous moment, the separate worlds of Los Angeles and Celadores bleed together at the edges.

"Hello," the woman smiles.

Frank croaks, "Cassandra Parker?"

"That's me."

"You're the tarot lady, from the bookstore."

"Yep."

"And you're Sal—" Frank corrects herself, "Diana Saladino's daughter?"

"Yeah," she says, puzzled until she sees Frank's badge. "Oh my God, you're the detective Mom told me about."

Frank nods.

Parker laughs. "What are the odds?"

"Indeed."

Frank folds the badge away, trying to slow her ricocheting thoughts. "I guess we were never properly introduced. I'm Lieutenant Franco, LAPD."

"Homicide." Parker nods. "That makes sense."

"Glad it does to someone. Mind if I ask a few questions?"

"I'm so sorry. Please."

Parker holds the door wide. She shows Frank into a cozy living room cluttered with cowboy decor. Two mutts wag their tails and slobber on the outside of a sliding glass door.

"I just put the kettle on for tea. Would you like some?"

"Sure."

"Have a seat. I'll be right back."

Frank studies the photographs ringing the room, pictures of the same three kids at various ages, a young Parker beaming between her mother and father, one that appears to be Sal with a baby in her lap.

Parker reappears with two mugs. "Green tea," she says handing one to Frank. "Hope that's okay."

"Great." She tips her head to the pictures. "These your kids?"

"Yep."

One of the dogs barks, but Parker silences it with a look. She makes a downward motion and both dogs sit.

"You're good with animals, just like your mother."

"One of the few things we have in common."

Parker settles into the couch and Frank perches on an old, leather recliner. "You don't get along?"

"I didn't say that," she answers without rancor. "We've just never been close. She's not exactly the maternal type."

"What type is she?" Frank asks, suddenly more interested in Sal than Sal's father.

Parker tucks her legs beneath her—like her mother, Frank notes—and plays with a swirl of sun-streaked hair. Knowing her age, Frank guesses the sun comes from a beauty parlor, and decides this acorn has rolled a bit from its tree.

"If Mom were a tarot card," she reaches to the credenza behind her and flips through a deck, "she'd be this one." Parker slaps down the picture of a red-robed man flanked by three sticks, standing on a promontory with his back to the viewer, watching three ships sailing on a golden sea. "See how alone he is? High up on his mountain? He has his staffs, they're creative and budding, but basically he stands alone and watches the world go by."

"Do you think she spends a lot of time watching the world go by?"

"No." She slips the card back into the deck and shuffles it absently. "She's cut herself off from it. She stays isolated on her mountain while life goes on despite her."

"Why do you think she does that?"

"I think she made a decision a long time ago not to have much to do with people. I think losing her immediate family in such a short time frame pushed her into a sort of self-imposed exile. I don't think she's ever gotten over all that."

"How difficult was that for you?"

"I get it now that I'm older, but as a kid . . ." she shrugs.

Frank sips at her tea. "But you have dogs in common. And you're both apparently . . . gifted."

Parker twists her hair and gives the ceiling a rueful smile. "Something else I hated about her when I was a kid. I just wanted a normal mother, not one the whole town whispered about."

"Seems like you have that in common, too." Frank clarifies, "Having a parent that embarrassed you."

Parker stops twirling her hair. "Did she say that?"

"Said it was hard having a father that drank so much. What do you remember about your grandfather, hearing about him?"

The fortune-teller frowns and resumes twirling. "Let's see. That he drank a lot. That he was incredibly handy. Apparently he could fix anything. That he didn't have the best temper. I guess he used to hit my grandmother, but I hear he was good with the horses and dogs." She smiles. "Guess we got that from him."

"When you say he hit your grandmother, was that a regular thing?"

"I don't know how regular it was, but apparently it wasn't unusual."

"So he had a habit of beating her."

She squirmed in her seat. "I don't know that I'd say a habit."

"What was his relationship like with your mother?"

"You know, it's funny. She never talks much about him. Never has."

"Is she evasive?"

147

"I wouldn't say evasive. More like uncomfortable. Like it hurts to talk about him."

"Even after all this time?"

"I think so. I think it just devastated her, his leaving and all. Apparently now we know why, but it didn't help then."

"What has she told you about your grandmother?"

"Not much about her either, other than she was a terrific gardener, had the original green thumb. I know Mom wishes she were as good a gardener. I think she loved her a lot."

"Why do you say that?"

"From what I've been able to glean over the years, it sounds like they did a lot together—pruning, canning, sewing, baking, reading. Apparently my grandmother read to her and Aunt Cass every night. That was one thing I loved about my mother," she adds. "She used to tell the greatest stories." Parker eyes her shrewdly. "You should get her to tell you about the *zopilote*."

Frank steers the conversation from storytelling back to the Saladinos. "Do you think your grandmother was as close to your aunt as your mother?"

"You know, I couldn't say. I think Cass was more of a tomboy, less domestic. I think she spent more time tooling around with my grandfather doing ranch things."

"I understand there was bad blood between the Saladinos and Mazettis, yet your family was allowed to stay on. Do you know why?"

With a warm glint, Sal's daughter teases, "I don't think you'd believe me if I told you."

Frank grins. "Oh, you might be surprised."

"Alright. It goes back a long way. The Saladinos were the first owners of the ranch, other than the Native Americans that used to live there. We've always had a relationship with that land. When we're there, it seems to thrive. When we're not, it fails."

"So it was a barren wasteland before the Saladinos got there?"

"Not at all. Apparently it was always very productive land. Where the cabin is? That's where one of my great-great-grandmothers was born. She was Native American, one of the last of the Esselen tribe. You know the Esalen Institute? That's what it was named for. Anyway, she married whichever great-great-grandfather it was that settled there, and the rest is history. They say the land needs a Saladino, but what I really think it needs is that old Esselen blood."

"You believe that?"

Parker chuckles. "You're a detective. It's hard to argue with the evidence."

"What happens to the ranch when your mother dies?"

A crease plucks the fortune-teller's brow. "I couldn't say."

"Do you ever plan on going back to stay?"

"I don't think so. I'm not that monastic."

Frank nods. "She said you stopped going when you were a teen."

"Yeah, my life was in town. I didn't want much to do with her, or the ranch."

"And now?"

"Now that I'm a little older, a little wiser, and a lot more scarred, I appreciate them both, I know it hurt her that I didn't want to be with her. And at the time—rotten little shit that I was—I was glad it hurt."

"How so?"

Suddenly Parker gets cagey. "I thought you came here to ask about my grandfather."

Frank grins into her tea. "Sorry. I did. I just find your mother fascinating. And the ranch. Celadores. What your mother does, which I'm still not even sure what that is."

"I thought you were a skeptic," she teases again.

"I thought so too."

"Have you used the deck I gave you?"

"Can't say I have." Frank's not even sure where it is.

"Well, like I said, I'll be glad to finish the reading any time you want."

"I'd like that."

"Really? Let's do it right now."

Parker starts to get up, but Frank stops her before she can blur the line between the personal and professional even further. "I really am here on official police business." Setting her tea down, she continues, "Miss Parker, do you remember anything about the time your grandfather disappeared? I mean, anything you may have heard about that time?"

"Miss Parker," she laughs. "Please. Call me Cassie."

Frank nods.

Cassie only reiterates what little Frank already knows about him and when she asks how her grandmother died she confirms that, too.

"Why do you think no one ever looked into her cause of death?"

Cassie flips her hair over a shoulder. "What could they do? He wasn't even around to press charges on. And it could have been an accident. She might have fallen. It's one of those things no one'll ever know."

"Did your mother ever tell you that she went down to LA looking for him?"

"Yeah, she and Aunt Cass went on a drunken wild goose chase to find him."

Frank tries, "Did she ever tell you what they did when they found him?"

Cassie looks momentarily startled. "I don't think they ever did."

"Can you think who might have wanted to hurt him?"

"Apparently he was an ass when he drank." She adds remorsefully, "And that was the gift I got from him. It could have been any number of people he was at odds with."

Frank prods, "Can't think of any family grudges, arguments with the Mazettis, anything?"

She shakes her head.

"Has your mother ever mentioned anyone who might have had more than a spat with him?"

"Not that I can recall. Sorry."

"It's okay." Frank snaps her notebook shut. "It was a long shot."

She stands and Cassie walks her to the door. "So you like the ranch, huh?"

"Yeah, it's . . . it's enchanting."

Cassie laughs. "That's a good word for it."

Frank reaches to shake her hand but Cassie wags her head. "I see things when I touch people."

"Like your mom."

"Yeah."

Cassie opens the door for her. "When would you like me to finish your reading?"

Frank smiles. "I'll give you a call."

"You do that. You've got my number."

The sun is down behind the canyon and they stand in the purple dusk. Frank thinks to give Cassie her business card. "Call if you can think of anything. No matter how trivial it might seem."

Cassie studies the card. "I will."

Neither woman says anything and neither seems inclined to move.

"Alright," Frank breaks the stupor. "Thanks for your time."

"Sure. Don't forget to call."

"I won't," she says, walking to her car. Bending to unlock the door, she glances back.

Under the bower of dusky greenery, Cassie leans against the railing, her gaze steady on Frank. For an instant in the twilight she looks like a young Sal. Déjà vu overcomes Frank and she clings to the car; she has already been here, in the narrow, gravel drive, unlocking her car, glancing up at Cassie on the porch beneath ghostly pale blooms, the sun a shadow behind the hills.

Of its own accord her hand lifts to Sal's daughter. The gesture is returned, and this too has already been lived.

Chapter 24

For the next two weeks, Pintar is on vacation. Frank and Lewis run out of local leads, and it is late October before Frank can get back to Soledad. The tumbling, happy hills east of the highway are steeped the color of aged malt whiskey while the western mountains remain unchanged—an impenetrable, evergreen maze of cliff and canyon. Frank leans over the steering wheel to take in as much as she can of the craggy range, and is filled with a hunger, an almost erotic longing for them. She shakes her head at the incomprehensible desire and sits back, eyes on the road.

When she checks into her hotel, the young woman behind the counter greets, "Well, hi, welcome back."

"It's good to be back."

In her room she places a chair at the window, props her feet on the sill, and eats a sandwich in front of the darkening mountains. Content to share the evening with them, she doesn't bother with lights. After the sun is well and truly set, she brushes her teeth in darkness and slides into the crisp-sheeted bed. The window remains open.

First thing in the morning, she tracks down the leads Gomez gave her. Two of them are Domenic Saladino's pals from grade school, and as Gomez warned, neither is particularly interested in cooperating with the Five-Oh. Her third and last lead is the owner of Soledad's oldest bar. He is retired but likes to work the lunch shift. Frank hopes as she walks into the tiny, windowless bar that he will prove more fruitful than Saladino's friends.

Though it's barely noon, regulars in ball caps sit at the bar nursing beers. Behind them, four men walk around a pool table with barely enough space to line up their shots. The barkeep, as round as a cue ball and just as bald, gives Frank a cold eye.

His voice issues thick and phlegmy from beneath a silver handlebar mustache. "Whatcha want, hon?"

"Frankie Avila?"

"Yep."

She flashes her badge. "I need a couple minutes."

He doesn't move from his straight-armed stance against the bar. "License is on the wall."

"Nothing to do with your business. I'm Homicide, LAPD."

The drinkers all look up from their glasses and the men at the pool table lean on their sticks.

"Don't know nothin' bout any homicides."

"I know." She takes the next stool down from the drinkers. "But you do know about Domenic Saladino."

He grunts. "That's going back a ways."

"I hear he was a regular."

"Regular as that chair you're sitting on."

"Every night?"

Frank orders a Coke and softens Avila up with questions she already knows the answers to. The men next to her return to their conversation and the pool balls crack. She gets the barkeep telling stories.

He asks, "I figure you know our Chief of Police?"

"I've talked to him."

Avila chuckles. "He mention the night ol' Dom dressed him down, right about where you're sitting?"

"Larry Siler?"

The old man's chuckle turns into a deep cough. When it clears, he smoothes his mustache and launches into another tale.

"We used to be a lot more flexible with the drinking age back then. Hell, we knew these boys, where they came from. They weren't no trouble. Just liked to have a drink or two with the men now and then, made 'em feel growed up. We'd serve 'em as long as they had the cash and kept their cool. So ol' Larry and a couple of his pals are in here playing pool one night when in comes Dom, madder 'an a bull comin' outta the chute. He walks right up to Larry, taps him on the shoulder,

153

and decks the poor son of a bitch. No warning or nothing. Larry's laying there on the floor wondering what the hell just hit him and Dom tells him to stay away from his daughter. Ol' Larry's ear swole up about the size of a grapefruit and he—"

"Wait a minute. Which daughter?"

"The dead one. What was her name?"

"Cass."

"Yeah, okay. That one. Larry had the hard-on for her. Way I heard it, he proposed but she turned him down. Hell, prob—"

"Larry Siler proposed to Cass Saladino? Dom's daughter?"

"Yep. Made Dom madder 'an a pissed-on hornet. Told Larry to stay the hell away, that he had plans for her. Way I heard it, he wanted her to marry Pete Mazetti and get the ranch back."

"Did Larry stay away?"

"Far as I know. But I'll tell you something."

He leaned as close as his belly would allow.

"Tore him up when that one died. He'd just gotten his badge a couple months earlier, and he and ol' Huey were first on the scene. That was tough on Larry. Real tough."

She interrupts again. "First on what scene?"

"The accident. The one Dom's daughter died in. Him and Huey. What you call first responders nowadays. I can tell you he spent plenty a nights in here after that."

Avila shakes his head. "Tore him up."

Frank pays for the Coke she didn't drink and walks the couple of blocks to the police department. "Afternoon." She flashes her ID at the duty officer. "Chief in?"

"Uh, let me check. Hold on."

The cop comes back a minute later, the chief behind him.

"Lieutenant."

Neither extends a hand.

"I need a minute."

He tilts his head, indicating she should come back to his office. He shuts the door behind them. "I'm pretty busy."

"Understood. Why didn't you tell me you were first on the scene at Cass Saladino's accident?"

Siler walks behind his desk and sits. Frank settles into a hard chair. Pulling on his chins, Siler explains, "It's not something I like to talk about."

"Why is that?"

"She was a friend, for Christ's sake. A good friend. I went to school with Cass. I grew up with her. I was just a snot-nosed rookie when we got the call. It was my first fatality involving someone . . . I cared about. That's not an easy thing."

"No." Frank has had plenty of such fatalities. "It's not. But I need you to describe it for me."

"What in hell does the accident have to do with Domenic Saladino?"

"Something. Maybe nothing. I won't know for sure until I have all the facts. You know that."

"Well, I can't see how Cass dying had anything to do with her old man's disappearance."

"I can, but I might be wrong. How'd it happen?"

Siler gives her a hard look. "I told you. She was drunk."

"When you got the call, did you know it was her?"

His edge fades and Larry Siler looks like the old cop he is. Even from the remove of almost fifty years he saddens in the telling. "No, I did not. Donny Aliotti called from the pay phone at the gas station. Said he saw a truck out on 16, out in the wash by the Landons' place. My partner and I tore out there. I was excited as hell, thought it was probably some tourist on their way up to Carmel."

He strokes his chins.

"Boy, I can tell you, when we walked out that wash and I saw whose pickup it was, I didn't want to go anywhere near it. 'Course I had to. The cab was empty. We shined our lights around and just when I was thinking the girls must have just crashed and hitched home, we found her. She was thrown a good 150, 175 feet into some willow scrub. She was a mess. Still breathing, though. Couldn't be sure which girl it was until we found her purse. We called the ambulance, but she died before they could get to her. My partner was an old-timer name of Huey Caine. He insisted we be the ones to go up to the Mazettis and tell Sal. Boy, I'll tell you, that was a long drive. Only good thing was that the Mazettis

155

ended up breaking the news to her. I don't know that I could've done it."

She nods.

"Did she say anything before she died?"

"She never came to."

"Did Soledad help CHP with the investigation?"

"Wasn't anything to investigate. She was just a dumb kid all liquored up and driving too fast. That's all there was to it."

"So Soledad PD handled it alone?"

"No, 16 is CHP jurisdiction. They came and wrote it up. Nothing to it."

"They measured the skid marks, all that?"

Siler tugs under his jaw. "Weren't any that I recall. Drunk as she was, she just plain didn't see the curve."

Frank nods. "You loved her?"

"Look, I just said we—"

"You proposed to her."

"Who the hell told you that?"

"Apparently it wasn't a secret. And when Dom Saladino heard, he beat the crap out of you."

"Like I said, I was just a kid. I couldn't get near Cass, but I gave it a shot. Figured it might keep me from gettin' drafted."

"That's the only reason?"

"No." Siler sighs. "I loved her. Hell, half the boys in the Salinas valley did."

From the long reach of Siler's memory, she extracts the time frame of his proposal, Sal's refusal, and the beatdown he got from her old man. They all back up what Avila told her. "One more thing. You knew Saladino roughed his wife up from time to time."

Siler nods. "That was something we heard."

"So Saladino has a history of beating his wife, he takes off, and she dies a few days later. No one thought that was suspicious?"

"Hey, when all that was going on, I was just a snot-nosed, high-school kid worried about staying out of 'Nam. And besides, this was a small town with very conservative, independent roots. It wasn't as common as it is nowadays for the law to get involved in domestic matters. What a man did with his family back then was his own concern."

"Even if he killed her?"

"I'm sure if there was reasonable suspicion that he'd killed his wife the authorities would have investigated. One dead body's not enough, you've gotta resurrect another?"

"Not trying to resurrect anyone, just looking for motive for who'd want to whack him."

"So what have you got?"

Frank ticks names off on her fingertips. "The girls, for one. Pete Mazetti."

Siler grunts and shakes his head. She ignores him.

"And Mike Thompson. They were both crazy about the girls. And any of Mary Saladino's brothers. They all threatened to kill him."

"Says who?"

"Sal. Carly Simonetti."

"Ah." He flaps a meaty hand. "Doing and talking are two different things. Thank God. Else I'd be a hell of a lot busier than I already am."

Frank continues, "John Mazetti. I hear things were strained between them."

"Strained doesn't lead to homicide."

"You."

"Me?" Siler laughs. "You think I killed Old Man Saladino because he punched me in a bar?"

"I'm just telling you who has motive."

"Well, you keep looking, Lieutenant."

"Oh, I will."

Siler stands and opens the door.

"Anything else you've kept back?"

"You're the big city detective. You tell me."

She considers a minute. "You don't really give a shit who killed Saladino."

Siler sighs. "It's not that I don't give a shit, it's just that you're missing the mark. What happened is, he was probably drinking in

157

some dive after work, pissed off the wrong guy, and ended up dead. Saladino was a drunk and a pain in the ass. If you want motive, Christ, probably half this town had motive at one time or another, me included."

Frank nods. "Half the town, indeed. Appreciate your time."

Chapter 25

The day has been productive and Frank wants to get her thoughts down while they're still fresh. She takes a taco combo back to the hotel room and writes while trying not to get *carnitas* grease all over. When she has her ideas on paper, she gets up and watches college football for a minute. But even the classic UCLA/USC rivalry can't keep her attention. Frank wanders to the window, where the sun bleeds out behind the mountains. She stands in the last of the russet glow. The eastern flanks of the Lucias are already shrouded in darkness. In concealed dens and hollows, coyote and cougar stretch the day from their bones, ready to feed. The mountains gather the twilight close. Occasional lights hold the night back, but mostly canyon and ridge blend into a single stygian hue. Wind from the Pacific has threaded its way steadily through gap and pass to find its way to her window. It blows softly upon her cheek and as if it is a lover's kiss, Frank closes her eyes to receive it. The breeze caresses her overheated skin and she lifts her shirt to feel more, then steps back. She removes her clothes and stands with the smooth, rushing hands of the wind upon her—and she is in the dark on a bed of pine leaves under a blanket of stars. A sickle moon cleaves the branches overhead and washes her clean in its silvery light. She turns her head to see many figures stretched and sleeping near.

Beyond the window out on the freeway, a truck sounds its basso horn. Frank shivers and rubs her arms. She shuts the curtains and turns to her room, to the game playing silently on the television, the papers arranged on the shiny bedspread. Highway sounds seep through the curtain, tempting her to return to the window, but she picks up her clothes and folds them. Contemplating the mute football players, she lets the starlit ridge ebb from her system. When she has fully returned to the present, Frank takes a long, scalding shower. She dresses in an old T-shirt and sits propped against the bed pillows. Pulling binder and notepads close, like papery talismans, she concentrates on the murder of Domenic Saladino.

Some cases have no clues and must be raked, scraped, and gleaned for even one lead to start working with. Others, like Saladino's, have an abundance that need to be sorted and winnowed. Frank takes a legal pad and rips a page out for everyone with motivation to kill Domenic Saladino. It makes her smile to think how Lewis would scowl at her scattershot, old-school approach, and how the detective would brandish her laptop—again—to show Frank her meticulously organized collection of folders and notes. And Frank would shrug— again—and reply, *I don't care how it works as long as it works.* To which Lewis would whine—

Her cell phone vibrates across the polyester bedspread and Frank catches it. "Speak of the devil."

"You talkin' ill about me, LT?"

"Nah, just lookin' at my notes spread all over the bed."

"Aw, man, what I—"

"—gotta do to get me into the twenty-first century?" Frank finishes. "I know, I know. I'm hopeless."

Lewis makes a disgusted sound and Frank asks what she called for.

"What did you say the uncle's name was that used to fight with Saladino?"

"Hold on. Let me check."

Lewis seizes the opportunity to point out, "You know, if you went digital all you'd have to do is type the name in and blam."

"Amazing," Frank murmurs. "Oh, wow, look. Somehow I found it. Blam. Roderick Dusi."

"That's it. I had wrote down Broderick."

"Why you want to know?"

"Could be something, could be nothing. What else you heard about him?"

"Nothing beyond what Sal's told me. But that's not surprising.

Nobody up here volunteers a goddamned thing. It's almost like they all know who did it and nobody wants to say anything."

"That Saladino musta been a bad dude, so many people hatin' on him."

"Should I follow up on Roderick?"

"Nah, keep it on the down low for now. A'ight, LT. Gotta go."

Frank stares at the dead phone, then the legal pages all over her bed, the muted TV. Finally she gets up and parts the curtains. Across the highway, the black wall of mountain climbs into a charcoaled sky. Lights from scattered farms and ranches blink across its flanks in earthbound imitation of the stars. She drops to her knees, crossing her palms over her heart. An urge to speak wells within her, but she hasn't words. At length she whispers, "Goodnight," and closes the window.

She gathers the papers into a folder, turns the TV off, then her phone. Undressing completely, she slides between the cool sheets and pulls the blanket over her head. The darkness complete, she drifts toward sleep, imagining she is held in the warm, lightless belly of the mountains.

After a dreamless night, she wakes with a gnarly headache. Getting up and dressed, she assesses whether this is a garden-variety headache or one of the killers she occasionally gets. If she lets it go and it's a migraine, the pain will end only when she can lie in a still, dark place and sleep. But the gift of sleep is dear and always paid for in hazy visions of blood-red battles, both ancient and new. In some, she recognizes the combatants; in others, not—yet she wakes from each dream with a disturbing sense of familiarity.

Not wanting to take chances, Frank eats quickly at the restaurant next door and swallows a fistful of Advils. She waits over coffee for the pills to kick in and studies her to-do list. She still has Mary Saladino's nephew to talk to and a guy the bartender mentioned that used to work at the ranch. With the headache reduced to a single, dull point behind her right eye, she pays and heads out to start knocking. By late morning she has added nothing new to her notes and is eager to get to Celadores.

She drives slowly from town, past empty fields waiting dryly for winter, over frowsy blond hills that yield to gorse-speckled cliffs funneling into Celadores. She parks on the street near the old oak. A dented but clean Civic and a late-model Chevy pickup rest side by side under the tree. Two women wait on the sunny bench, and today one is Caucasian. Frank strolls around behind the store. Sal's pickup is under the lacy shade of the pepper trees and, without thinking, Frank rests a hand on the hood, noting the metal is at ambient temperature. The windows are down and the key dangles from the ignition. Frank shakes her head, clearly in a different world.

She hears footsteps and the back door of the store creaks open. Moments later, the Caucasian woman comes around but won't meet Frank's eye. She passes through the gate and the latch catches softly. The quiet returns. Frank squats on the running board, wishing she had one of Sal's cigarettes. She presses the heel of her hand into her eye to ease the last bit of headache. It does nothing to blunt the dull pain, but the summer sky is lovely, the breeze sweet, and she finds herself humming an unknown tune.

She hears the back steps, the familiar screech of the door, and moments later Sal's last visitor passes through to the courtyard. Frank waits in the pleasant shade, humming her strange tune and swatting at flies. When the back door creaks again, Frank gets up and paces, grinding a hand into her eye. The gate opens and she stops. Sal walks toward her, plastic bags dangling from each arm.

"You're back."

"Yep."

"What's wrong with your eye?"

"Just a headache."

Sal dumps the bags in the bed of the pickup, then faces Frank. She lifts a palm to Frank's head, but Frank steps away.

"Hold still," Sal scolds. She holds her hand about a foot in front of Frank's face.

"Do you get these a lot?"

"Pretty regularly."

Sal's brows scrunch.

"What?"

"It seems like spiritual pain. I don't usually get that from a headache. Can you feel that?"

Frank nods at the warm pressure emanating from Sal's hand.

"Close your eyes."

Frank feels silly but complies. The pressure becomes stronger. It's soothing and Frank relaxes into it, listening to the wind push through the pepper trees and down the valley.

The rough bark of an oak digs into the base of her spine. Bits of dirt and rock press into her legs crossed on the ground. She sways in front of a circle drawn in the dirt and sings a small song. Her hair is long and dark and swings in front of her face. A fly flits around her head. Behind her a lizard scrambles down the tree and crashes onto dry leaves. The sky is blue, the wind soft.

"Better?"

Frank opens her eyes, slightly surprised to see Sal in front of her. She touches fingers to her head. The pain has faded to a memory. "Yeah."

"Good." Sal drops her hand. "I assume you're coming up?"

"Yes," she answers instantly. "I'd like that."

Sal scrutinizes her with an intensity that almost makes Frank squirm. She kicks herself for having answered so quickly, for being so plainly eager. Sal seems to arrive at a decision. "Let's go," she says.

Frank walks casually to the Honda, determined not to follow Sal like a piddling puppy. Past the gate she parks at the turnout and gets into the pickup with cool nonchalance. But her heart thumps and her cheeks are flushed. She can't explain her excitement nor the thrumming undercurrent in her blood as the truck bounces up the road.

Frank shouts over the engine, "Does this thing have shocks?"

"Used to."

The last time Frank was in the truck, she was so overwhelmed by the ranch she hadn't noticed the cracked dashboard or rust-rimmed windows.

"What year is it?"

Sal frowns. "You know I honestly can't remember. It's early 60s. Pete would know."

"She's been around."

"Pete's a great mechanic. He's kept her running all these years."

"This isn't . . . is this the truck your sister was driving?"

"Yeah. The front end was stove in, but the engine survived relatively intact."

"And Pete fixed it?"

She cocks her head. "I think he took it to a body shop for the front end, but I know he took care of the mechanical repairs."

"Was that hard, driving it later?"

"No. This old gal always makes me feel closer to Cass. Like I still have the best of her. She loved driving. Any excuse to go into town."

Deciding Sal is a captive audience, Frank asks the hard questions before she can get sidetracked by horses, storms, or snakes under her chair. "Something else I'm curious about. Was Larry Siler at your mother's funeral?"

"What?"

"Larry Siler," Frank shouts, repeating her question.

"Larry? I don't know."

"How'd he feel about Cass?"

"He was in love with her—just like every other boy in Soledad."

"What came of that?"

"Nothing."

"How come?"

Sal hefts a shoulder.

"Did your father have anything to do with it?"

"My father discouraged a lot of young men."

"How'd Cass take that?"

"She'd make a fuss about it, but for the most part she was indifferent. Cass didn't usually keep boyfriends as long as they wanted to be kept."

"Was she ever serious about anyone?"

"She was fond of Pete. She knew it was inevitable they'd marry, but until then she was determined to sow every one of her wild oats."

"How'd your dad feel about that?"

"It drove him crazy." Sal smiles. "That was half the reason she did it."

"Did they not get along?"

"No, I told you, they got on famously."

"How'd Pete feel about her going out with other guys?"

"He was stoic, but I think it bothered him."

"Who was she dating when she died?"

"She was with Pete then."

"No one else?"

Sal shakes her head. The silver plait slithers across her back. At the next gate, Frank gets out to open and close it. Reclaiming the sprung seat, she says, "I talked to your daughter."

"I heard."

"She looks like you."

Sal shakes her head. "She's much prettier."

"Younger maybe, but not *much* prettier." That earns Frank a slight smile, and she is ridiculously pleased. "She tell you we knew each other?"

"She mentioned it."

Straddling a deep rut, Sal says, "Where does your daughter live?"

"In Louisiana, with her father and his people."

"That's so far away."

"It is, but it's okay. It's good she's with all of them."

She mentions talking to Frankie Avila at the bar, and asks, "Is he one of the people your father owed money to?"

"He owed Frankie more than anyone."

"How come?"

"Gambling debts. He and Frankie bet on everything—who would walk in the bar next, who'd win the rodeo events, the Giants, 49ers. You name it, they bet on it."

"Big bets?"

"Big enough when he lost and couldn't pay."

"Did that happen a lot?"

"Fairly regularly."

Frank studies the rise to the ranch house, wondering why Avila hadn't mentioned that. Sal parks at the corral. Frank is glad to see there aren't any horses in it. Sal goes into the barn and Frank stretches in the mild sunshine, waiting to hear the four-wheeler start. But Sal comes out with halters and a feed bag.

"Come on." She motions around the corner. "We've got to catch our rides."

Frank groans. She trails Sal behind the barn, where four horses come trotting at a shake of the bag. She stands well away and lets Sal cut Dune and Buttons from the herd. The other horses crowd around, hoping for a shot at the feed bag, but Sal hands it to Frank.

"You know the drill. And get a hoof pick, too, it'll be with the brushes."

"I'm *not* picking anybody's hooves," Frank says, pleased again to see Sal's smile.

Frank grooms while Sal digs dirt from the horses hooves. They work silently until Frank thinks to ask, "How come you don't use the quad anymore?"

"It can't take us where we're going."

"And where's that?"

"You'll see."

"Up there?"

Frank points to the western ridges. Sal nods. "All the way up there? On a horse?"

Sal stops picking to stare at her. "I thought you wanted to go."

"I do. I just—"

"Don't worry. We'll take a shortcut. It's not as far as it looks."

Sal returns to the horses hooves and Frank steals a glance at the recondite mountains. Her heart knocks into her ribs. The ride up seems far and steep, but that's not what daunts her. She looks again at the toothy peaks and this time she is certain. The mountains are looking back.

Chapter 26

After a brief stop at the cabin to put away Sal's food and get the dogs, they ride across the sloping fields to the edge of the mountains. Leaving the soft foothills behind, they enter a vertical landscape of scarp and gorge. They ride single file, and talk is difficult without raising their voices. Sal digs into a saddlebag and bends back to hand her an apple and link of chorizo. Frank stretches nervously over Buttons' head to take them. She doesn't realize how hungry she is until she gnaws a hunk of the cold sausage and chases it with a sweet bite of apple. When Sal leans over Dune's neck to feed him her core, Frank warily does the same for Buttons. She wipes grease and horse slobber on her jeans, grinning at her equestrian proficiency.

The horses labor and the dogs plod single file behind them. Sal gets off to scoop up Kook, and Frank takes advantage of the break to stand in the stirrups and stretch out her kinks. They continue. The trail narrows to a flinty path on the cliff edge, barely wider than the horses. Stubborn shrubs grab Frank's right leg. Her left dangles over a sheer drop. Careful not to look down, she fights the urge to wheel for the relative safety of the ranch. But even if she gives in to her panic, there's no room to turn around. She imagines Buttons spooking and rearing, her back legs sliding over the crumbly ledge, scrabbling for purchase and not getting it; imagines the plunge from the mountain, how long it would take to hit the canyon bottom, all the time she'd have to think about dying.

Frank is dangerously near panic. Afraid Buttons will catch her fear, she forces herself to concentrate on Dune's tail swishing in front of her. She reasons Sal wouldn't have come this way if it wasn't safe—after all, she is ahead of Frank. Then it dawns on her Sal might still want to kill her. Shooting her instead of the rattlesnake was a good plan—but, by Christ, this is an even better one. It would be a tragic horseback accident that no one would question. They'd never find her body. Her broken bones would litter the far, far canyon below, and coyotes would feast on them, undisturbed.

"Here we go." Sal is angling Dune through a pass in the cliff. He leaps onto a boulder and Sal calls, "Hang on."

"Aw, Jesus." Frank wraps the reins in her fist, clutches the saddle horn, and without any prompting Buttons lunges. Somehow, miraculously, Frank hangs on. The horses squeeze through the gap out onto a small, grassy *portrero*. Sal stops and sips from a battered canteen. She passes it to Frank. Frank shakes her head, not sure if she could keep the water down.

"Can we get off for a sec?"

"We're almost there." Sal points to a lonely stand of pines on the ridge. "It's just a couple minutes." She looks Frank over.

"Then let's go," Frank says through clamped teeth. She kicks Buttons past Dune. He catches up and the horses trot side by side across the wheat-colored meadow. "Do we have to go back that way?"

"I'm afraid so."

"What happens if the horses slip?"

"They won't. They don't want to fall any more than you do."

Frank persists, "What if there's a rattlesnake on the trail? Or a mountain lion? Or whatever it is that scares a horse?"

"You control her. Don't panic and don't let her panic." She trains a judicious eye on Frank. "You spooked yourself, didn't you? It's easy enough to do. But Buttons is a good horse. She's been on this trail so many times she could do it blindfolded. This would be a lot easier if you'd just relax and trust her."

"Easy for you to say. You ride like you're part of the horse."

"Do you think I'd bring you here if I thought you'd get hurt?"

"I don't know." She brings Buttons to a quick stop. "Would you?" Sal stops beside her. "No. I wouldn't."

The horses shift their weight while the women hold each other's gaze. For no discernible reason, Frank believes Sal. The belief springs purely from instinct, from that whispery knowing of the blood and bone.

Frank nudges Buttons ahead. The *portrero* rises gently into a dappled forest of east-leaning pines. The horses step without sound onto a carpet of brown needles. Sal stops and drops from her mount. The dogs sit and pant, glad for the rest. Sal loops her reins around a branch and looks expectantly at Frank.

"Am I supposed to get off?"

Sal nods. "Do you need help?"

Her legs feel like wood blocks glued to the saddle and she grumbles, "A ladder would be nice."

Sal moves toward her, but Frank waves her off. Squelching a very natural fear of being neither on nor off an unpredictable quarter-ton beast, she loosens her right foot from the stirrup. With a deep breath she swings an aching leg over Button's rump and kicks her. The horse knickers but doesn't move. Frank starts to slide off, realizing too late that her left foot is still in the stirrup. She lands awkwardly, holding to the saddle and praying Buttons won't move as she works her foot free.

Sal chuckles. "Give her a good scratch under her cinch or saddle. That way, she'll start to expect something good when you get off."

Stifling a groan at the ache in her ass, Frank scratches the big horse with genuine appreciation. Sal feeds them each an apple. Frank starts to loop the reins around a pine, but Sal points to the dead tree in front of Dune. "Tie her there. You don't want to get sap on the reins."

She offers Frank the canteen. The water is warm and metallic, but Frank drinks greedily. She notices Sal takes a sip only before stashing the canteen back into a saddle bag. The dogs get nothing, nor do they seem to expect it. She looks around while Sal rolls a cigarette.

They are on the ridge, but not quite at the top. A wall of gray granite rising over the pines deepens the shade of the hurst. As if from memory, it comes to Frank that this is a good and safe encampment; no one is likely to approach from the narrow ridge above, nor from the steep slopes below. There is only the *portrero* to be watched. She frowns, wondering how she knows that. Sal offers the cigarette. Frank shakes her head. Wind sifts through the boughs, bringing the scent of sun-warmed pine and tobacco. And something else. Frank lifts her nose to the air. It smells faintly of the sea.

169

Sal toes a hole through the needles. She takes one more drag and spits on the cigarette. It goes out with a hiss and she pinches off the wet end and puts the butt in her pocket. She walks past and in the dim light of the copse she seems like an ethereal conjuring. Frank wants to touch her, to make sure she is real, but Sal is already disappearing through the trees. The wind brushes Frank's arm. She jumps and trots stiffly to catch up. Ahead of her, Sal boosts Cicero up onto a ledge, and after lifting Kook onto the boulder she looks back at Frank. Bone stands beside Frank and Sal tells her before clambering onto the boulder, "You'll have to help him up."

Frank looks at the head-high rock, then at Bone. "Not gonna bite me, are ya?"

He looks up at her, wagging his stump. Frank pats the rock like she saw Sal do, and Bone stands against it. She shoves him up and over the ledge, then pulls herself up using cracks and footholds. Boulders clog the way, but none Bone can't maneuver himself. He hops over the bare granite and she follows, emerging into a shallow bowl at the top of the ridge. A solitary bush grows on one side and the dogs sprawl in its sparse shade. Sal scrambles onto the far lip of the bowl and holds a hand to Frank. She takes it. It is rough and brown and dry and Frank has the crazy notion that Sal is more of the land than of human origin.

"Whoa." Frank is on the dizzying verge of the mountain. It falls away below her, down hundreds of feet through brush and boulder, gradually fanning into jagged folds of ridge and canyon. She backs from the edge. Cicero leaps onto the granite bench and stands proudly, chest puffed like he's posing for a hunting magazine.

Sal sits on the edge of the world, legs dangling. She pats the flat rock. "Come sit."

"I'm good right here."

Sal fishes the half-smoked butt from her pocket and lights it. She takes a drag and holds it out. The cigarette is tempting. Frank is reminded again that with one quick shove Sal could disappear her so that even the coyotes and crows couldn't find her. Still she steps forward. She sits cross-legged, a couple feet from the edge, and takes the cigarette. The smoke is cool and tastes sweetly of mint. She takes a second drag before passing it back. "I'm really not much of a smoker—a pack'll last me a year—but this is good stuff."

Sal nods. "It's my julep blend."

"You make your own tobacco?"

"Yes. It's easy. It grows wild near the ranch house."

"You have everything you need here, don't you?"

"Pretty much."

The wind races up the flank of the mountain face, carrying the scent of salt and rainless brush. It kisses Frank's head and ruffles her hair. She shades the westerly sun from her eyes and points. "That purple on the horizon, is that the ocean?"

"Yes."

Impelled by the endless vista, she scoots closer to the edge. "It's so wild here."

Sal nods, mashing out the cigarette. "Down there it's too foggy and up here it's too dry. The Lucias are just miserable enough to keep most people out."

"But not you."

Sal cocks her head at Frank, and it's hard to tell where her eyes leave off and the sky begins.

"This place is wild until you get to know it. Then you can never leave."

Cicero settles behind them with a sigh. The breeze sifts through a small pine above the bowl. Frank squints at the smudge of sea and far canyons crowded with redwood and fir, the sere, wind-burned peaks dotted with only the hardiest shrubs.

Sal nudges and points. "Look. A condor. Two of them!"

A pair of plank-winged birds skim into view below them. Frank's head swims with déjà vu. She places her palms on the rock to steady herself. Sal is saying she has seen them only once before. "When I was young. Before they had tags and radio wires."

The big birds glide north and disappear.

"Do you know why the vulture family is bald?"

"What?"

"They don't have feathers on their heads. Do you know why?"

"Uh, to keep their heads clean because they stick 'em in dead things?"

171

"Nope. It's because a long time ago the sun started falling to earth. It was getting so close that it was burning the people that lived here and they cried for someone to carry the sun back up into the sky."

Frank relaxes back on her elbows, taking some of the pressure off her aching ass.

"Fox jumped up and grabbed the sun, but it was too hot and he dropped it. That's why he has a black mouth to this day. Raven said, 'Give it to me' and started to fly off with it, but the sun charred all his feathers and he finally dropped it. After a while Vulture said, 'I'll give it a try,' and she picked up the sun and off she went, straight up into the sky. Higher and higher she flew. Her feathers started burning, but Vulture kept flying up and up.

"Her feet caught fire, and all the feathers burnt off. But Vulture held onto the sun. The feathers on her head burst into flames and turned her skin red. But Vulture held on to the sun. She flew higher and higher, until she was just a speck in the sky, and when she couldn't go any farther Vulture finally let go off the sun, But she'd flown so far and so high the sun stayed right where she dropped it. Poor Vulture. She was so badly burned that her head feathers never did grow back. And she is still so exhausted from that long-ago trip that she has to glide wherever she goes instead of fly."

Frank claps and Sal smiles.

"I haven't told that story in years. It was Cassie's favorite. She'd make me tell it over and over."

Frank remembers, "She said to get you to tell me about the *zopilotes*."

"She said that?"

"Uh-huh. Said you were a great storyteller."

Sal hugs her knees and looks toward the ocean. Clearing her throat, she starts. "I told you the Santa Lucias aren't hospitable to most people, but long before there were roads and cars along the coast, there were always a few intrepid souls called to scratch out a living between the mountains and the sea. They were hardy folks, as tough as the land. For the most part they lived in shacks at the foot of the mountains, on bluffs above the ocean just wide enough to grow beans and corn on and keep a few chickens, maybe even a cow."

172

Frank lies back and closes her eyes, the sun a benediction upon her face.

"They worked hard on their little plots of land, scratching out a meager living between the storms that battered the coast in winter and the fog that shrouded it in summer. They had simple wants and means, but a couple times a year they would saddle up their horse, if they were lucky enough to have one, and make the journey to one of the few towns along the coast. If they didn't have a horse—well, then they walked. There was no smooth paved highway back then, just a muddy or dusty horse trail, depending on the season, that hugged the edge of the sea. It was no path to be traveling in the dark or a storm.

"But one day a man did just that. He'd been in town to get the flour, salt, and a bolt of cloth his wife had asked for. He'd purchased all his supplies and still had a little money left over, so he thought it couldn't hurt to have a whiskey at the bar before the long ride home. Well, the one drink turned into two, and then three, and when he was finally out of money the man toddled out of the bar and started climbing onto his horse.

"It so happened that a scoundrel who'd been watching the man lay his coins on the bar followed quietly behind. Just as the man tried pulling himself up into the saddle, the scoundrel grabbed his reins, pulled a knife, and demanded the man empty his pockets lest his throat part sides.

"Now, a man who lives alone with the Santa Lucias at his back and the Pacific Ocean at his feet is hardly going to be intimidated by a rascal with a knife. So, pretending to empty his pockets, the man reached into his coat and in a flash of gleaming steel he slit the scoundrel from navel to chin, and off he galloped into the falling night. Though home was a hard half-day ride, the man didn't slow. He whipped his horse, following the trail by a sliver of moonlight. He rode and rode, and as he rode the fog crept in. It gathered off the ocean and crawled toward land, keeping time with the horse and rider until at last it pulled ahead to lay as thick and heavy over them as a brand-new blanket.

"The man slowed his horse to a trot, then a walk, until the horse balked and would move no more. Certain he could hear the pounding of hooves behind, the man kicked his horse and whipped him on. The horse took one faltering step, then another. The man gouged his spurs into the horse's belly, urging him on, and the horse complied. Too late the man realized his mount was slipping. The horse tried to scrabble back to solid ground, but all its hooves could find were air. With a horrible screaming, beast and rider fell onto the broken, wave-swept rocks. The horse ceased its struggle, but the man was alive and in great pain. He tried to stand, but his legs twisted under him and he knew, in the darkness and wet salt air, that he would rise no more."

Sal stops to pull out her pouch and roll a smoke. After it is lit, she continues.

"Throughout the night, the dawn, and the next night, the man lay on the rocks in his terrible pain and screamed, but even if someone had been passing by the edge of the cliff, he was too far down and the ocean too loud for them to hear his cries. Yet cry he did. He howled piteously in his pain and thirst. On the second sunset, the man began to lick the salt spray on the rocks. He knew it would hasten his end, and the wet saltiness did little to slake his thirst, but he had to speak once more before his black and swelling tongue forever filled his mouth.

"So with his last breath he cried out to his animal gods, begging forgiveness for killing the scoundrel who had tried to steal his horse and hard-earned goods. He begged for mercy—not for himself but for his wife and children back home, that the gods might keep them well and free from harm despite his sins. And the man fell back upon his broken legs and as he looked up into the clouded sky he saw a patient line of *zopilotes* gathered upon the cliff above, and as he watched, a lone vulture took flight from the cliff and flew south, toward his wife and small children, toward his humble cabin in a sheltering arm of the mountains. The man closed his eyes and flew with the *zopilote*."

"Legend has it that upon the next storm the man's wife gave shelter to a doctor traveling between the lonely coast towns. The doctor was so impressed by her kindness and apparent plight that he left the woman with his horse and a bag of gold, promising to return in the spring with more. And for many years after, the doctor was true to his word, visiting every spring and every fall with gifts for the woman and her grown children. When the doctor at last died, his journals went to a local museum, and there the curious notation was discovered that upon each of his visits to the woman's cabin, the doctor was unfailingly accompanied by a single *zopilote* following lazily overhead.

"To this day the abuelas swear that spirit vultures circle the Santa Lucias searching for lost souls, and that if you are ever in trouble you can call on *zopilote* and he will come to your aid."

Frank claps again and sits up. "Your daughter's right. You *are* a good storyteller." Then she asks, "Have you ever called on *zopilote*?"

Sal only smiles and drags on her cigarette. Frank admires the sprawling vista, swats at a persistent gnat.

"Do you know what *jhator* is?"

Frank shakes her head. The gnat buzzes away.

"It's the Tibetan practice of burying the dead. It literally means 'giving alms to the birds.' The Tibetans dismember their dead and leave the bodies out for the vultures to feast on. I think it's a beautiful concept. I'd love to be returned to the world like that, when it's time. Right here. Wouldn't that be lovely?"

Frank doesn't find the idea particularly "lovely" but can see the symmetry for Sal, who seems such a part of the landscape.

Sal stands. "We should get back."

Cicero and Kook stretch and follow her down the rocks, but Bone watches from his strip of shade. "I'm with you," Frank confides. "I've got to get on that goddamned horse again."

Frank regrets cursing Buttons, who has been nothing but patient with her. Sore from the waist down, she grunts and limps toward the ladder of boulders. She turns for a last look at the ocean. It's still there. It will be there, along with the rolling peaks and canyons and blue, blue sky long after she is gone. Frank turns and steps into the cleft. With a grunt and gimp to match, Bone climbs down after her.

Chapter 27

As if Sal has used all her words back at the pass, they don't speak until they are in the corral, and then it is only to murmur praise to the horses. After they are brushed and turned loose behind the barn, Sal and Frank walk to the truck. The dogs are passed out in its shade, and it occurs to Frank she has barely asked any questions about the investigation. Sal kneels and checks Cicero's feet for foxtails. Without looking at Frank, she says, "You're welcome to spend the night, if you want."

"Really?"

Sal nods. The shadows of the barn drape round her like a mantilla and Frank glances around to see that the western half of the ranch is already twilit. Figuring Sal isn't as much generous as she is tired and reluctant to drive Frank to her car, she kicks herself for having fallen once again under the ranch's spell. She has no intention of spending the night again. The freak storm last time made the overnight stay somewhat plausible, but this time it would be impossible to justify. She searches for a reason to stay and is unable to find one, other than she wants very badly to be part of the coming dusk, to see how it steals over the rest of the ranch and creeps up on the cabin and across the yard into the trees until all the land is washed in gray and the last traces of color are swallowed by velvet night.

"I really should go."

Sal stands and wipes her hands on her jeans. Neither woman moves toward the truck.

"Why did you come all the way up here?"

Frank shrugs, glances helplessly around her. "I have to ask you more questions."

"You haven't asked any."

"I know."

"Then you may as well at least come up for dinner."

Sal stalks behind the barn. A moment later she drives the quad around and parks by the truck. She drops the short tailgate and the dogs rise slowly, leaping one by one into the small bed. Frank glances into the cab of the truck. The keys hang in the ignition. She should drive herself to town. She's pretty sure she knows the way. Just hop in and tell Sal she'll leave the truck at the gate.

That'd be the right thing to do. Just leave.

Sal sits behind the wheel of the idling quad and Bone stands in back. Both stare at her. The mountains' shadows grope for the eastern edges of the ranch. Frank looks there, toward Soledad and the highway. Soon it will be dark and she will be shut in her hotel room, studying the star-sprinkled mountains from behind the curtains.

Swearing, but hiding a smile, she jogs to the quad and hangs on as it lurches up the meadow. They get closer to the creek and the sycamores grow in the dimming light, yet their bulk seems incorporeal. Frank lifts her nose to the air. She can smell their greenness, their sap-running life, and the smile that has been threatening busts loose. Sal stops just shy of the tree line. The dogs jump out and run across the bridge. Frank follows her hostess, pausing to peer into the unfathomable water. A bird calls plaintively. She can't see it in the graying leaves but knows the bird is seeking a roost out of the wind, safe from nocturnal hunters. If it picks a poor site or is forced to flee in the unnavigable darkness, it may well not live through the night. Frank leaves the sinuous bower, unsure where she has learned that.

Sal is in the cabin getting the dogs' food ready and tells Frank, "It's a little chilly. Do you know how to build a fire?"

"I do."

Sal appears doubtful, but asks her to start one in the fire pit while she heats their dinner.

"Where's the wood?"

Sal points to a neat stack between the sheds.

"Are there snakes in there?"

"Possibly. Take the pieces on top."

177

Frank calls Bone to her, but he is fixated on his bowl.

"Traitor," she says.

The yard is shadowy. Frank crosses it slowly, searching for snakes. She gingerly gathers an armload of wood and totes it to the fire pit, relieved the dogs have finished eating and are prowling the yard. Frank arranges the kindling, then pokes her head into the cabin. Whatever Sal is cooking smells good. The dogs must think so too, for they push past and arrange themselves in a semi-circle around the kitchen. Watching the homey scene, Frank is overcome by another déjà vu. She clings to the doorjamb until the sensation passes.

Sal asks, "Are you alright?"

"Yeah. Matches?"

Sal tosses a box. Frank lights the fire just as the sun falls into the hungry ridge tops and is swallowed whole. The frisson Frank feels isn't just from the fading heat. The dogs burst through the door again, but this time she doesn't flinch. Sal sets down a plate of fresh tortillas and heavy bowls of chili verde. They sit near the fire, tucking silently into the spicy stew. The dogs lay at their feet waiting for spills.

Swabbing her bowl with a tortilla, Frank casually asks, "You ever have déjà vu?"

"Sure," Sal answers around her spoon.

"What do you think it is?"

"I couldn't say. Maybe a thinning between worlds. A place where the edges of time overlap and bleed through."

"Parallel universe kinda thing?"

"Maybe. Have you ever heard of universal wavefunction or Everett's many-worlds interpretation?"

"*What?*"

Sal smiles. "They're quantum mechanics theories. Remind me before you go, I've got some books you might like."

"That's funny, my daughter's father just suggested I read some physics." She chews thoughtfully on the last of her tortilla. "You remind me of his ex-wife."

Sal wrinkles a brow and sets her empty bowl on the hearth. "Why?"

"She's a physicist at UCLA but also a voodoo priestess. You

know about physics and are obviously an intelligent woman, yet you're a . . . *curandera*. I don't get how either of you reconcile intelligence and blind faith."

"It's not blind at all, we see just fine. But because you can't see what we do, you think it doesn't exist." Sal pulls out the tobacco pouch. "Besides, physics and faith are just different routes to the same source."

"What source is that?"

Sal shrugs. "God. The unknown."

Frank thinks about that as she watches stars blink on in the purpling sky. The sycamore leaves stir as if to watch too. The fire dances and from the creek little frogs sing down the darkness. Bone sighs at her feet and eases into contented sleep. Frank's fingers drop to his flank. "You get to see this every night."

"No." Sal shakes her head. "Every night is different. The sun falls a half-second sooner or later. The wind blows cooler or warmer or not at all. The animals change their songs according to the season. Even the grass is different. Stems bent under the weight of the stars last night were eaten or trampled today. Somewhere there are new eyes seeing the night for the very first time, and somewhere another pair of eyes have closed forever. Every night is different. Brand-new. I'd hate to miss a single one."

Frank digs her fingers into Bone's coarse fur as she understands that this night is subtly altered from the night that preceded it, and the night to come, by her very presence. It will be different by that slight degree and that difference is her home in the world, her place among the stars and sun and earth and sea. Frank flattens her palm to Bone's warmth. He lifts his head wonderingly, then drops it back to the dirt. He grunts and squirms his hip into her hand and she wonders if he wants reassurance as much as she does. She wants to talk to Sal, to hear words, but the enchantment of the gloaming is greater than her need for comfort. She remains silent and the night continues its wizardry.

Sal breaks the spell by holding out a cigarette. Frank takes it. Remembering why she is here, she sets reluctantly to work. "Why did you wait so long to file a missing persons report?"

Sal exhales a fragrant plume. "My father wasn't exactly in anyone's good graces. We felt we'd done enough by leaving him messages that his wife was dead. When he didn't show up or call after that, I don't know what we thought. I guess, that he'd show up eventually. It wasn't unusual for him to go off on a bender, so at first we didn't think much about his absence; it was just my father being a drunk. Believe me, that wasn't odd."

"What about weeks, or months later? Did his benders usually last that long?"

She admits they didn't.

"Wasn't anybody the least worried then?"

"We were, but I think we all assumed he'd still turn up. You have to remember that he'd fought with my mother before he left. She said she fell into the table—but he knew, and we knew, that she didn't. We thought he might have been afraid to come home, and rightly so."

"Why? What would have happened to him?"

"He'd have had to face a lot of hurt and angry people. In light of that, you couldn't blame him for staying away."

"Did he ever say anything to his uncle about his plans, where he was going?"

"Not that I'm aware of."

"The uncle never thought it odd that he just disappeared?"

"I can't remember. I know we spoke at the funeral, but I talked to so many people that day."

"When was the last time you saw him?"

"His uncle?"

Frank nods.

"It must have been my Uncle Carl's funeral. He was still alive then, but very old. I'm sure that was his last trip here."

"And that was . . . ?"

"I couldn't say. I'm awful with dates. They don't mean much living out here. Sometime in the 80s. My daughter would know."

"Did he ever offer any ideas about where your father might have gone?"

"The whole family kicked ideas around, but there was never a way to prove anything. And that's when Aunt Ellen filed a missing persons report, when Carl died. She was the executor of his estate. She wanted to settle it, and to do that she had my father declared legally dead."

"How large was the estate?"

"Not enough to kill someone over, if that's what you're thinking."

"How much?"

"I think it was around $20,000, divided between her and my father. Hardly a fortune."

"Didn't Carl have a wife, or kids?"

"He married, but it ended badly. They never had children and he never remarried."

"So your aunt got all of it?"

"Uh-huh."

Sal's right—twenty grand is hardly worth killing someone over. Nonetheless, she'll have Lewis look into it.

"Did he leave you any money?"

"Oh, sure, plenty. Let's see, the money he owed at Pasquales'. At Ven a Mexico. A tab at the 101. The hardware store. And don't forget the hospital."

"If he was so broke, why'd everyone let him keep tabs?"

"He was always good for them. When he got paid, he'd settle up, then start a new one."

"You didn't have much money growing up?"

"We didn't. But we got by."

Frank nods, commiserating more than Sal knows. "How'd you feel about your aunt having him declared dead?"

"I didn't care one way or the other. It made sense by then."

"You must have been pretty angry to be so ambivalent."

Sal shrugs. "Maybe. It was a long time ago."

A bat swoops and glides at the edge of the clearing where fire and night meet. Frank would rather focus on the tiny aerialist but dutifully asks if her father always stayed with his uncle.

"Usually, but sometimes his cousins took him in if his uncle kicked him out."

"Why would he do that?"

"Because he'd get drunk and mean. His wife wasn't very patient with that in her house."

181

Frank retrieves a notebook from her back pocket. It is bent and damp. The little pencil stuck in the binding is snapped in two. She turns the book so that it catches the light and scribbles the names of cousins and spouses. When she looks up, the eastern sky is glowing over the outline of trees.

"What's that light?"

Sal looks where she points. "The moon, silly."

The sky continues to brighten, such that it seems dawn must be coming. As they watch, a full white moon creeps over the backs of the trees. It rises imperceptibly yet soon clears its leafy moorings and drifts into the sky.

"I don't know that I've ever seen the moon come up."

"Never?"

"I must have. I guess it just looks different in the city, like a Hollywood prop."

Placing another log on the fire, Sal says, "I take it you're spending the night."

"I should really get back."

That is Frank's cue to get up and leave, but she stays in the comfortable Adirondack chair. A pair of bats dive and twirl in the swaying light. The moon sails farther into the night and Cicero wags his tail, deep in a dream.

"I'd like to stay."

Sal nods. "Inside or out?"

"What?"

"You can sleep inside if you want, but I sleep out here."

Frank looks around. "Where?"

Sal pats the dirt with her bare foot. "Right here."

"On the *ground*?"

"Uh-huh."

"Why?"

"I don't like sleeping inside. I won't go in until the weather forces me. Try it. I'll lay down some sheepskins for you. It's cozy as can be."

"Sounds hard as can be."

Sal stands over her. "Your choice. What'll it be?"

"What about snakes?"

"I've been sleeping outdoors all my life and have yet to wake up with one."

"What about that one under my chair last time? It must have relatives somewhere."

"Tell you what," Sal says walking to the cabin, "I'll lay out a bed and you can try it. If you don't like it, you can go inside."

Frank asks Bone, "You wouldn't let a snake get me, would you?" She can make out his black stub wiggling. "Is that a yes or a no?"

The screen door bangs. Sal strides into the circle of light with an armful of woolly skins. She drops two by Frank's chair and two by her own. A second trip to the cabin produces a pair of sleeping bags. She arranges the thick sheepskins end to end, unrolls a bag over them, and pats the pile. "Lie down."

Frank casts a dubious eye but oozes from her chair onto the makeshift bed. It is surprisingly well-cushioned and she stretches along its length.

"How's it feel?"

"Not bad."

"I'll get you a pillow."

Frank lies back under the impartial night. Bone edges onto the fleece, and she wonders what in hell she is doing. Enthralled by the land and all its enticements, she's abandoned all perspective and persistently overlooks the possibility that Sal may be implicated in, or actually responsible for, Domenic Saladino's murder. Instead of conducting a professional homicide investigation, she's acting like a kid invited to her big sister's slumber party. Worse, she doesn't seem inclined to stop herself.

Bone sighs and snuggles closer. Frank pets him, vowing to turn in her retirement papers as soon as she gets back. The wind waltzes with the fire, the stars keep time, and the creek sings from its long and wandering bed. Frank is asleep before Sal can bring the pillow.

Chapter 28

She wakes twice in the night. The first time she is afraid, but Bone presses against her and she goes back to sleep. The second time, she lies staring at the sky. She finds Orion's star-studded belt, saddened that she knows only one of the hundreds of constellations above. Hands pillowed beneath her head, she studies the stars, wondering what else she hasn't bothered to learn. And if it's too late.

Dawn begins as a grayness less than night. The sky becomes an orange smear over the black outline of land, then a translucent, eggshell blue. Plants take form in the dark light, all the same shade of muddy brown. As orange and blue fade to the white of an aged eye, the greenery grows distinct; olive and yellow leaves appear, tipped with sepia and red. Farther away, oak and chaparral and pine assume their blue-green mantle. Remnant patches of night cling to their feet.

Sal is awake, watching too, and Frank asks, "Is it always this beautiful?"

"Always."

"But different. Every morning."

"Yes."

Quail cluck down the hill. Bone stands and spreads his forelegs flat to the ground. His butt wiggles in the air. He comes to Frank and she lets him greet her with a lick to her check. Dragging an arm from her sleeping bag, she scratches his chest. "Good job keeping the snakes away."

Pressure squeezes Frank's chest. She wonders if it's a heart attack, then realizes she is just happy. Ridiculously, rarely happy. Yet close on the heels of her joy comes sorrow. Dawn's palette, Bone's affection, the cool silhouette of mountains—they are gifts she can't keep. Borrowed presents she has no more claim to than a street urchin looking in the window of a warm, well-lit home.

Sal slides from her bag, prompting the dogs into a tail-wagging dance. All four of them stretch and shake the night from their bones. Frank recognizes it as their morning ritual and rolls toward the mountains, feeling very much the outsider. Hunkering deeper into her bag, she studies the sharp-planed faces etched beyond the barn. Strands of mist filigree the canyons and hollows like strands of hair. Frank wants to tuck the gray strands neatly back behind ridge and knob. She wonders if there is an inch of the mountains that Sal hasn't traveled.

Sal bangs out of the cabin carrying the dog bowls and sets them down. She is about to go back inside but stops with a hand on the door. "Do you have to leave right away?"

"Not necessarily."

"Good. Get dressed. I want to show you something."

Frank covers her surprise. "Does it involve horses?"

"Not today."

"My ass thanks you."

Sal smiles and bangs back inside. Frank eases her saddle-sore bones from the sleeping bag. Getting dressed is easy, as she fell asleep with most of her clothes on. She is tying her tennis shoes when Sal plunks a mug next to her.

"Where are we going?"

"Not far. I won't keep you long."

"That doesn't answer my question."

"Neither will my telling you where we're going. Come on."

Frank makes a token, guilt-induced protest. "You know I'm supposed to be investigating your father's murder, right?"

"Aren't you?"

"Hardly," Frank murmurs into her coffee.

Sal leads straight up the hill behind the cabin along a clear but crooked trail defined by chamise and boulder. Sweating and breathing hard, Frank leaves her cup on a rock and struggles to keep pace. She thinks she is in good shape, but Sal puts the lie to that. Just as she wonders if riding wouldn't have been better after all, Sal veers onto an outcrop. The ledge is a couple yards wide but tangled with thick scrub. Watching Sal inch sideways against the prickly brush, she gauges that a tumble from the ledge wouldn't kill her but it'd be damn uncomfortable.

"How 'bout I wait here?" she calls.

Concentrating on her footwork, Sal waves for her to follow. The dogs have already crawled through the underbrush, out of sight. Frank debates if crawling after them would be too cowardly. Sal rounds a clump of brush and disappears too.

"Shit."

Frank steps onto the ledge. Manzanita and buckbrush poke her belly, but she clutches the shrubs and toes the edge of the shelf. Salt stings her eyes and the tough little branches scratch her arms, but Frank clings to them as if they are her best friends. After a couple dozen feet, the ledge suddenly widens into a long, bare balcony. Sal sits with her legs dangling over the edge and the dogs lie panting in a strip of shade at the base of the cliff behind them. Frank glances at the smooth wall, then squints at a tall, crooked gash concealed by a spindly bush. She steps closer. Her mouth goes dry and her heart beats in her ears.

"This is a cave."

"It is."

The dizziness comes and Frank grabs at a buckbrush. Thorns pierce her palm, but she doesn't notice. Afraid she will stumble off the ledge, Frank's last conscious thought is to fall to her knees. When she comes to, she is rocking on them. She hears a woman keening. Realizes she is making the sound and stops. Sal squats on her heels in front of her. She appears concerned but not alarmed. For some reason, that relieves Frank. She runs her tongue over cracked lips tasting of blood and wipes her hand over her eyes. The sting of sweat brings her fully back. The dogs pant in the shade, the sky remains an impassive blue, and scrubby little trees still guard the cave.

"What is this place?"

"Come. I'll show you."

Sal helps her stand. Frank lets her part the bushes and lead her to the passage. The entrance is tight, and they squeeze through sideways. The southing autumn sun filters in behind them, illuminating painted deer running on the walls between leaping dogs and banded snakes. Charcoal birds soar across the limed ceiling down the opposite side. Chalked lizards and many-legged bugs climb from the bottom of the cave. Painted in ghostly daubs of black and white, a wispy, winged human curves from floor to ceiling. Its head is beaked and fiercely red.

High over the crack are a row of handprints. Dimly aware she shouldn't, that the art is fragile, Frank stretches to place her palm in the center of an ancient hand. It fits perfectly. She lays her cheek upon the cool, rough stone. Her arm vibrates like a tuning fork.

She whispers into the rock what she has seen: women and children huddled in the cave. Air made solid with smoke and ash. Coughing and gagging made almost inaudible over the crackle of brush and roar of fire. Parched skin cracking and oozing in the searing heat. Lips splitting and tongues swelling in spitless mouths.

Sal's hand is on her shoulder. She says, "You see all that?"

Too big to slink through the skinny entrance, Cicero whines alone outside the cave. Frank drops her arm. The thrumming ceases. She rubs her hand. It's as cold as if it's been packed in ice. She squeezes from the cave, blinking in the mellow autumn light. Bone pads behind and Cicero greets him, leaping and fawning. Kook prances around the big dogs on his hind legs. Dust lifts in the air, like the ash that once sifted in the cave. Frank sits on the edge of the ledge, Sal beside her. They look out over the cabin far below and the meander of creek and sunny field, and brooding over them all, the watchful Lucias.

Sal rolls a cigarette. "What else do you see?"

With rushing relief, Frank describes all the visions. When she finishes, Sal passes the cigarette. Frank takes it with a trembling hand. "It's like they're are all related to the land here. Even in Morro Bay it was connected, the way the harbor was sheltered by the very last of the mountains."

Sal nods and rolls another cigarette. "Angelo Saladino—the first Saladino to live here—married an Esselen woman."

"Cassie told me. Said the woman was born where the cabin is now."

"That's right." Sal smiles. "I'm surprised she remembered. At any rate, every spring the Esselen burned around the oak trees to get rid of bugs that might otherwise infest the acorn crop that was a goodly part of their diet.

"One spring the men went out and set the fires as usual, but the wind shifted halfway through the burn and started blowing back to the camp, where all the women and children were. The girl who would eventually become Angelo's mother-in-law was the first to see the smoke bending toward the camp. She heard the men shouting, trying to contain it, and when she realized it was out of control she ran around the camp and gathered everyone and herded them here. The fire overran the camp not long after she got everyone into the cave. Some of the men died, but everyone in the cave lived, and for as long as the people were alive they left gifts here—deer, quail, baskets of acorns, whatever they had. The girl became the leader of her clan, and legend has it that when the Spaniards began rounding up the Esselen for slave labor, she fled into the mountains with the last of her people."

Sal contemplates the far, dark chine of mountain. "Some say they all turned into great birds and flew away. Others say they're up there still."

A chill courses through Frank. She can't take her eyes from the ridges. Sal scratches a match and Frank leans to the flame.

"How long have you been seeing all this?"

"Not long. Seems to have started about the time we found your father."

Sal nods as if that makes sense. They smoke and study the land below.

"Did you see this when you touched me?"

"Not quite."

"But you're not surprised."

"No. Down there," Sal waves in the general direction of civilization, "people have forgotten how things are. They've created a new normal and think it's real because it's all they know. The things that happen here happen down there too, but here they're concentrated. This is where the last of the rough old gods live—the gods people down there only remember in half-buried dreams." Sal grinds her cigarette carefully into the dirt. "Do you know what retro-cognition is?"

"Nope."

"It's the ability to see the past. I've always been more clairvoyant, but Cass had a great talent for past sight."

"What's the difference?"

"Clairvoyance is seeing the present."

"You can't do both?"

"You can, but usually one is dominant."

A breeze riffles the tough manzanita leaves and tickles Frank's cheek. She looks reluctantly at her watch. "I hate to, but I have to get going."

Frank steps onto the ledge, crossing fearlessly and without effort. The dogs crawl through the thorny cover and are waiting when she comes out onto the trail. She follows them down the hill and Sal trails behind. At the bottom, Frank starts for the bridge, but Sal stops her.

"Just one more thing."

"I really have to go."

"I know. It'll just take a second."

In the cabin, Sal picks books from the shelves and hands them to Frank.

"Whoa. That's plenty."

She piles more into Frank's laden arms. "I don't expect you to read them cover to cover. Just skim the interesting parts."

"Okay, okay. I can barely carry 'em all."

Sal adds one more. "There. That ought to keep you busy."

"For a decade or so."

Sal helps her carry them across the bridge. Frank wants to stop and study the water, but she's already lost enough time on the ranch. The dogs load into the quad, and when they get to the ranch Pete is bent under the hood of the truck, a quart of oil in hand.

He gives Frank a suspicious eye and asks Sal, "Everything alright?"

"Fine. Lieutenant Franco's just leaving."

To Frank he says, "I'm assuming this is the last we're gonna see of you."

Her smile is chilly. "You know what they say about assuming."

"Big city cop like you might not know it, but Sal's a busy woman. It'd be best if—"

"Pete," Sal breaks in brusquely. "It's fine. Is the truck alright?"

He slams the hood and stalks to the house.

Frank mutters, "I hope that's a yes."

The dogs jump from the quad to the pickup. They lean over the side of the bed as Sal drives, and Frank keeps a worried eye on her side-view mirror. They hit a rut and the dogs scramble for footing. "They ever fall out?" she shouts.

Sal nods. "Once. That's how they learn not to."

They drive without speaking the rest of the way. There are probably questions Frank should be asking, but she wants to absorb as much of the mountains as she can. When Sal pulls up next to the dusted Honda, she leaves the engine idling. Frank reaches and turns it off. Except for the shrill alarm of squirrels, the silence is sudden and deep.

"Pete seems awfully possessive."

"He doesn't know you. He thinks you're bothering me."

"Am I?"

"No."

"Do you sleep together?"

Sal sucks in a small, alarmed breath, but recovers quickly. "No."

"Never?"

The question hangs in the cab. Sal gets out and drops the tailgate. The dogs leap out to chase a squirrel into its hole. Frank joins Sal against the back of the truck. Cicero and Bone take turns digging for the squirrel, but Kook trots back to them and Sal picks a dried stalk out of his tail. Her brown fingers work the stem into a row of knots.

"You know most of this. Pete and Cass dated in high school. She never went steady with anyone, never wanted to be tied down to one beau. Pete was her fallback guy, always there when she needed him or wanted him. He loved her. He proposed after our father disappeared, but she turned him down. Then a year after she died, he married Linda Seelig. I think she always felt like he'd settled for second best. But they got on well. Linda was old Salinas, a farmer's daughter. She was a good match for Pete. They were better friends than lovers. I used to spend a lot of time at the house. Linda and I would plant a big garden every year. If it grew, we planted it. Okra, eggplant, raspberries, strawberries. Everything."

Sal smiles. "We kept the orchards up back then, too, and Linda and I would spend all summer pickling, drying, canning. Come fall, the shelves in the pantry would be sagging with all the food we'd put up. It was hard work, sweating over a stove in the middle of summer, but we had fun." Sal lifts Kook onto the bed and picks stickers from his fur. "She was only forty-six when she was diagnosed with breast cancer. She fought it for a couple years, but the cancer eventually won."

Frank nods.

"There was a night after she died, Pete opened a bottle of plum wine that we'd made. It was warm and sweet and tasted just like the summer we made it, and we drank the whole bottle. The next thing I knew, we were in bed. Their bed. It was awkward and embarrassing, but I think it was a way for both of us to feel like part of her. That summer Linda and I made the wine was the last time we were close, until she was diagnosed." She teases a bur from Kooks' foot.

"What pushed you apart?"

Sal straightens and looks toward the ranch as if she can see it. "I did. We were pickling cucumbers. It was hot, but there was a breeze from the window over the sink. We were standing in front of it, and Linda's hair had fallen across her face and I pushed it back so she could catch the breeze. Then I kissed her." Sal takes a deep breath and crosses her arms. "She laughed and asked, 'What was that for?' I told her it was because I loved her. And I kissed her again, but she pushed me away, very politely, saying we had to get finished so she could start dinner. She acted like nothing had happened and we never mentioned it again."

"Did Pete know?"

"I don't think so. He knew things had cooled between Linda and me but I never told him why, and I doubt she did."

Frank nods. They watch the dogs, buried up to their chests in the hole they've dug.

"But he still carries a torch for you."

"No, we're just old friends. More like brother and sister." Shoving off the truck, she says, "Don't forget your books."

"Right."

Sal helps her load them into the car and Frank says, "Thanks. I'll bring 'em back."

"No need."

"I'd like to."

Frank shuts the trunk and moves to the door, but she can't make herself open it.

"Something happens to me here. Every intention I have to question you vanishes—poof. I don't know any more about you than when I first started."

"You know a lot more."

"How do you figure that?"

Sal tips her head toward the mountains, the direction of the ranch. "You know all that, and that's all you need to know."

"That's not what I came here for."

"Isn't it?"

She calls the dogs and turns the truck around.

Frank watches the pickup until it rounds a curve and the dust has settled onto the empty road.

Chapter 29

At a truck stop north of San Luis Obispo, Frank gets coffee and a piece of ollalaberry pie. She eats it standing over the trunk, looking at her books. She brings a couple up front with her and riffles through them on the long drive home. In Oxnard traffic a truck behind her has to honk to get her to look up from *A Natural History of Big Sur*, and in Thousand Oaks she almost rams into the back of a BMW while thumbing through a pictorial history of the Salinas Valley. Finally home, she lugs the books inside and stacks them reverently by the bed. Over the next few days she plumbs the geology and geography of the Santa Lucia range, delves into the histories of the area (human as well as natural), then moves on to the daunting physics and philosophy texts.

On Wednesday Caroline spends the night, and as they lie in bed reading she glances at the title in Frank's hand. "Seriously? Quantum mechanics?"

With a sheepish grin, Frank defends, "It's complicated but fascinating."

"Since when? I've never known you to read anything deeper than *The Da Vinci Code*."

"I didn't know you thought I was so shallow."

"Not at all. I just never knew you were interested in—" Caroline laughs. "I don't even know what morphic resonance is."

Frank loves the creases at the corner of Caroline's eyes. She traces them with a fingertip, moves down the line of her jaw to lift her chin for a kiss. "Let's forget about physics."

She lays the book down and sets about her seduction. It is not a repeat of their last wild abandon, but rather a slow, amiable satisfaction of desire. It is pleasant and distracting, but when they turn the lights out Frank can't sleep. The bed is too soft, the room too close. Switching from side to side doesn't help. Neither does pushing the covers off. The bedspread slides to the floor and gives her an idea. She tiptoes to the guest room. Taking the bedspread from there, she unlocks the patio doors and steps into the city night. Cocooning herself, she lies on the chaise lounge and searches for stars. The city lights eclipse most of them, but she finds the brightest and wanders between them. She wonders if Sal is sleeping outside, and if she looks up at the soft black night and sees the same stars, only sharper and closer. Frank shuts her eyes, pretending Sal sleeps nearby and that the murmur of the freeway is the lullaby of creek and wind.

"Frank."

She comes awake with Caroline's face blotting the stars.

"What are you doing out here?"

"I couldn't sleep."

"Why didn't you go into the guest room?"

"I don't know. What time is it?"

"It's five. Your alarm just went off."

Caroline stalks into the house. Frank showers quietly, but Caroline is sitting up when she comes into the bedroom. "Frank, is something wrong?"

"No. Why?"

"It just seems that half the time you're not here and when you are here, it's like you're somewhere else."

The somber mountains bloom in her heart. The sky hugs them, lucid and endlessly blue. Frank sits next to her girlfriend.

"You're right. It's this case. My mind's always in Soledad. Probably will be until I nail it shut."

"What if you don't?"

"Oh, I will. Don't you worry about that. Look, I know I've been impossible. I'm sorry. Cops are horrible girlfriends."

"Not always," Caroline kisses Frank's forehead just as her phone rings. Caroline picks it up and makes a face. "I should talk." She answers, then promises to be at the hospital within an hour.

Before she leaves, Frank warns, "I might have to go up again this weekend."

"You just got back."

"I know. Just trying to tie up loose ends before they unravel any farther. Then I can be done with it."

But Frank dreads the case being closed and harbors the nasty hope it will go cold so she can keep making follow-up visits to the ranch. She makes it a point to corner her boss as soon as she comes in and asks if she can cover the weekend.

"*Again?*"

"You sound like my girlfriend."

"I think I feel like your girlfriend. I just wonder which one of us likes this less."

"Toss-up probably."

After decades of manipulating suspects and witnesses, lying comes as easily to Frank as blinking. She doesn't like doing it to Pintar, yet does so with only a twinge of guilt.

"I found a couple more people I have to talk to."

Describing the tangled leads and how she plans to tease them apart, Frank decides she's not lying as much as telling a partial truth. Pintar remains skeptical.

"What about the rest of your workload? I still don't have a schedule forecast, and unless I'm mistaken," she makes a point of looking through the papers on her desk, "I haven't had any 60-days from you in a month."

"I've got 'em," Frank fibs again. "They'll be on your desk tomorrow morning."

Pintar purses her lips.

"Last trip. I promise."

Her boss sighs. "Alright. But only if everything's on my desk by the time I come in tomorrow, wrapped up and tied with a bow."

"Deal."

Back in her office, Frank lets out the breath she's been holding. Even the promise that this will be her last trip isn't enough to tamp her enthusiasm. Seconds later Lewis lumbers in.

"Got a minute?"

"Of course. Sit."

Lewis settles heavily onto the old Swiss modern couch that is modern in name only. The vinyl is cracked and duct-taped in places, the thin metal arms flaking to bare steel, but the couch doesn't take up much space and has given Frank many hours of desperately snatched sleep.

"What's up?"

"I don't know." She flaps a beefy hand. "This Saladino thing startin' to look like a real whodunit."

Tilting back in her chair, Frank grins and laces her hands behind her head. "Body that old, you didn't expect anything less, did ya?"

"No," Lewis pouts. "But still."

"Girl, you givin' up on me?"

"Nah, I ain't givin' up. You know better 'an that. Just we got off to such a hot start and I hate to see it fizzlin' out."

"It ain't fizzling, just settling. Go work some other cases. Let this one simmer down."

"Yeah, okay."

"You alright?"

"Yeah, just tired. Baby thing gettin' to me, frustrated I can't go up there, work it myself 'stead a you having to do it all." She heaves off the couch and the metal squeaks back into place. "I been checkin' provenance on the uncle's house where Saladino stayed at. Hattie Saladino was the wife. She died in '92 and left the house to her niece, Gail Hendry. I tracked Hendry down to an assisted living over to Silver City. I'mma head over there, see if she got anything to say. You wanna come?"

"Nah." She nods at the messy desk. "I promised Pintar I'd take care of all this. And don't sweat it about me going to Soledad. I'm digging it. Nice change a pace, and I need that. I'm gettin' stale."

"You ain't stale, LT. You still the best in the game. You want, I can go up wit' you and see it fresh, maybe shake somethin' outta the tree?"

Frank instinctively lies, "Ain't much to shake right now. You're welcome to go, but I think you'd be wasting your time."

Lewis is visibly relieved. "You probably right."

"Hey. It's not over yet. I'mma keep workin' it there. You keep workin' it here. If nothing comes up, we'll just let it ride a little bit. How's Halliday coming?"

She encourages Lewis on the progress of other cases, and when the big cop finally leaves her office, the tiny room seems to expand. Frank's hands remain locked behind her head. She's lied to her best cop; there's plenty to shake on the Saladino tree. But she won't give Lewis the mountains or cabin, Sal or Bone, the creek, the sycamores, even the old store. None of it.

Frank gets up and closes the door. She finds the white card in her wallet and dials the number on it. She is relieved when Marguerite answers, and Frank tells her everything—flying over the dark mountains, seeing trails that aren't there but are, passing out at Sal's, the fire at the cave—all of it. "They're like—what's that word when part of a painting's drawn over another?"

"Pentimento?"

"That's it. The visions are like little flashes of history, like what used to be on the land is still there and bleeds through sometimes, and even though you can't always see it, it's still there." Frank pauses. "Do you remember telling me I'd have guides, or helpers?"

"Yes."

"Can a place be a guide?"

"It's possible."

"And what happens if I can't get to that place as much as I want to?"

She hears Marguerite thinking. "Help takes many forms. As much as we'd like it to remain the same, to look the same every time, energy like that is tremendously fluid. It's dynamic and constantly shifting from one form to another, depending on our needs."

"What if I need that place?"

"Then you'll have it. If you don't, it may have outlived its purpose and the help will manifest elsewhere. I'd caution you not to become so fixated on one form that you overlook another. And why can't you get to this place?"

"It's private property. I can't go whenever I feel like it, but the damn place is seeping into my bones."

"Maybe it has always been in your bones and is finally seeping *out*. Can you hold the line a minute?"

197

"Sure," Frank sighs, irritated to be put on hold. But as she waits she can hear the mambo breathing. Frank drops her head into her hand, listening to the steady rhythm of Marguerite's breath. She sways in her chair to the gait of a horse and hears the steady clop of hooves, the ring of an iron shoe on rock, a gnat's complaint. Sun heats her back. She touches her tongue to her lips, taking away a salty grit of sweat and dust.

"This place," Marguerite says. "It's very much with you. Even when you're not there. It has many animals?"

"Yeah. Dogs, chickens. Rattlesnakes. Bears. You name it."

"Yes. I can feel them. I think they're touching your heart, that through them you're opening to the larger energies of this place, this land."

"And the woman, is she—"

"Yes?"

"Nothing. Never mind."

"If it's any consolation, your estrangement from this place seems temporary. I feel your time there isn't over, that you have much more of a relationship with that land than you can even begin to imagine."

"You're right. I can't imagine."

"Don't despair," Marguerite encourages. "If I know you, you're trying to put this all behind you, to close the door on your experiences as if they never happened. If you can't have them, you'll deny them. Am I close?"

Frank has to smile. "Center mass."

"Don't do that. Don't deny them. Remember the land as clearly and as vividly as you can. That will keep it connected to you. Distance doesn't matter."

"That's what Darcy said. Called it 'spooky action at a distance.'"

To Frank's surprise, Marguerite chuckles. "Yes. That's exactly it. Lieutenant, I know this is difficult, but I'm proud of you for keeping such an open mind."

Frank can't remember the last time she made anyone proud and deflects the praise. "I don't know how proud you should be. I'm a terrible cop."

"That may be. But your heart is opening, and that is far more important than being a good cop. I'm glad you called me."

"Thanks, Marguerite."

The mambo tells her to take close care, and Frank hits End. Determined to keep at least one promise to Pintar, she settles to her paperwork. It takes a grinding, concentrated day, but she gets it all done.

"Tatum!" she yells.

He pokes his head in the door.

She waves a bill at him. "I need you to run up to the CVS Pharmacy, get some wrapping paper and a bow."

"Me?"

"Is there anybody else in here?"

"I was just about to leave."

"Alright, forget it. I'll just tell Pintar you couldn't get her paper."

"It's for her?"

"Yeah, but don't worry about it. Go home."

He reaches for the bill. "Nah, I got it. What type you want?"

"Doesn't matter. Just something bright and girly."

Lewis barges past Tatum, a grin slicing her face. "Who's your number one detective?"

"Uh . . . Tatum?"

He looks on with interest.

"This boy here?" Lewis scoffs. "He couldn't find a clue if it was stapled to his willie. Check this out." She waves a faded green ledger and Frank flaps a dismissive hand at Tatum.

"I found Miss Henry, 'member the niece I was telling you about this morning?"

Frank nods, hiding a yawn. She wants to go home and get on her treadmill for an hour.

"She a sweet old thing, lonely, and well, you know how charming I can be." Lewis bats her lashes. The delighted grin returns. "Turns out she got all Saladino's old records. Boxes of 'em. Full of these old notebooks. 'Fraid the minute she throws 'em out, ol' Uncle Sam gonna want to know something about the house or her uncle's business. Keeps 'em all in storage. And she gimme the key.

"1968," she says, brandishing the register. "Got notes of everyone Louis Saladino paid and how much. Some of it legit, but mostly like it's under the table. But three times there's a record of payment to one Roderick Dusi, and the last one?"

She slaps the ledger down and points to a line on an open page. "December 17, 1968."

Frank thinks. "That's the day before Mary Saladino died."

"Uh-huh. Why the uncle be writing out a check to this Roderick unless he be down here to collect?"

"Maybe Saladino was gonna take it back for him?"

Lewis shakes her head. "You do temp work, you get paid by the day or as soon as the job's over. You don't get your money later."

She taps Roderick's name. "Mary Saladino's brother was down here the same time her husband was. Right after he put the beatdown on her."

"Son of a bitch."

Frank pulls the notebook close. Studying the entries Lewis has tabbed, she mutters, "What else aren't you telling me, Sal?"

Chapter 30

Frank is waiting next Saturday when Sal leaves the store. She looks drained and her shoulders slump even more than usual. Frank opens the truck door so Sal can stash her bags. "Rough morning?"

Sal nods.

"I'd offer to buy you a cup of coffee, but I know the dogs are waiting."

"Yeah."

"Could I ask a couple quick questions?"

"You're welcome to come up."

"You sure? You look beat."

"I just need to eat. I'll be fine."

Frank isn't convinced but Sal urges, "Hop in."

"How 'bout I drive? You can sit back and relax. Survey your kingdom."

Sal gives up a wan smile. "That'd be a treat."

Frank slides in behind the wheel, hoping she remembers how to use a clutch. "Don't forget to tell me where to turn."

Sal nods. Except for directions, they drive without speaking and Frank is surprised how much she has missed the companionable silence. She thinks of all the people in her life and how much they talk. There is never silence in her ears. Not like here, where even the truck straining at the top of its gear is a kind of silence. Frank parks at the barn. "Quad or horses?" she asks before getting out.

Sal thinks a second. "Horses."

They saddle up and ride the worn track to the cabin. Frank sees as they approach the creek that the sycamores have changed from emerald to a brassy green. Riding into their embrace, she wonders why they ever gave her the willies. The dogs bark as the horses clop across the bridge and Frank smiles at the water tumbling below.

Sal opens the corral gate and Frank offers, "How about I take care of the horses and you fix something to eat?"

Sal lifts a brow. "Last week you didn't know what a hoof pick was and today you're a regular Annie Oakley."

Frank grins. "I had a good teacher."

"Actually, I want to take a ride after we eat, so just leave them saddled."

"Where to?" she asks, trying to copy Sal's fluid dismount. While lacking grace, she manages to get off without kicking Buttons and scratches her belly.

"You'll see."

Frank mutters, "Why'd I even ask?"

They feed the dogs, then themselves. Sal finishes her coffee and asks, "Ready?"

"I guess. How far are we going?"

"Not far. We'll be back before dark."

Frank checks her watch. Sunset is around 7:30 and it's not even three o'clock now.

"Four hours?" she protests, but Sal is already out the door.

They ride north, paralleling the toe of the mountains until Sal suddenly turns up a dark green canyon. Madrones and maples filter the light. Soft, leafy branches swat them. A layer of duff muffles the step of horse and dog alike. The only sound is the swish of cloth upon leather, the occasional note from a bird. The leaves on the ground thicken. The trees lengthen into shaggy-barked redwoods that blot the sun. Sal weaves Dune between the somber spires. They cross and re-cross a dry, ferny stream at the bottom of the canyon. Dune hops up a series of boulders, and before Frank can protest Buttons clambers after him. Frank clings to the horse's neck and manages to stay in the saddle. She rubs under Buttons' bridle and whispers what a fine beast she is.

The cobbled streambed leads deeper into the mossy cool. Sal stops at a cliff rising straight from the creek. They lift their heads, looking to where the wall disappears in an apse of needle and bough.

Sal insists, "You'll have to come back when the water's running."

Almost afraid to break the churchly silence, but glancing at the tight sides of the canyon, Frank asks, "How do you get up here if the creek's full?"

"There's another trail. It's longer, but it comes out at the top of the falls."

To Frank, the mountains are an impenetrable tangle, and she marvels, "You know this place as well as your own face in the mirror."

Sal shakes her head. "Much better than that." Turning Dune toward a jumble of boulders, she calls, "She won't want to, but you have to make Buttons jump up here. Hang on when she does." With that, she digs her heels in, bends over Dune's neck, and sails onto a flat ledge.

"Oh, sure."

Sal wheels to watch. "Walk her up to it, then give her a big kick in the ribs. She'll go."

Frank rides up to the boulders. "How 'bout I get off and walk her up?"

Sal shakes her head. "She won't go that way. Just give her plenty of rein and a hard kick. Bend over her neck and hold tight with your knees."

"This is crazy," she says more to herself than Sal.

Frank pulls in a deep breath, savoring it as if it might be her last. She lets it out with a loud "Yah!" and jabs her heels into Buttons' ribs. With a great gathering of haunches, Buttons launches into the air and Frank loses a stirrup. She squeezes her eyes shut as Buttons lands with a jolt and clatter. Giddy with relief, Frank grins and feels for the loose stirrup. Before she can find it, Buttons shakes herself and Frank slides out of the saddle. She tries hanging on, but her other foot slips through the stirrup up to her shin.

The crack of bone on rock knocks her breath loose. She waits for Buttons to bolt and drag her to a gruesome death, but Sal has the reins and is twisting Frank's leg free. Her foot drops to the ground and Sal crouches next to her. "Are you alright?"

Frank studies the sky beyond the dome of trees. She murmurs, "I think you ask that every time I'm here." Bone licks her cheek.

"Does anything hurt?"

Almost everything, Frank thinks. Shifting her gaze from the sky to Sal, she grumbles, "You're the psychic healer. You tell me."

Sal rolls her eyes. "Do you really want me to sit here and take the time to do that?"

"Yeah. I think I do."

Sal shakes her head, but she gets up and ties the reins onto a sturdy bush. She sits back next to Frank and closes her eyes. Frank does too. She braced her neck to keep her head from slamming on to the rocks and it aches like a sonofabitch. The shoulder and hip she fell on, too. After she inventories the rest of her parts, she decides nothing's broken and sits up. "I'm okay," she whispers.

Sal opens her eyes. "You seem to want proof." She touches the stiff muscle in Frank's neck. "It's hot here." Her hand falls to Frank's shoulder. "And a little bit here, but more right about. . . here." She holds her hand a couple inches from Frank's hipbone. "We'll get some ice on that when we get back to the cabin, but for now . . ." Sal stands and reaches for a handful of bay leaves over her head. She crushes them between her hands, pours a little water on the mix, and rolls it into a loose ball. "Hold this on your hip. You're going to be sore, but this'll help with the swelling."

Frank stuffs the fragrant mash into her jeans, wincing when she presses it in place.

"Can you ride?"

"I'm not getting back on that horse."

"It's a long walk down."

"I'll crawl." Frank slaps dirt from her pants with a bloody palm. "What the hell's up here anyway?"

"You'll see."

"And why's everything always such a goddamn mystery with you?"

Sal turns Buttons sideways to a boulder. "You're a detective. You should like mysteries." She pats the rock. "It'll be easier if you get on from here."

Frank swears but eases herself gently into the saddle. They climb a series of boulders that top out onto a wooded plateau and the dogs break into a run. She hears splashing, and rounding a fern-covered cliff sees them swimming in a pond as black and round as an eye.

After the horses drink, Sal hobbles them near a patch of swordlike grass, then sits and tugs her boots off.

"Don't tell me you're going in there."

"Why not?"

"It's dirty. There's snakes and bugs and . . . *things* in there."

Sal is out of her shirt and unbuttoning her jeans. Frank looks down until she has splashed into the water. She yells after her, "You're going to get a disease!"

Sal's laugh floats to her in a silvery tinkle. It echoes, rare and lovely, from the cliff on the other side and Frank wishes she could hear it more often.

"I've been swimming in this pond for sixty-two years and haven't caught anything yet."

"That's a long time," Frank admits.

"It is," Sal answers. "Come on. You don't know what you're missing."

Yes, she does, because before she's even left them Frank is missing Sal and the trees, the pond, and cabin, dogs and mountains, even Buttons.

"Come and soak for a minute. It'd be good for your hip."

"Oh, for Christ's sake."

Toeing her sneakers off, she shucks her clothes and limps into the pond before she can talk herself out of it. She dives, eyes squeezed tight, and surfaces gasping. "It's cold!"

Sal laughs while Bone and Cicero splash in circles. Kook barks and races around the rim of the pond. The big dogs tire and join him on shore. Cicero and Kook play a frenzied game of tag while Bone keeps a worried eye on his women. Copying Sal, Frank floats on her back. The dark water holds her, offering her tenderly to the brilliant blue bowl of sky between cliff and leaf. Frank is a willing sacrifice.

She turns over and watches Sal swim out, appreciating that she is as graceful in water as she is on a horse. Frank follows her, skimming beneath the surface. It is quiet under the water. Peaceful. If she drowned in the still, blackish pond, she would become the mud and trees and rain and sky and stay forever a part of the land. Her lungs pound for air and she rises. Bone wades out to meet her.

They dry themselves with their shirts, and when they are dressed, they sit in a patch of sun slanting through the trees.

Sal tells her, "You should see it when the lilacs and buckbrush are in bloom. Promise you'll come back in the spring."

"You keep treating me like I'm some kind of tourist when I'm supposed to be investigating your father's murder."

Sal pulls the tobacco from her pocket and Frank asks, "Who would want to kill him?"

"Who wouldn't?" She folds a paper, sprinkles tobacco in the crease. "He wasn't a bad guy, he really wasn't. He just—I think he truly believed that somehow, some way he'd get the ranch back into the Saladino name. He had so many ideas about the ranch, so many things he wanted to do with it, but he could never interest John in them. He was a dyed-in-the-wool rancher and didn't have any interest in converting rangeland into fields of broccoli or sweet peas. It drove my father crazy."

The cigarette is rolled and sealed. Sal twists one end and tamps the other against the bag.

"My mother didn't help. She'd nag that he was always going to be John's hired help and that he should just get used to the idea. I think his dreams made them both miserable. And it was only when he drank that he was bad. When he was sober, he was really very nice. Very kind. Almost as if he were trying to make up for his drinking."

"Do you know if he ever had an affair?"

Sal shakes her head adamantly. "It's a pretty small town. I'm sure we'd have heard."

"How about your mother?"

"What about her?"

Frank shifts her attention from the pond to Sal. "Did you know she was having an affair with John Mazetti?"

Sal studies her unlit cigarette. "Where'd you hear that?"

"George Perales."

Frank stopped by his place last night. Actually his daughter's place, in Greenfield. Twisted with arthritis, Perales sat in a wheelchair and watched his grandkids while his daughter was at work. "Useful even in this," he'd said, patting the chair. And he was.

"Gonna smoke that?" Frank asks.

Sal hands it to her and fixes another.

"Did you know?"

Sal nods.

"How old were you when you found out?"

"I don't remember."

"Did you know during or after the fact?"

"During."

"How old were you?"

"I just told you, I don't remember."

"A girl or a teenager?"

"A teen. I think it was my sophomore year. We'd have been seventeen."

"How'd you find out?"

"We caught them in the barn together. They weren't doing anything blatant, but it was obvious we'd interrupted them. I think we'd kind of suspected anyway."

"Did your father know?"

Again Sal gives a firm shake. "He was always jealous of John—they both courted my mother. My father would throw that in her face when he was drunk—accuse her of wishing she'd married John instead of him, how she could've been proud of her husband, and be the wife of a ranch owner instead of a ranch hand. But his jealousy came more from his failings than her deeds. With his temper when he drank, he couldn't have known, he'd have killed her."

"That was pretty risky of her. Do you think she might have wanted to get caught?"

"Why would she want that?"

Frank shrugs. She keeps to herself all the homicides she's investigated, where spouse and lover provoke the other spouse into a rage so violent they can turn murder into a justifiable homicide. "Why do you think she was playing with fire like that? I mean, she must have known the consequences."

"I'm sure I couldn't tell you. It's not the kind of conversation a teenage girl has with her mother."

"No," Frank agrees, considering her own mother's eccentric behavior.

Through gaps in the redwood needles, the sun shimmers across the water. A fly lands on Frank's arm and she leaves it to whatever delights it can find. The dogs nap, as still as the cliffs around the pond. Dune and Buttons munch their patch of grass. The air is languid. Time stretches. They might have dozed, Frank isn't sure. Redwood shadows reclaim the pond. Sal stirs and the dogs lift their heads.

"Why are you showing me all this?"

Cicero stands, shaking off dead needles and bits of rabbit dream.

"Someone has to remember it."

"Why me? Why not show all this to someone who can stay here? Cassie or someone?"

"Because I trust you."

"To do what?"

Sal won't answer, and Frank swats at a fly.

"This is ridiculous." Frank stands, ignoring the throb in her hip. "You live this hermetic existence in this rarified air and have given me a very generous taste of it, but it's nothing I can ever make a meal of. I can't have any of this. I have to go back down to the real world. I can't just saddle up a horse anytime I feel like it and trot on up here. You're showing me things I never even knew I wanted until I came here, but I can't have them, so I don't know why you keep showing me."

She stalks to Buttons and yanks the reins over the horse's head, but the hobbles thwart her. "How do you undo these goddamn things?"

Sal comes and unbuckles them. Too angry to be afraid, Frank swings painfully into the saddle. She trots from the glade, then stops. She has no idea which way to go.

Chapter 31

The return to the cabin is in chilly silence. When they drop from their horses, Frank says, "Look. I'm sorry. I have been incredibly unprofessional, and I just want you to know that my shortcomings are in no way representative of the LAPD. I am a rogue cop acting completely on my own."

"That's too bad. From what I've heard, they could use more like you."

"Not the way I've been lately. I'm starting to think you've put ranch crack in my food—this place is magical. It's all I can think about lately. And then the minute I'm here, my brain flies out the window."

"Maybe that's not such a bad thing."

After they feed the animals, Sal slices apples and puts a small wheel of cheese on the table. Frank is browsing the bookshelves, and says, "Hey, I've got all your books. Remind me when we get to my car."

"Did you read them all?"

"I did. I really liked them. But it kinda freaked my girlfriend out that I was reading up on morphic resonance."

She taps a tarot book, asking Sal if she reads cards like her daughter.

"No, I'm just curious how they work."

"And how is that?"

"I think the images and symbols, all the archetypes, speak to our souls. They stimulate our deepest, most innate intelligence."

"So they're not magic."

Setting a plate of tortillas on the table, Sal says, "No more magical than your soul. Sit. Eat."

Frank pulls out a chair. "Does everything in your world have a soul?"

209

"Everything."

Frank tips her head to the window. "Even the mountains?"

Sal smiles. "Especially the mountains."

"How do you know?"

"How do you not?"

They eat in silence, the dogs asleep under the table. Mindful of the deepening shadows, Frank drags herself from pleasure to business. She asks about her father's work with his uncle, how often, was it always in LA? "Did he always go down alone?"

Sal nods.

"How often did your uncle Roderick work with him?"

The question catches Sal raising her tortilla. She pauses, lowers it back to the plate. "I don't know. I don't think very often. Louis didn't like him. I think he only used him when he was desperate. I'd forgotten he used to work with my father."

"He was down there the day before your father was."

"Was he?"

"You didn't know that?"

"If I did, I don't remember."

"Did he ever talk about that time down there?"

"Not that I recall."

"Never said anything about your father before he disappeared?"

Sal pushes her plate aside. "No."

"Did you ever go down to LA to look for him again?"

"What would have been the point? Where would we have started? He just vanished."

"Did Roderick keep working for Louis?"

She cocks her head as if to a far sound. "It was so long ago. We lived up here, everyone else was in town. We didn't keep track of everyone. We were living our own, suddenly very different lives. I really don't remember much about that time. It all seems very foggy." Sal carries their empty plates to the sink and pours coffee. "Let's go outside."

They take their seats by the fire ring and sip coffee. Along the creek, birds begin squabbling over night perches. A tree frog croaks, then another. They watch as the great black snake of the ridge catches the sun and swallows it alive. It is a beautiful, bloody business. Wholly frightening and wholly necessary.

As she bears witness to the vivid death, Frank's limbs grow heavy, as if the mountains have stolen under her skin to replace blood with dirt and bone with granite. From the darkening mountains comes the sound of sticks being hit together, then a woman singing. "Who is that?"

Sal looks from the sunset to Frank. "Who's what?"

"There's someone singing out there."

Sal listens intently. "I can't hear anything."

"That." Frank points in the direction of the sound. "You can't hear that?"

Sal shakes her head. "Is it just one woman?"

"Yeah. And sticks clapping. Who is it?"

Sal's gaze returns to the ridges. "It's the mountains. They're singing to you."

"The mountains."

Sal nods. "I've never heard them, but my mother used to. After she put the food out for the hosts, she'd sit here and do chores and watch the sun set. Every now and then, she'd get an odd look on her face and start humming. If we asked what she was singing, she'd say it was the song of the mountains and that not everyone could hear it. When we asked her to tell us the words, she said there weren't any. It was just the sound of a woman crying and beating sticks. The Esselen didn't have drums. They used sticks."

Frank insists, "Somebody lives up there."

"No. It's just the mountains. You're lucky. I've always wanted to hear them."

Frank shakes her head. "It's a recording or something."

Tucking her knees up under her chin, Sal asks, "Isn't there a paint or a compound you use to find blood?"

Without taking her eyes off the mountains, Frank answers, "Luminol."

"And don't you need a black light to see it?"

"Yep."

"That's how the mountains are. There are things in them that not

211

everyone has the ability to see with the naked eye. It doesn't mean they don't exist, it just means not everyone can see them."

Frank is tired and her hip aches. She snaps, "Does anything up here have an explanation that's not supernatural?"

Sal laughs. "I hope not. There's nothing supernatural at all. Everything is natural and normal, but we each have different detection ranges. Bone can hear a mouse digging a foot underground. Just because you can't hear it, doesn't mean the mouse doesn't exist. He can smell a man walking up to the house from a couple hundred feet away. Just—"

"Okay, okay." Frank finishes, "Just because I can't, it doesn't mean the man's not there."

Frank likes the idea that there is an enclave of hippies living out in the hills, growing dope, playing sticks, and chanting their oneness with the earth, but is resigned to the possibility—no, at this point the probability—that this is just the auditory version of a vision.

"Has anybody else heard this, besides your mother?"

"Yes."

"Who?"

Sal studies her in the gathering twilight. Frank repeats her question. Twisting back toward the outline of her rough, old gods, Sal promises, "You'll see."

"Jesus," Frank breathes. "Why do I even bother to ask?" As she glowers west at the brooding mass, her frustration transforms into fascination. "They're not unfriendly, are they?"

"The singer?"

"No. The mountains. Gomez said Steinbeck called them unfriendly."

"Gomez said that?"

"What, you don't think cops read?"

"I'm sure I don't know enough cops to judge."

A bat glides through the purple sky and frogs croak from the creek. Tiny movement catches Frank's eye and she watches a cottontail hop at the edge of the trees.

Frank clears her throat. "What did your father like to do besides drink?"

"He played a fair guitar. He liked music. He loved this."

She sweeps a hand toward the dusk-covered land. "It would have been confining for some men. They'd have wanted to see the world beyond the Gabilans and Santa Lucias, but not my father. There was nowhere else he wanted to be. It makes sense he's dead. Death is the only thing that could have kept him away. Sometimes I wonder if even that's enough."

"Are you your father's daughter?"

A slash of pain rearranges Sal's normally placid features, only to be replaced by a joy so fierce it makes Frank's breath catch to see it. She looks up at the night, embarrassed at having spied such naked love. The first stars are winking on and a chill slinks up from the creek.

Sal stands. "I assume you're staying?"

It's wrong, but Frank is past caring. "If you'll have me."

"Of course. I'll get a fire going."

She brings kindling and blows it to life from ash-covered coals. When the small sticks catch, she adds larger ones, then a hatch of logs. They turn their chairs to face the heat.

Sal makes a cigarette and offers it to Frank.

"Thanks."

She rolls another and they smoke as night settles upon them like an old favorite sweater.

"Am I one of your suspects?"

Frank studies the half of Sal's face she can see. "Should you be?"

"Isn't everyone until they're ruled out?"

"Yeah. But you've got lots of company."

"Who?"

Frank blows smoke, smiles. "I can't tell you that, even though I've busted just about every rule in the rulebook."

"Whoever it is, I know you'll find him."

"Him?"

Sal shrugs. "Him, her, them."

Frank turns to her. "In your heart of hearts, who do you think killed him?"

The blue eyes, turned black to gather the light, reflect only the fire.

"In my heart of hearts, I couldn't say." Sal pitches her burning stub into the pit. "Are you sleeping inside or out?"

"Out," Frank says to the star-bright sky. "I wouldn't want to miss a minute of this. There are only so many, aren't there?"

"Only so many," she agrees, and Frank is certain she hears Sal's voice crack.

Chapter 32

The wind rises up in the night. It is restless and swirls from the north, the west, then north again. Switching around, it comes briefly from the east, scattering leaves from the creek. Frank lies snug in her bedroll, thinking what a good thing it is to hear the strong, fine instrument of the wind playing its symphony against tree trunk and leaf and round the corners of the cabin. It sings clear and clean through the barbed wire and over bent grasses, blowing hard off the black, star-speckled ocean and across the wild humpback of the mountains. It is a noise that makes Frank want to throw off her covers and howl like a beast to its kin. She lies a long time listening and when she sleeps, she dreams of the sharp mountains and fires glowing like eyes.

The next time she wakes, the waning moon is rising through a raft of clouds. One thin cloud crosses the hilt of the moon and together they hang like a shining scimitar. The cloud drifts and the moon becomes the moon again. Frank looks to Sal. Her hair glimmers against the still dark ground, but Frank can see from the way her head rests on her forearm that she is watching too.

They stay in their bags until the sun has leached all the drama from the night. Then Sal frees the chickens and goes inside to make coffee. The dogs follow for their breakfast. Frank is left alone with hens scratching in the leaf litter and a covey of quail trundling down the hill for water. Frank puts on her shoes and pisses behind the sheds like Sal does.

The screen slams and she hears Kook barking for his bowl. She meets Sal carrying two mugs. They wander to the bridge and drink coffee. Their legs dangle over the coming and going water. The dogs

215

press between the women, Bone close to Frank. She strokes his flank, noting the browning sycamore leaves.

"I can't believe it's fall already."

Sal nods. "It won't be long before we get the first hard cold. Just a couple weeks."

"How do you know that?"

Sal shrugs. "It's in our bones."

"You mean Saladino bones."

"No. Our bones."

Frank wags her head. "I'm a city girl. The only thing in my bones is glass and concrete."

"That's what's in your brain. This—" Sal indicates everything around them "—is what's in the hold of your bone."

Quail approach from the ranch side of the stream. A male scouts the way, topknot bobbing.

"Do you ever eat them?"

"Pete will give me a couple when he goes hunting."

"Do you spend a lot of time with him?"

Sal rolls them cigarettes. "Depends on the time of year. I see him a lot when we're branding and gathering."

"Is this a pretty profitable spread?"

"It's good enough for Pete, but it could be better."

"How long did he and your sister date?"

"I couldn't say. Off and on, a long time."

"Why'd your father want Cass to marry him instead of you?"

Sal is lighting her cigarette and chokes. "Why wouldn't he? Cass and Pete were pals, even as kids. They were the daredevils, the risk-takers, the ones that always had an idea up their sleeve. The rest of us just bobbed along in their wake."

They smoke and listen to the water. The quail come closer.

"You said John let you stay because it would look bad if he tossed two orphans out, but why does Pete let you stay?"

"I also told you John let us stay because the land needs a Saladino. Pete lets me stay for the same reason."

Frank remembers the old clerk in Celadores saying something like that. "What's that mean exactly?"

216

"Just that. The land needs a Saladino. Things don't go well if we're not on it."

"What sort of things?"

"Blackleg. Scours. Drought. Fire." Sal lifts a shoulder. "Things."

"So. Your being here changes the weather?"

"It seems to."

Frank wags her head. "I'll admit I can hear mountains singing, and that you knew exactly where I was hurt yesterday, but you really think you can change the weather?"

"I didn't say we change it, it's just that it's different when we're not here, more destructive. In 1872, when John's grandfather turned us off the land, he was struck in the course of three months by an outbreak of brucellosis, drought, and a wildfire that came over the mountain and burned down his barn but didn't touch the neighbors on either side. The rains came a week after he hired Mateo Saladino back, and that spring the Mazettis had a record number of calves that survived and made it to market. In 1914 Mateo's son Paul was working the ranch. When he got drafted, there was another drought, worse than the one in '72."

She tips her head back toward the mountains. "Springs that had held water even in the driest years went bone dry. There wasn't enough grass to get the cattle to market, and ninety percent of the herd died of starvation or were slaughtered and left for the vultures. In August, a month after Paul came home, the rains started. The next year, the Mazettis shipped out seventeen hundred head of cattle. He made more money than anyone in the valley that year. And next year and the next. The only other time there wasn't a Saladino on the ranch was after I married Mike."

"And what calamity happened then?"

"We had a windstorm that spring that toppled a perfectly healthy oak tree into the ranch house. Pete and Linda were out branding, so they didn't get hurt, but their twin boys were killed. A month later, an outbreak of swamp fever wiped out every horse on the ranch."

"No drought?"

"Not that year, but the winter was drier than usual. They had to sell the cattle early, and all summer they were plagued by lightning

217

fires. I'd sit in our living-room window in town and watch the storms come in. The clouds were like wild, black animals licking the mountains with tongues of lightning, starting fires everywhere they touched. It was terrifying, watching the lightning strike and not being there to do anything about it."

"What would you have done if you were here?"

"I don't know if it would have happened if I'd stayed."

"If you're such a storm master, why'd you let us get soaked the first time I came here?"

"Why not? The land was thirsty. I'm glad the rain came."

Sal flicks the head off her cigarette and crumbles the rest over the water.

Copying her, Frank asks, "Are there trout in there?"

"Um-hum."

"Do you catch them?"

"Sometimes. But not from here. Pete keeps a pond stocked behind the ranch."

"Speaking of which, I better get going."

As they walk, Sal asks if Frank can stay longer next time. "I have to show you one more thing. It's the last."

"You have to?"

"Yes," Sal answers soberly. "Can you?"

"Thing is," Frank says to the mountains, "this is probably my last trip for a while. My boss is getting tired of covering for me."

"I see." Sal's eyes pierce Frank and she gets the feeling Sal sees more than she lets on. "Well, whenever the next time is, make it a couple days."

"What is it you have to show me?"

"You'll see. But it takes time to get there."

"On horseback?"

Sal nods.

"My ass is already starting to hurt."

And already Frank is pondering how to break her promise to Pintar.

Chapter 33

Leaving Soledad, driving south on the 101, Frank refuses to look at the mountains. She senses the Lucias' long, doleful stare but will not meet it. It's best to forget the watchful range, to pretend she was never held in its arms.

In Gonzalez she stops at a liquor store. The smell of stale booze and spilt beer is reassuring. She buys Buglers and a bag of Drum. In the car, she rolls a clumsy cigarette. She smokes without glancing west. Back on the highway, she returns Caroline's call. The conversation is stilted and disengaged. Claiming fatigue, Frank wriggles from their tentative date.

At home, after miles of pressing Sal and Bone and Buttons from her mind, she lights a fire in the barbecue and chars a steak. Slicing bloody chunks right off the grill, she eats without benefit of plate or napkin. A muddled dusk settles over the city. She rolls a smoke and watches the night's benign arrival. When the sky is as dark as it's going to get, she drags her mattress into the yard and lies under the few stars bold enough to compete with the city lights.

She wakes cold and shivering. Instead of crawling into bed, she retrieves more blankets and falls deeply into dreams of high mountains and black pines. Traffic wakes her before the alarm. She lies a minute, pretending the susurrus is wind in sycamores. The spell is broken by a horn blast.

In the morning meeting she is vague about the weekend, explaining once again that she has come back with more questions than answers. As the meeting breaks up, she motions Lewis into her office. Frank hasn't typed up her notes yet, giving Lewis the opportunity to crack, "Fred Flintstone's more plugged in than you are."

"Got a prettier wife, too," she says, shuffling through papers. "Got nothing on Roderick Dusi. Sal seemed surprised when I mentioned he was down here. Said she forgot he worked with her old man. The uncle only hired him when he was desperate. Didn't tell me shit about him. But we know he was there. We know he fought with Saladino. Know the uncles," she quotes the air, "wanted to kill him. Had a history of mental illness. I want you to dig deeper on him. Everything you can find."

Lewis is nodding, writing, not waiting for her boss's notes.

"Gets better. John Mazetti—the guy who owned the ranch? Saladino's boss? He was having an affair with Saladino's wife."

Lewis whistles. "Saladino know?"

"Don't think so. Bad as his temper was when he was drinking, I think Mazetti'd have been a dead man if Saladino knew. He was already jealous of Mazetti—"

"How you know?"

"Sal—the daughter—she said he used to accuse his wife of wishing she'd married Mazetti instead. They had a history. All grew up together—"

"Damn. S'like *Bonanza* meets *Melrose Place*."

"Mazetti knew where Saladino would be. Big, strong guy. Angry. Motivated after his lover was beat. Again. Saladino wouldn't have defended himself if Mazetti caught him unaware or came on him all friendly-like. Have you accounted for him yet after Mary Saladino died?"

Lewis wags her head. "None of the auction places in Merced keep records that far back, and if he didn't buy anything they wouldn't a had a record of him being there anyway."

Frank lifts a finger for each point. "Opportunity. Motive. Means." She stops to scratch a note to herself. "I should've thought to see if I could find who handles the Mazettis' books. Might be something going back that far, about his trip that week. Okay. Here's another thing's been rolling around in my head. His daughter Cass, Sal's sister.

"Cass is drunker than Stingy Jack when she dies, but she's a good driver and can handle her liquor. She's been on that road her whole life. She'd have known the turn was coming, even blind drunk she'd have known to slow for it. The old cop on the scene, the sister, neither remembers skid marks in the road. There's no obvious cause of accident other than a postmortem .16 Blood Alcohol Content. Which could have been exaggerated postmortem results, and if it wasn't, if that really was her BAC while she was alive, that would have been nothing for her. By all accounts, she could drink anyone under the table."

Frank tosses her pad on the desk and kicks back with her feet on it. "I'm not buying it was an accident. I think she killed herself."

"How come?"

"That's the question. What makes a pretty, talented, popular young woman drive herself through the windshield? I'm betting something drastic, like maybe you killed your father, or you know who did, like maybe your uncle, but you can't say. That'd be hard to live with, wouldn't it?"

"Yeah, but you ain't got nothing to back that."

"Don't I? People don't just wake up one morning and decide to kill themselves. Things happen that lead to the decision, that build up to it." Frank counts on her fingers again. "Her mother's dead. She did nothing to stop the beatings. She's furious with her father. Blames him. Supposedly can't find him. I think that's bullshit. If you're that angry, that's incentive enough to live, to find the bastard and hunt him down. They don't do that. The girls give up right away. Why? 'Cause they know where he is. No sense in looking. One of them killed him. Maybe Cass. She's the wild one, the reckless one with the temper. They find him that night, they argue, things get outta hand, Cass grabs a two-by-four and connects in a rage. She doesn't mean to, but now what are they gonna do? They've got a dead body on their hands. Bury him quick. Right there. The girls are smart enough to know they gotta be pouring a foundation soon. Dig him down. Hurry home. Pretend nothing ever happened."

Lewis looks skeptical. "Possible," she admits. "But what about the boyfriends? See, this is the way I'm feeling it. They go down there. The uncle tells them where the girls are. They get there, and one of 'em takes on the old man. Get into a fight."

"No defensive wounds."

Lewis waves. "An argument. It escalates. One of the boys pop him. They all four bury Saladino. They all in on it. That's why Cass kill herself. Can't handle the pressure. 'Specially girl drink like she do? She know she gonna spill it, get someone she love in trouble. Don't make sense, the girls popping they old man. 'At's something a boy up in his blood about a girl would do."

Nodding, Frank says, "Maybe Pete. He's a shystie bastard. Real possessive of Sal. Might be Thompson, but I'm not feelin' him. Sal says he's an awful liar. Or—" Frank drops her feet onto the floor and turns back to the paperwork on her desk "—could be we're both fulla shit and some long-dead wino popped Saladino for pocket change."

"Maybe so," Lewis agrees, standing to go. "Maybe so."

"Close the door, please."

She does and Frank stares at her phone. She owes Caroline a call and a date. She wonders what Sal is doing, how cool the morning is, and what the creek will look like when all the leaves have fallen. She wishes she'd thought to take pictures. Going online, she scrolls through images of the Santa Lucias. None look right. They don't fill the craving in her heart.

The retirement papers catch her eye. She pulls them out and calls Caroline. "Hey," she tells her voicemail. "It's me. Nothing on the agenda tonight. Holler if you'd like to do something."

But right after lunch the squad catches a drive-by. Tatum is next on the rotation and Frank rolls with him. The victim is an eight-year-old girl riding her bicycle home from school. The bullets sprayed into a quiet Dalton Street home were meant for her older brother. The bicycle has pink tassels on the handlebars. They match the girl's anklets and the barrettes in her hair.

Pintar arrives on scene to deal with the media. It's a small crowd, as even pretty eight-year-olds don't rate much South-Central airtime. Frank goes inside the house, where the mother and father and younger brother huddle on the sofa. The son who was the intended target has fled. She steps carefully around shattered glass in the front room, listening as Tatum asks for a photograph of the boy.

"He didn't do anything. Why do you want him? Why you don't go find the punks that did this to my baby girl?"

Tatum starts to explain that their son can lead them to the shooter, but Frank interrupts. "Whoever did this to your daughter is going to know your son's coming for them and they'll be waiting for him. We want to get to your son before they do."

The mother nods and goes into another room. She comes out with three freshly printed pictures of her son, his arms around his mother and sister, all grinning for the camera.

Tatum puts out an APB while Frank takes the brother aside.

"What's his street name?"

"I dunno."

"Yeah, you do. It'll help me find him faster, and maybe keep him alive. Who's he claim?"

"I dunno."

Frank sighs. "Do you love your sister?"

He nods.

"Your mom and dad?"

He nods again.

"Do you have any idea how hard this is gonna be for them, how much it's gonna hurt that they've lost their baby girl?"

The boy tears up and tries to choke them down.

"Can you think how it'll be if they lose their baby girl *and* their oldest boy? I don't want whoever did this to your sister to kill him, too. You know they're gonna be lookin' for him. If I can find him first, I have a chance to protect him. If I don't, your parents are gonna lose two of their babies. You want that, to be the only one they got left?"

He shakes his head at the floor. Frank squats next to him and leans in. "Who's he claim?"

The boy is staunch in his brother's defense.

"Nobody's gonna know you told me, and the longer you hold out, the more time you give for the guys who shot your sister to find your brother. Trust me, little man, you don't want that on your head. Who's he claim?"

He mumbles, "One Bloods."

"What's he go by?"

"Lil' Hook."

"Alright."

She stands. Her leg is cramping. She gives his shoulder a squeeze and leaves to find Tatum. "I'mma take the car. You finish up here."

"Where you going?"

"Find their boy."

Frank idles through late afternoon traffic, pausing next to the furniture store she pointed out to Braxton. Every 1Blood and F13 tag is crossed out with a 59 HCG tag. "Shit." She turns around and heads for the Rec Center.

An ex-banger and old street friend runs the center, and she's glad to find him in. "Colgate." She pumps his hand and they catch up briefly before Frank hands him the print. "You know this boy? One Blood, goes by Lil' Hook?"

Colgate squints at the grainy print. "Yeah, I know him. He just a tagger."

He hands the paper back. "What you want with him?"

"I think he's jumped in. Someone—I got a hundred bucks on a 59 HC—iced his baby sister, and Lil' Hook's gonna take me right to him."

"Last I heard, Ones be kicking over to a *casita* somewhere by Roosevelt Park."

"That's east side."

"Yeah, you know the lines blur all the time. Street word is F13 making a big push into 18th turf and scooping up all the little sets, promisin' a nibble of the eMe pie."

"Hm. Tasty. Hollah at me if you hear anything?"

Colgate nods somberly. "Will do, Frank."

She places a call while driving east. The sergeant at the bureau Gang Enforcement Unit is out and she speaks to another GEU cop, trying to narrow the *casita*'s location, but the guy is clueless. She hangs up, staring at her phone, wondering what in hell he gets paid for. Scrolling through her address book, unconsciously reading the surrounding street traffic, she presses the number of a Newton Division cop. "Stacy Vandewort. Frank Franco. How you doing?"

"I get any better, I'm gonna be dancin' with the stars. How about you? Long time no see."

"Nothing's changed. Same shit, different day. Stacy, tell me what you know about a Florencia *casita* somewhere on Central, might be starting to blend with One Bloods."

"Yeah, I can think of one or two. Why, what's up?"

She explains how Lil' Hook is probably gathering his posse even as they speak and that she'd like to preempt a payback. "The Warthog," as the overlarge woman is called, promises to meet her in forty. Frank cruises into the neighboring division, slowing to check out Newton's graffiti.

She calls Caroline to tell her she won't be able to make it after all, and is oddly relieved. Not wanting to know what that's about, she concentrates on a west-side tag over an east-side click, surprised the westies have expanded this far. A woman walks a dog on the other side of the street. The dog is black and thin, like Bone, with only a stub for a tail. She double-takes the owner, certain it's not Sal, and then she is sitting on the shore of a gold-dappled pond under green trees and blue sky.

There are women before her, younger women, laughing and splashing in the cool water. The sun is a comfort to her old bones. Her fingers blindly work long stems into the start of a basket. Beside her rests a grizzled hound, head on its paws. Spying a spot in the circle of blue sky, she glances up with a greeting for the vulture whirling there. The younger women laugh at her. She accepts the harmless derision with a warning that they will see, they will see.

A truck honks and returns her to the black tar and brown air of South-Central. She takes a breath to clear her head and looks for the dog. It is gone.

The afternoon is spent surveilling *casitas* with The Warthog, checking in with Tatum and later the GEU sergeant. He doesn't have any intel on Lil' Hook or who capped his sister, but he assures Frank he will keep his ear to the ground. Back at the station, night is coming hard. Frank pushes away the purple mountains that rise in her head. She grabs Tatum and they start running down sources and snitches. Colgate calls just before midnight with a name. They run it through the system and by four a.m. have enough information on the 59 Hoover Criminal to wake a judge for a warrant.

By 0730 hours they are assembled with backup at a derelict home under the Harbor Freeway. At Tatum's announcing knock, bangers in boxers and T-shirts leap from windows like fleas from a dead dog. One is the 59 they're looking for. The rest of the day, she and Tatum take turns breaking him in the box. The case is only thirty hours old when Braxton comes into the squad room waving a plastic bag with a crappy Raven MP-25 recovered from the banger's baby momma's apartment.

Disgusted and exhausted, Tatum asks the 59 what the hell he was thinking. "What makes you keep such a piece-of-shit gun when it's so hot?"

The dissed banger is exhausted, too. He looks at the wall and yawns.

Frank chimes in, "Yeah, you can replace that junk for a hundred bucks, easy. What you such a cheap ass for?"

"Ain't cheap," he argues, then says proudly. "I'm prudent. Ain't rich like you policemans."

Frank nods. "You got a point. We get new weapons every six months whether we want 'em or not." Tatum twists his head toward her, but she continues, "Guess if I was buying my own I'd be prudent, too. But, man, couldn't you have got nothing better than a Raven? I mean, if you're gonna be keeping 'em and all, why not step to something dope, get you'self a *real* gun?"

"Shit, motherfucker, that ain't my only piece. I got others way better 'an that."

Frank gives him a big smile. The 59 has just tied himself to the weapon. With luck, ballistics will tie his weapon to the murdered girl. Frank steps out of the box and lets Tatum finish. On the way downstairs she calls Pintar with the update.

"Nice work," her boss says. "You must be one happy detective."

"Yeah," she lies. "See you tomorrow."

Frank unlocks her car. She sits, scrolling through messages. Two are from Caroline. Frank puts the phone down and reaches into the glove box. Extracting Drum and Buglers, she slowly rolls a smoke. The October evening is chilly. Lights wink at the dusk and encourage night to come along. She fights onto the freeway and drives with the window down, cigarette balanced in the corner of her mouth. Ash falls into her lap. It would be so easy to keep driving north into the dark hold of the mountains, to sleep under their quiet watch.

The cigarette burns her lip. She squints through the distracting smoke and pain. Disappointed she can't bear the heat anymore, she flicks the butt away. The phone rings into the passenger seat. She flips it over, reads Caroline's number, and switches it off. A couple miles later, she relents, texting Caroline that she has to get some sleep and will call tomorrow.

Caroline texts back, *Are u avoiding me?*

Don't be silly. Beat. Up 36 hrs. xxoo.

Frank hits Send and powers the phone off again, satisfied that at least the middle of the text is true.

Chapter 34

There are no new cases during the week, but Frank stays busy. She cruises with her cops on their cases, visits with Colgate, Miss Lacy, and a dozen other contacts. Out of respect for the family, she attends the funeral of a Rollin' 60s banger, and stops in at Drew Memorial to see an old informant dying from AIDS. She stays in touch with Mary and goes to lots of AA meetings because that helps keep her from thinking about Sal and the mountains.

When Caroline calls, Frank makes excuses not to see her. But the weekend looms, and she can't put her off anymore. They make a date for dinner at Caroline's. Frank arrives with flowers and Caroline's favorite chocolate truffles. She goes through the prescribed motions, by turns gracious, attentive, and charming. It is only after they are in bed that Caroline wonders, "If I ask you something, will you promise to be straight with me? No pun intended."

Frank smiles thinly in the dark. "Sure."

"Why do I feel like you are a million miles away?"

"Not a million," she admits. "Just a couple hundred."

"In Soledad?"

"Afraid so."

Caroline removes her hand from Frank's thigh. It leaves a cool spot the same temperature as Frank's insides.

"Is there someone else?"

"No."

"Not that woman up there, your victim's daughter?"

"No. Absolutely not."

"Then what is it?"

Frank snaps the light on. She pushes her pillow against the

headboard and sits up. "It's crazy. I don't even know how to tell you."

"Start at the beginning."

Frank does, repeating everything she told Marguerite. "I feel like I've suddenly come alive up there. Like my whole life's been fake up to this point and all of a sudden I've discovered my real one. I know that doesn't make sense. I don't expect you to understand."

"That's good," Caroline murmurs. "Because I'm not sure I do." She stares at the ceiling while Frank traces the pattern on the bedspread. Finally she says, "I feel like you've told me you're seeing a man. I don't know how to compete with something like this."

"You can't. There's nothing to compete against."

"That's my point."

They lie in the strained silence until Caroline sighs. "Seeing as you're not really here anyway, it might be better if you went home."

"Yeah."

Frank tries not to bolt from the bed. She dresses patiently while Caroline looks on. Zipping up her hoodie, Frank sits on the edge of the bed. She takes Caroline's hand.

"I'm sorry it's not working right now."

"So am I. I miss you."

"I know. I'm sorry. I wish I could give you more to hang your hat on, but I don't have it to give. I've got to see this through. I don't know why, I just do."

"And I wish I could help you but I don't feel like you need my help. Or want it. Do you?"

Frank shakes her head. "I think this is something I've got to do alone."

Caroline nods. "It looks like that tarot lady was right."

"Maybe."

She kisses Caroline's cheek with a twinge of remorse. But her lover's comfortable familiarity is no match for the mystery of the mountains. As she lets herself out of the condo, she feels like a prisoner stepping from jail. She drives fast through the red darkness, windows down, fog wrapping in her hair. At home she drags her mattress and blankets out to the backyard. The night settles her cool, damp hair on her face, and she ponders the insanity that drives her from the warm bed of a desirable woman. But it's an idle question, because Frank already knows the answer.

Chapter 35

Frank gets to the squad room early on Friday, but Lewis is already there. Before Frank can even greet her, Lewis grins and waves a sheaf of papers. "Guess what I got?"

"Winning lottery ticket?"

"Almost as good," she gloats. "Remember all those ledgers I found? I've been working them steady, running down names, making calls."

Frank lifts a finger. "Hold on."

Her detective has switched from casual ghetto slang into an Ivy League idiolect. Frank thinks it's an unconscious habit, but it always signifies Lewis is onto something hot. She pours coffee and perches with it on Lewis' desk. "Alright. Tell me."

Lewis is almost bouncing in her seat. "Jim McKinley. In 1968 he was an apprentice plumber and he worked for Saladino Construction. He's retired now. I talked to him last night. He remembers Domenic Saladino."

Frank nods.

"McKinley remembers working with Saladino. Said that he was a good worker but he drank too much. Recalled that he usually came on in winter, that he lived somewhere up north. Never stuck around too long. I asked him, did he recall the last time he worked with Saladino, and he said yeah, at a block of commercial buildings they were building on Western."

She pauses, unable to keep the grin from splitting her face.

"He says he remembers because Saladino's daughters pulled up to the job site one night and started screaming at him that he'd murdered their mother."

Frank sets the cup down. "What else did he say?"

"That ain't enough?"

Frank shrugs. She keeps her hands in her lap so Lewis won't see them shake.

"He left after the girls got there. It was almost dark. He was helping Saladino do some framing because they were gonna pour concrete the next day. They were almost done when the girls pulled up. Saladino told him to go home, that he'd finish up. So McKinley did. Said he was un-comfortable with the daughters being upset and screaming, so he got the hell out of there."

"Where's this guy at?"

"West Covina."

"Guess we better go for a ride."

She gets up and carries her coffee into her office with two hands. Not bothering with the light, she locks the door and puts her back against it. She is unmoved when a wave of dizziness warns a vision is imminent. She surrenders to the oncoming flight, spiraling high like a condor over the sunset-bloodied mountains. The canyons flicker below her in golden orange and red flame. The sea washes blackly to shore to break ruddy on the sand, and all of it—mountains, fire, sky, and ocean—is forever a great endless circle of beginning and ending, leaving and coming, birthing and dying, and always, always, always—"Fuck."

Frank drags a hand over her eyes to wipe away the endless whirl. She slaps the light on, takes her chair, and sets to furious typing. A knock summons her to the morning meeting. She finishes what she is typing and starts the meeting late. She hears only half of it. When it is over, Lewis is excited to roll to Covina.

"Half an hour," Frank tells her. She returns to her office, finds two pictures on classmates.com and hits Print. Then she pulls the retirement papers from her drawer, seals them in an interdepartmental envelope, and drops them in the mailbox. Picking up her prints, she slides them into a cell-frame with four other pictures.

"Ready?" she asks Lewis.

"Just been waiting on you."

Lewis grins and grabs keys, but Frank says, "I'll drive."

This gets a raised eyebrow from Lewis, but she answers, "Ten-four.

You know what? I'mma use the little girls room 'fore we get stuck in traffic."

Waiting in her car, Frank rolls a cigarette and smokes. Lewis comes out of the station and Frank pitches the cigarette. Her cop gets in, fanning the air.

"Damn, LT, it stink in here. That why you wanna drive, so you can smoke you nasties?"

Frank's only answer is to swing out of the lot. Lewis is in a good mood and chatters like a songbird. Frank doesn't contribute to the conversation. Eventually Lewis ventures, "You sweet on that Saladino chick?"

Franks cuts her with a glance. "What are you talkin' about?"

"You just looked sad this morning when I told you. Like you disappointed or somethin'."

"Surprised, more like it. Disappointed I didn't pull that outta her, that my young Turk's sharper than I am."

"Yeah," Lewis jollies, "that'll be the day. What you wanna do about this?"

"Go back up and talk to her."

"Let me go with you."

"No."

It comes out sharper than Frank intends.

"You sure?"

She speeds under a yellow light.

"I'll take care of it."

The next light is red. Each cop studies her side of the street. As Frank accelerates, Lewis mentions, "My aunt's birthday party is next weekend. I could invite you. I'm tellin' you, you'd like her."

"Lewis, don't." Frank warns. They've had this conversation before.

"A'ight, I'm just saying."

Frank shakes her head at Lewis's unceasing effort to hook her up with a dyke aunt. "If this woman's such a damn prize, why isn't she taken already?"

"She selective, is all. Don't want just anybody."

"Then I'm sure she'd be thrilled with a broken-down, old cop."

Lewis turns on her. "Whatsa matter, you sayin' shit like that? Young

Turks," she mimics. "Broken-down old cop. Why you all Gloomy Gus on me?"

"Ain't Gloomy Gus."

"The hell you ain't. Your face so long it be leavin' drag marks here all the way back to the station."

Frank has to tell Lewis about her papers before they get back to the office. But not before the interview. She doesn't want her distracted for that, and indeed, McKinley precisely reiterates everything he's told Lewis. How it was cold and almost dark when the girls drove up, how they jumped out of the car crying and screaming at Saladino. Frank asks if both girls were screaming, or just one.

McKinley is grizzled and chain-drinks black coffee. He looks at the ceiling, trolling memories. "Just the one was screaming, as I recall. The other was more like she was crying. But they were both fair upset."

Frank shows him the six-pack of black and white photos. He squints at the page a moment, then picks out a young Sal. A second later he taps a finger on Cass.

"It was these two girls. At least, it looks like them."

"Which one was screaming?"

He leans over the pictures, studying them. "Can't say for sure. Like I said, it was getting dark, and they look alike, don't they?"

Frank nods. "Do you remember what the girls said?"

"Sure I do. Not every day a guy's daughters drive up accusing him of murdering their mother. That's what the one girl kept saying. She kept screaming, 'You killed her. You killed her. You killed my mother. You sonofabitch. You killed her.'"

McKinley shivers and rubs his arms. "It was spooky, and I don't mind telling you it gave me the creeps. Saladino was holding the one girl off, and he turns to me and says to go on home. That he'd finish up. I can tell you he didn't have to say that twice. I was out of there like I'd been shot out of a cannon."

"What's the last thing you remember seeing before you left?"

McKinley sucks at his coffee, shakes his head. "Just Saladino talking to his girls. Like he was trying to calm them down."

"Did it work?"

"I don't know. I didn't stick around long enough to find out."

They drive back to Figueroa, Lewis crowing and Frank glum. Before they head into the station, Frank touches her cop's arm. "Hey. I want you to hear this from me. I turned my papers in this morning."

"What papers?"

"Retirement."

"You're shittin' me."

"Nope. I'm done."

Lewis leans against the car, fingering the cross at her neck. "Why?"

Frank nods her head at the binder Lewis is holding. "For that. I'm tired of being lied to every day, dumped on. Been at it almost longer than you are old, and I'm over it. I'm all done."

"You can't be," her cop protests.

"I can and I am. Just wanted you to hear it from me first."

Frank walks away. Upstairs she types a quick synopsis of the Saladino evidence. Finding Pintar in her office, she presents her notes. "I need to go back up there. Just one more time."

After scanning what Frank has given her, Pintar agrees. "But it's got to be the last time."

"Oh, it will be. And by the way, I've turned my papers in."

"*What?*"

"Yeah. I'm done."

"Since when?"

Frank shrugs. "Been meaning to do it for a while. It's time."

"I thought you liked your work."

"Used to. Don't much anymore."

"I'm so sorry to hear that. Can I do anything to make it better?"

"No." Frank makes an effort to smile. "You've been great. Mind if I leave now? I'd like to get up there before dark."

Pintar shrugs. "Guess I may as well get used to you not being around."

Feeling a sad wave of affection for her boss, she assures, "I'll always be around. You can call anytime."

"That's not the same—and you know it."

Frank nods. She checks in with the squad to let them know Pintar's on call and that she's headed back up north. Lewis ignores her, but Braxton and Tatum nod blandly. She knows Lewis hasn't told them yet. She thinks about doing so but decides she doesn't owe them like she did Lewis. She pauses by her detective's desk. "Sister Shaft."

Lewis stops typing but doesn't look at her.

"Hold the fort down?"

"Somebody got to," she mutters darkly.

After a quick stop at the house to pack a bag, Frank creeps onto the 405. Traffic is awful, but Frank takes her time, rolling cigarettes and thinking. She expected to be thrilled about retiring but is only slightly relieved, as if she's turned in nothing more important than an overdue expense report. Even that is overshadowed by disappointing Pintar and Lewis. She calls Mary. "Hey. Congratulate me. I put my papers in."

"Oh my God! That's terrific. Congratulations, kiddo. You must be ecstatic."

"Not really."

"Give it time to kick in. You'll wake up one morning at o-dark-thirty and that's when it'll hit you that you never have to do any of that shit again."

"Yeah. Maybe. Just wanted to check in. I won't be at the meeting tomorrow. I'm heading up north again."

"Alright, kiddo. Congratulations. Enjoy the ride."

"Yeah."

But there is no joy in the long drive, and halfway to Santa Barbara Frank realizes that Lewis' and Pintar's disappointment is the perfect mirror for her own. She's hoped without even knowing she's hoped that Sal wasn't involved in Saladino's death. Now, at the very least, she knows Sal has withheld evidence; at worst, killed her father or was an accessory.

Fog reaches in from the ocean, gathering the blue with long, grey fingers. Frank shakes her head at the disappearing sky. "Hey, guides," she speaks to the windshield. "Where the fuck are you now?"

No one answers. At least not that Frank can hear. The fog swallows the last of the day.

Chapter 36

She is leaning against her car, smoking, when Sal comes down off the mountain. She parks the old truck and gets out.

"I didn't expect you back so soon."

Frank shrugs. "Me neither." She pitches the cigarette. "You said you had something to show me."

Sal considers. Frank holds the steady blue gaze. The women gathered on the bench watch the wordless struggle. Sal nods. She walks to the women. One protests as Sal explains she can't stay, but Sal touches each woman in turn and whispers in her ear. A squat *abuela* hugs her tearfully, as does a younger woman. They leave or walk to the cars parked under the oak tree. All except the one who argued have pressed a bag upon Sal. She carries them to the truck, and Frank drives after her through the gate. They leave the Honda at the turnout and jolt wordlessly to the ranch.

"Can you get the horses? I have to get something from the house."

"Sure."

Dune and Buttons are already in the corral. Frank easily halters and ties them. She is brushing Buttons when the truck rumbles back to the corral. Sal silently joins in the work without speaking. She ties saddlebags to the horses, and when they leave the corral she loads them with ten-pound sacks from the back of the truck. Frank knows better than to ask what is in the bags or where they are taking them. Not that she even cares to ask, for she has learned that her questions are best answered in the showing. They ride the cropped trail to the cabin. The morning sun is warm and the mountains loom almost cheerfully. Frank wonders if they mock her.

At the cabin, Sal ties bedrolls onto the horses and fills the remaining saddlebags. The dogs cry and bark from the pen. They cannot go, she tells Frank. It is too far. After stocking them with food and water, she makes one more trip into the cabin. She comes out with the shotgun and slides it into the empty rifle bag.

"What's that for?"

"It's a long ride. You never know when you'll need it."

They swing the horses toward the mountains and trot over the easy pasturage. Frank is uncomfortable with the pace. She glares at Sal's back and rides with one hand on the pommel. They begin the climb through buckbrush and manzanita. Frank recognizes the trail; it's the one they took to the pass. Thorny branches grab at her legs and she has to pay attention to keep Buttons clear of the hungry shrubs. The sun is hot for October and beams with lusty vigor. Frank is glad for the baseball cap she wears. Sweat dribbles from her temples. Dust puffs under the horses hooves and lizards skitter out of their way. The trail rises and narrows. Somewhere Sal has turned off the pass trail, and now the horses pick their way with dainty precision.

Noon comes and passes in front of them. The horses rise steadily into the heart of the mountains. The rough old gods watch with clasped hands and heads bowed. Frank shivers under the obdurate gaze, certain she will be found wanting.

They gain a lean ridge and Sal pauses in a scrawny patch of shade. She unscrews the canteen and passes it to Frank. After a long swallow, Frank gives it back. At the barest flick of the reins, Dune moves out. Frank follows into the blunt mallet of the sun. She wishes she'd drunk more water. A cold beer sounds good, too. She imagines reaching into an icy cooler, the tangy spray of hops as she pops the cap, then the bitter, malty taste and rush of bubbles down her throat. She'll chase the beer with a tumbler of belly-burning scotch.

Frank is so engrossed in alcoholic dreams she almost runs Buttons into Dune's ass. Sal is stopped, staring into a thicket of boulders and thorny brush. Dune whinnies and dances in place. His nerves are contagious, and Buttons shies from the brake. Frank reins her sharply, but is sympathetic with her urge to bolt. Sal slides the shotgun from its scabbard just as a flock of vultures erupts from the thicket. They flap desperately, barely clearing Frank's head. Buttons leaps sideways, but Frank keeps her seat. She yanks the reins to keep the horse from getting her head and Sal yells, "Not so tight. She'll rear."

Sure enough, Buttons is gathering her haunches and Frank drops the reins. The birds wing heavily into the sky and the sun returns. Sal dismounts, motioning Frank to do likewise. Sal hands Frank her reins and creeps around the tangle of brush. Crouching, she presses through and disappears. Frank watches nervously until she reappears with the Winchester crooked in her elbow. She takes Dune's reins and tells Frank, "Go look."

"At what?"

"You'll see."

"Jesus!" Frank shakes her head. "Always with the mysteries."

She gives Sal her reins, and nods at the shotgun. "Can I take that?"

"You won't need it," but she hands it to Frank anyway.

Approaching the concealing brush, Frank catches the familiar whiff of high blood. She parts branches and peeks in. The sound of flies leads her eye up to to a broad boulder. Splayed across it is a deer's head and what's left of a torn carcass. She backs out and gives Sal the shotgun. Without thinking she takes Buttons' reins and lifts effortlessly into the saddle. Her feet instinctively find the stirrups.

"What the hell did that?"

"What do you think?"

"I don't know. Something strong enough to drag a deer around. Bear?"

Sal shakes her head. "A bear would eat it out in the open."

Frank sighs. "I don't know, Sal. Just tell me."

"Mountain lions like to drag their prey up and cache it."

"Aw, Jesus." Frank scans the scrubby glade and cliff above. "Is it coming back?"

"Maybe. Maybe not. There's not much left."

The horses are still spooked and Buttons dances in place. Sal notes, "You've turned into a fair horseman."

"I should be with the amount of time you've made me spend in a saddle," Frank grumbles, but the compliment pleases her. They ride out, around the cliff and up. The horses reach and climb in loud, labored grunts. When they gain the top of the bare ridge, Sal lets them rest. She hands Frank the canteen.

"Finish it."

She does, greedily. Sal stashes the empty canteen and they plod on. The sun slants fiercely into their faces. Frank rolls her head around her shoulders and squeezes the muscle bunched in her neck. Sweat stains the horses and she is sure they are as miserable as she is.

Their climb levels out onto another mean, stony ridge, but this one falls west to a series of dark canyons and beyond them is the purple smudge of sea. Frank waves at a persistent gnat. The horses step in alternating rhythm along the wide ridge. Occasionally one gives a snort and shakes its bridle as if rousing from the verge of sleep. Their saddles make the creaking sounds of old leather. Frank sways drowsily to Buttons' step, her attention returning as they drop into sudden, cool shade on the lee side of the ridge.

Sal stops and slides from her mount. "We get off and walk from here."

She leads Dune across a steep slope of broken rock and shale. Frank hesitates. Buttons wants to follow, but Frank grips the reins. Loosening her feet from the stirrups, she swings a leg and slides free of the saddle. Buttons nickers for Dune but stands still. Frank scratches under her belly band and starts across the scree. Buttons rear, hooves slip, and Frank scrambles to get on the uphill side of the beast. Ahead, a little higher on the slope, Dune skews sideways. He slides a couple feet before finding purchase.

Frank swears as Buttons does the same. She gives the horse plenty of rein, figuring she knows more about traversing the gravelly slope than Frank does. The horse lunges a dozen feet upslope to more stable footing. She is breathing hard and Frank pats her shoulder. They pick their way slowly over the loose rock. She glances up, hoping to see where the slide levels out, but sees only the tall wall of ridge curving around to block them.

"Oh, for Christ's sake."

Sal's about a hundred feet ahead. Frank is about to call out to her, but she and Dune disappear into the granite face of the mountain.

"What the fuck?" Frank stops, but Buttons pulls her on. She staggers but breaks the fall with her scabbed hand. The cuts from last week open and weep red, but she doesn't feel them. She stumbles closer to the wall. What had seemed a shadow in the rock slowly becomes a fissure wide enough to allow a horse through. Frank's breath rushes into her lungs and her knees wobble; if she weren't so eager to leave the slope, she'd have sunk to them, rocks and all. Cursing for following Sal on this last, harebrained adventure, probably the one that will kill her, Frank steps into the crack's quick gloom. She starts to lead Buttons through but the horse balks.

Frank coaxes, "Come on, girl."

Buttons takes one step, but backward. Her rear hooves begin to slide. Frank tugs on the reins but is dragged along the dusty fissure floor. Buttons scrabbles for traction in the loose rock and can't find it. She makes a panicky scramble, only to lose the little footing she had. She slides slowly down the slope, and Frank slides with her. Her ankle knocks against a sharp rock, and Frank plants against it.

"Yah!" she encourages, pulling with all she's got on the reins. Buttons slips and gains her footing, but she is still sliding. Frank is pulled out of the skinny chasm out onto the treacherous slope. She yanks the reins, screaming, "Yah! Yah!" With a desperate lurch, eyes rolling white, Buttons heaves past Frank only to start slipping back again. Frank drops her ass into the loose rock and braces her feet into it. With every last ounce of strength, she pulls on the reins, praying they won't snap. Buttons' hooves ring and skid, but for a second she finds traction. It is enough for a final lunge past Frank, up and into the safety of the fissure. Frank crawls in behind her, using the cool, rough walls to stand. She squeezes between rock and horse, knowing Buttons could crush her and knowing she won't.

They stand head to head, catching their breath in sweet, long draughts. Frank reaches down and drags her nails through Buttons' hot, greasy hair. Her big chest heaves. The horse trembles, and Frank does, too. "Shhh." Frank smoothes a palm over the sweat-slick coat. "Good girl. Good girl."

Dune's nicker drifts into the crack and Buttons lifts her head to answer. She bumps her nose into Frank's shoulder. Frank nods and leads her through the cleft. Sal waits just outside in a copse of short, wind-bent pine.

"Everything alright?"

"Yeah." Frank looks at her horse. "We're good."

They continue on foot across a much more reasonable slope. The pines give way to a *portrero*, strewn on its far side with house-sized boulders. They cross the soft, round hill bending tall, yellow grass before them. The horses snatch mouthfuls, and Frank absently picks at ticks that brush off from the waist-high grass.

As they approach the boulders Sal croons in a low voice, "*Hola, Abuela. Es Saladino. Vengo con una amiga.*"

Frank is surprised Sal's Spanish is so good, but more surprised that someone might actually live here. Sal and Dune stop as one. Coming up alongside them, Frank sees why.

A woman beyond old waits between the towering boulders. Dry and hunched, she has less substance than a stalk of the yellowed grass. Eyes blued with age peer from folds of skin as dark and creased as the mountains. A wild spume of hair cascades around her shoulders. She wears a colorless cloth that might at some point have been a dress.

The old woman asks something in a croaky, thin voice.

Sal responds, "*Si, Abuela. Si. Saladino y una amiga.*"

The old head bobs like a dried apple in a pond, and a clawed hand waves Sal forward. Sal steps slowly to the grandmother, stopping just short of her. The crone cups her hands. Sal takes the hide-covered bones and guides them to her face. The ancient claws pat briefly, then fall away. The woman speaks in a language that sounds like Spanish but not quite. Sal motions Frank over.

She leads Buttons next to Dune. The horse shies at the old woman, startling Frank, and she grips the reins tighter. Frank winces—not at the scent of old urine and flesh, but at the smells behind the woman, of rancid grease and rotting meat. The hag reaches up.

"Go on," Sal urges.

Frank bends her head to the wizened hands. She stumbles and drops the reins. On her knees, she hears the voices of women raised in high keening. She tries to stand, but bony fingers grip her head. There is the smell of smoke and dust and sun in small green pools.

The voice of the old woman joins in the wailing. Frank tries again to pull away. The *abuela* holds her easily. A cacophony of sticks clack in time to the voices. Columns of gray smoke twist to the sky. They reach Frank, high in her dizzying flight over mountain, dusk, and winking fire. She grabs the crone's gristly wrists to keep from toppling.

The *abuela* releases her and Frank sits back. The singing stops, the clacking sticks and twilit flight, too, but Frank is still dizzy. The old woman cackles. She chatters and finds Sal's hand, following it to the reins and loaded horse. She feels the full bags and nods.

Sal leads the horses past. Frank doesn't watch where. It doesn't matter. Nothing makes sense. Not the sticks or singing or familiar flight, or that an old woman lives, alone and blind, at the top of a remote mountain range. None of it makes sense—yet all of it makes sense. As if it's always been, layer upon layer of time and stone, wind and plant, humans and animals.

A hand on her arm tugs her to stand. Sal says, "Help me unpack."

Frank follows mutely to the hobbled horses. She takes the weight handed her, as silent and patient as another horse, and trails Sal just as obediently between the tall boulders. After two trips back and forth, they sit on random rocks within the stone nest. A pit in front of Frank holds the ashes of countless fires. The old woman rustles inside a hollow in the boulders. Frank can hear the shuffle of naked, calloused feet. A bitter smell assaults her and she looks for the source. On a rock opposite her, across the cold ashes, Sal smokes nonchalantly.

The beldam steps nimbly from her cave. She waves a smoldering bundle of leaves and smoke grays the air. She circles the rocky enclosure, waving the bundle at each uneven corner and around the entrance. All the while she sings. Encircling Frank and Sal in smoke, she sings. Her voice is preternaturally young and strong. Her song rises in Frank's chest, ancient and wordless. The old woman sings the breath from her, and just as Frank thinks she can bear the song no longer, the *abuela* stops. She sways in front of Frank. Eyes sightless yet seeing, she intones a low and liquid song. Frank yields to the incantation as a sleepy child to the murmur of a parent. Her eyes close.

A lightness falls upon her hair, her face. She opens her eyes to find the *abuela* sprinkling ash upon her. Frank wonders dimly if Sal understands the chanted words. The old woman reaches. Frank allows her head to be cradled. A calloused thumb grinds between her brows. The *abuela* shifts her sinewy hand to Frank's shoulder, then the other, before pressing her palm to Frank's chest. It is warm where she touches. Quite clearly, Frank hears Marguerite James say, "Trust here."

She opens her eyes, sure she will find the *mambo* in the circle of boulders, but there is only the wizened, chanting grandma. The *abuela* removes her hand. She turns to Sal in a waft of salt and smoke and sage. Her song becomes soft and mournful. Frank's eyes drift shut again. She listens, dreaming. In her blood and bone, she understands the story of the song.

Chapter 37

"Come on."

Sal is shaking her knee. A small fire lightens the rocky surround. The *abuela* is gone. Frank stumbles after Sal. A fresh quarter moon clears the *portero*. The dark shapes of the horses stand out against the paler grass. They chew and watch the women come toward them. Sal undoes their hobbles and the women lead them past the boulders. The beasts nicker, and Frank knows they have smelled water. She smells it too. The ground becomes soft and the horses step forward to a small pool glazed with night.

Frank has been here before. She knows the source of the pool is a seep in the cliff that rises blackly to the stars. It is cloaked now in layers of night, but come morning the rock will sport the ferns and mosses that crave water. They cover the source of the spring to the edge of the deep green pool. She knows this without knowing how and accepts the knowledge calmly.

Sal kneels in the darkness and splashes her face. The horses suck quietly beside her. When they have had their fill, the women walk across the *portero* to the sentinel stand of pines.

"We'll camp here."

They tie and unsaddle their mounts. Sal hands Frank a nose sack. She buckles it on by feel while Sal hobbles the horses. After they roll out their beds, Sal offers an apple and hunk of dry cheese. Frank refuses and slides into her bag. She listens to Sal eat, then rustle a cigarette. When a match splits the darkness, Sal's features leap in peaks and hollows that seem carved from the mountain. The match dies and Frank settles deeper into her bag. Before she closes her eyes, she notices there seem to be twice as many stars as usual. She blinks, but the silvery lanterns remain steadfast. Wearing them like a magic cloak, Frank sleeps.

She wakes to the quarter moon scything through the boughs. The light glimmers on her face. She closes her eyes and listens to the voice of the pines. Needle and bough whisper to the wind, of roots and dirt and water, and grasping, reaching, always yearning for the sky and of the sky but never free to roam it like the gypsy wind. She looks once more to the twinkling stars, then sleeps until all but the most stalwart have faded.

She wakes as the dawn begins its kaleidoscope. Sal watches too. They rise when the blue stakes a permanent claim to the day. The horses whinny greetings, and Frank leads them to the spring. In daylight it is exactly as she knew it would be. She cups the water from its source in the rock. It is cold and soft and tastes faintly of earth and stars. She returns to Sal and they drink coffee while the horses munch grain. Sal shakes her empty cup clean and Frank swallows the dregs. They saddle up and walk to the cleft. Frank watches Dune and Sal negotiate the steep talus. When they gain the other side, Frank steps from her solid hold. She thinks she should be scared but is not. Hugging the cliff as closely as possible, she lets Buttons trail behind. The mare skitters a couple of times, but they cross the shifting rock and are soon pointed down the mountain.

They ride east into the sun. Frank has questions but no desire to ask them, trusting the answers will appear when needed. They arrive at the cabin just as the sun bends to the mountains. Sure it is the last sunset she will see here, Frank volunteers to stay outside and start a fire while Sal makes dinner. Bone accompanies her to the woodpile, and after she lights the fire he sits beside her. She is petting him when Kook sidles near. Sweeping the ground with his tail, he stares inquiringly at Frank.

She pats her lap and the little dog leaps in answer. He settles happily, and Frank gives him a few pets before returning her hand to Bone. Coyotes call from the hill behind them. Bone howls a reply and Kook jumps down to join him. Abandoning all self-consciousness, Frank howls too.

Sal brings tamales and steaming bowls of chile. Frank retrieves the coffee pot and cups. They eat with the day's last light spread before them and the fire glowing behind. When they are done, Sal rolls cigarettes. The dogs sleep contentedly by the chairs.

"Who is she?"

Sal twists to prop another log on the fire, then settles to the purple-black mountains.

"No one knows. My father took me there when I was twelve. She was old even then. He brought food like we did. Like his father had."

Frank quickly does the math.

"Some claim she's the last Indian, that she led her people up there to escape the missions. Some of the *abuelas* say she's a Mexican woman who ran away from a *gavacho* husband that was going to kill her for cheating on him."

The cigarette flares as Sal draws on it.

"How long has she been blind?"

"Years. But I don't know that I'd call her blind. She sees things you and I can't."

"How often do you go up there?"

"Fall and spring."

Frank blows smoke at the risen moon. "Why'd you take me there?"

"The same reason I've taken you everywhere."

"So I'll remember."

Sal nods beside her.

The evening has inked imperceptibly to night. Paled by moon and starlight, the sky hangs jealously over the true, solid black of the mountains. An owl screeches from the barn. Another answers from the creek. Frank leans her head back. Night seeps into her bones, and when Sal rises to turn her chair to the fire Frank does the same. Sal stirs the coals with a log, then lays it down to burn.

Frank doesn't want to ask what she must, but it is time. She hunches closer to Sal so that she can better read the answers when they come. "There's just one thing I don't know."

Sal turns fire-lit eyes upon her. Frank holds them with her own, knowing the fire dances within hers, too.

"The thing I don't know," she says slowly, "is if it was you, or if it was Cass, that killed your father."

Sal stiffens. She drags in a long breath and faces the leaping flames. "I knew the minute I saw you in the store that it was just a matter of time." She hugs her knees and leans toward the heat. Her hair catches the fire and throws it back, darkly red. Frank flashes on the Beretta in her pack but doesn't think she'll need it. She watches and waits patiently. The fire snaps. Cicero whimpers in a dream.

"His uncle told us he was working at a building over on Western Avenue. That they wanted to finish the framing so they could pour concrete in the morning. When we got there, it was almost dark. Only my father and another man were there. He turned when he heard us pull up, and then when he recognized the truck he broke into a big smile. Then Cass fell out of the truck—she was dead drunk—but she got up and ran over to him. She was crying and screaming that he'd killed her, our mother. He grabbed hold of her, to try and calm her down, to make sense of what she was saying. I told him that Mother was dead. At first he didn't believe it. He kept asking, 'What are you talking about?'

"Cass was hysterical. She was screaming, sobbing, 'You hit her, you killed her. You're a murderer. You killed her.' Then you could see it dawn on him, what had happened, and he started to shake Cass. 'Hold on a goddamned minute,' he said, and that was that. I literally, truly saw red. I wasn't going to let him start hurting us the way he did our mother. There was no way I was going to let us become his new punching bags. I didn't think at all. It just came to me in a flash that I wasn't going to let him do that and I picked up a shovel and swung it. I just wanted to hurt him, to get him to let go of Cass. I never meant to kill him. I knew the way he fell, the way he just crumpled, that I'd done something awful."

Sal stares through the fire. Frank waits for her to surface from the hold of her memory.

"Cass was rocking and moaning, 'My God, what did you do? What did you do?' She kept saying it over and over. Then we just sat a long time, staring at him. It was dark. And cold. And finally Cass stood up and found the shovel and started digging. I asked what she was doing, and she said no one would believe us that it was an accident, and that we had to bury him. I didn't argue. I couldn't."

"We dug a hole and dragged him into it. We thought to take his wallet, but not his wedding ring. Cass built the framing out over the hole. We had to do it by the truck headlights. I was terrified sick someone was going to call about the noise and that the police would come. But they never did. Not until you."

Sal slumps back into her chair. Frank watches the flames of the fire rise and die, rise again, fall.

"I've kept that secret for forty years."

"And Cass," Frank says softly. "It wasn't an accident, was it?"

"No. She couldn't stand the lie anymore."

She feels in her shirt. Frank tenses, but Sal's hand comes out with the tobacco pouch. She rolls a cigarette, passes it to Frank, and makes another. Frank puts a new log on the fire. A rabbit creeps at the edge of the black-red light. The women smoke.

"What happens now?"

"I take you in and we get you an attorney. There'll be an arraignment. Depending on the judge, you might be able to post bail or be released on your own recognizance."

"If not, I go to jail?"

"Yeah."

Sal nods. She drops her cigarette into the fire and sits with her arms wrapped around her knees. The fire snaps. A jet drones many miles above. Frank wishes she were up in the blackness with only moon and stars for company. She is glad she's turned her papers in.

"Do we have to go tonight?"

"No. He's been dead forty years. I don't think one more night'll make a difference."

The fire slashes Sal's features, reddening, then darkening the planes and hollows. In an effort to still the shifting mask, Frank breaches the distance between them, resting the back of her fingers against the lean, brown jaw. The weathered skin is soft there, much softer than Frank expected.

"I'm sorry it has to be this way."

"Don't be," Sal murmurs. "It's right."

Her hand covers Frank's, brings it to her lips. She rests it there a moment. Frank unfolds her fingers, cupping the side of Sal's face, running her thumb over the ridge of cheekbone. Sal clings to her wrist. The fire lifts a question in her eyes. Frank answers it with a kiss. Their lips linger, touch, merge again. Frank tugs Sal to her feet and tilts her head toward the cabin. This time, she leads and Sal follows. Frank undresses Sal and guides her to the bed. She strips and lowers herself beside Sal, who lies as still and cool as the sliver of moon peeking in the window.

Frank strokes and soothes her as if she is a spooked horse, and Sal softens beneath her. She presses into Frank's touch, tentative at first, then eager. Frank stokes the burning hunger. She leads Sal to the edge of satiety, then backs her down, only to climb her back to the brink and keep her there, quivering but silent, until Sal breaks and floods against her, into her and upon her, and Frank lets go and falls, falls from a great wine-dark height over mountains down through fire-glowing canyons and red-breaking sea, falling down, down deep into the lightless, soundless hold of the bone.

For a long moment, Frank is nothingness. Not thought, sensation, sight, or sound. She floats in dark and empty fullness. Slowly she surfaces to the moonlit room. Sal is motionless beside her, eyes on the ceiling. They glisten in the little light. Frank reaches, but Sal moves away. She sits on the edge of the bed. The moon holds her in silhouette. "I need to be alone."

She rises and finds her clothes, closes the door softly behind her. Frank falls back, needled with doubt, but she doesn't believe that Sal is dangerous or a flight risk. To be safe, she finds her pack and feels out the Beretta. She lays it on the bedside table and tugs her clothes on. Sal can have her privacy, but Frank will keep vigil. She fluffs the pillow against the wall and leans into it. The room is cold, and she flips the bedspread over her legs. Determined to keep watch with the stars, Frank is asleep within minutes.

Chapter 38

"Shit!"

Frank throws off the bedspread. Though stiff from the saddle and mantling over Sal, she is instantly on her feet, taking in the silence, the fact that it is still dark. Pulling on shoes she glances at her watch. Almost four a.m.. Frank swears again.

The door to Sal's room hangs wide, the bed smooth and unused. Sal isn't in the cabin. Frank peers through the window at the fire. It has burned to a bed of coals. The chairs in front of it empty. None of the dogs are around, and she feels a prick of alarm. She opens the cabin door quietly, but it's enough for Bone to hear. He whines urgently. Hair rises on the nape of her neck as she realizes the dogs are in the pen.

She jogs the moon-swept ground between cabin and barn. Buttons lifts her head and nickers a soft inquiry. Dune is gone. She runs her hand along the wall where the Winchester hangs. There is only rough wood and an empty nail.

She runs back to the cabin, slapping a light on as she enters. Only then does she see the envelopes on the table. Three, laid in a row. Addressed *Pete*, *Cassie*, and *Frank*. She tears her envelope open and reads the folded letter. She reads it a second time, then shuts off the light and returns to the still dark yard. The dogs whine as she paces the fire pit.

Frank runs to the barn. She saddles Buttons and trots her across the yard to the restless dogs. She turns them loose and mounts. The five of them cross the light-bled field at a gallop. As they near the hulking foot of the mountain, Frank slows to let the dogs lead the way. She gives Buttons rein, urging her at a trot behind the dogs.

The landscape is black and blacker, yet the trail gleams a lighter black between brush and rock. The dogs strain to keep ahead of Buttons, their breath pumping and ragged. Kook struggles to stay alongside but falls behind. Frank swears and reins the horse. She jumps down, scoops the heaving dog and plants him against the pommel. Buttons sidesteps, rearing her head in protest, but Frank keeps a tight hold. The horse steadies and she lifts herself into the saddle. Settling Kook in her lap, she tells the big dogs, "Go on! Go!"

They turn and run ahead. The trail narrows into the side of a cliff and she recognizes where they are. One foot dangling the verge, the other bumping into brush, she hopes to Christ that Buttons' night vision is as good as Sal says it is. It appears to be—until a rock clatters beneath a hoof. Buttons stumbles, quickly righting herself, and Frank almost pisses in the saddle. Her hand is cramped white on the pommel, the other wets Kook with sweat. Suddenly Buttons pulls up short. She lifts her head and whinnies. An answering whinny comes, then the sound of hooves striking rock. The dark shapes of Cicero and Bone back toward her as the bulk of a horse materializes round the cliff face.

"For fuck's sake."

The horses stand at an impasse.

"Go on!" Frank waves an arm at Dune. "Go on! Hyah! Git! Go!"

Dune nickers uncertainly and steps toward her.

"No!"

She pushes Buttons a step forward. Caught between the two horses, Cicero tries to slink between Buttons' legs.

"Cicero, no!" Frank yells. "Stay!"

Remarkably the dog stops and sits. Frank grabs a bush sprouting off the cliff and snaps off a branch. She brandishes it at Dune and forces Buttons to take a step. The dogs squirm in a tight circle.

"Yah!" she screams. "Goddamnit, move!"

The horse whinnies but doesn't budge. Swearing again, she leans into the cliff and digs out a crumbly handful of rock. She hurls it in Dune's direction, and the horse takes a faltering, backward step. She grabs another handful of rock and flings it, yelling for the dogs to go. They each make a nervous move toward Dune. Frank spurs Buttons behind them. Dune whinnies his fear and tries to come forward, but

Frank screams and throws her branch. The horse hesitates, feeling his way into reverse. She yells Dune into a tentative step, then another, recalling Sal's assurance that horses don't want to die any more than she does.

Dune is making slow but steady progress, until he slips. His rear end slews from the trail and his hooves clack on bare granite. She hears them drag and scrape and Dune heaving in loud, heavy grunts, but the dark mass of him continues sinking over the verge. He makes a final lunge but can't gain the ledge. Dune falls, screaming, and Buttons echoes his scream. She dances on the skinny trail and Frank weakly kicks her, turning her reins into the cliff. Buttons takes a reluctant step, then stops and screams again. Frank jabs heels into her ribs and Buttons dances backwards.

Vomit rises to her throat and Frank gags. "Come on, girl, *please.*" She kicks lightly and Buttons inches forward. "Good girl, good girl."

Frank strokes and clicks, urging her ahead, keeping her going. She is shaking so hard she's afraid she's going to fall out of the saddle. There is nothing she can do but hang on and trust. All she can do is push ahead. Her life is suddenly out of her hands, and she gets with sharp, implacable clarity that if she is meant to live, she will—and if she's not, she won't. It's so dreadfully, mercifully simple she almost laughs. Her fate is as fixed as the mountains and the moon. Nothing will alter the outcome either way.

Frank closes her eyes. She gives herself over to the beast beneath her. Her grip relaxes and the shaking slacks. Buttons picks her way doggedly. After a span of time that seems to elongate into an eon but is probably no more than a few minutes, Buttons turns into the cliff. She gathers her haunches and vaults effortlessly onto a low boulder. In a few strides they have passed through the gap and out onto the broad *portrero.*

The shakes reclaim Frank. She stops and leans, retching until she is empty. Kook licks her face when she straightens back into the saddle. With a firm hold on him, she kicks Buttons into a gallop. She sees as they fly over the meadow that the trees ahead are gaining definition. Night is yielding to yet another perfect, pearly dawn. She kicks Buttons again. And once more. The mare strains beneath her, hooves punishing the mountain silence. Bone and Cicero struggle to keep up.

As they close in on the pines, she slows to let the animals find the path. They plod while she silently curses and wills them on. The sky pinks as they enter the tall pines. Frank drops from the saddle and ties Buttons. She breaks into a jog, urging the dogs on until they get to the ladder of boulders. She lifts Kook onto the rocks and gives the big dogs a boost. They scurry up the cleft and out of sight. Cicero howls, and Frank bloodies her palms again. She pulls herself up onto the pass to see the dogs wiggling joyously around their master.

Sal sits naked on the ledge. Her hair is loose. The Winchester lies across her thighs. Sal smiles. She is relaxed, happier than Frank has ever seen her. "I thought you might find me. You're a good cop."

"Come on home, Sal. It doesn't have to be this way."

"No. It does. The land's yours now. I felt it go at the *abuela*'s. You felt it, too, didn't you?"

"I didn't feel anything," she lies. "Come on. Put your clothes on. We'll go home."

Sal smiles at her. "I am home."

"Look. We'll get you a good lawyer. I know lots of 'em. We'll get you off. It was an accident."

"It was, but lying about it for forty years wasn't." She shakes her head. "I can't leave, Frank. You understand that."

"You won't have to." Frank steps toward her. "I promise we'll get you off."

Sal rests a hand on the shotgun, her finger curled around the trigger. She arches a pale brow. "You can make those kinds of promises?"

"I can. I swear it. Look, who's to know? You could even say Cass did it, that—"

"No. No more lying. I'm all done with that."

"Okay. Fair enough. But if you knew I was gonna find you, why'd you wait?" Frank indicates the gun. "Why didn't you do it already?"

"I had to wait for that." Sal points her chin and Frank turns to look into the round, red eye of the sun. "I had to see it one more time."

Sal stands. The sun flames her body. The sky behind her is translucent. She lifts the shotgun. The barrel rests under her chin.

"Don't do it, Sal. Please."

Frank takes a step. Sal smiles and tosses the gun. Frank reaches for it, and Sal spins. She pivots slowly on one foot, a ballerina in a timeless music box. But this ballerina plants both feet on the edge of the bench and as Frank lunges, crying her name, Sal executes a perfect swan dive into the fresh, new morning sky.

Frank staggers back. The dogs stand with their heads hanging over. There is no sound but their panting. Frank drops to her knees. One by one, the dogs leave the edge. They arrange themselves around the shallow saddle. The sun climbs and the sky ripens to its true, fat blue. Frank removes her clothes. She folds them next to Sal's. She does not look over the edge.

A black shape slices the azure. A second joins it. With a great flapping the birds land across from her, higher on the curving ridge. They sink into their ebony plumage and settle to the waiting.

"*Zopilote*," she whispers.

She is small, in a hut of bent willow, caring for a younger child and a baby. Then grown to a maiden, dancing barefoot to a clamor, unaware of the elders watching, murmuring ascent. Dancing again, an older woman in a cloak of great black feathers with a soft, red-painted hide upon her head, and while her body dances her mind soars over the mountains, gathering dreams and wisdom that she may carry them to her people in their fire-bright canyons, and she is old, old, very old, plaiting reeds by a black and depthless pond, smiling at the dark watchers in the air, and she is air and earth and fire and ocean, and forever has been and will ever be.

Bone stands over her, his breath upon her face. Her cheek is wet where he has touched it. Frank stands. She bends and feels in Sal's shirt pocket. The pouch is there. She sits. Bits of rock and twig dig into her skin. She rolls a cigarette and smokes. The sun forges down and her skin reddens.

When she stands, the dogs stand with her. They stretch languidly. Across the way, the featherless heads turn to watch. Frank steps to the ledge and looks down. It is a far, far drop. She stares into the fathomless brush, then west at the black canyons stretching to sea. She closes her eyes, feet side by side, toes over the edge of the warm rock. But for her heartbeat there is silence. Then a soft stirring, and silence again. She opens her eyes. Bone stands beside her, ears cocked, nub wagging.

Frank steps back. She puts the shotgun on Sal's clothes and tucks her own under her arm. She turns with a lingering look. The birds wait like twin stones. Frank lifts a hand to them. As she does, a small weight settles on her shoulder.

"I'm here."

She whirls. There is only rock, a scraggly bush, and three dogs waiting to go home. Behind her the dark watchers drop from their perch. They float and turn, rising in slow circles, high over the guardian mountain and sea.

About the Author

Baxter Clare Trautman is a Lambda finalist for her *LA Franco* mystery series. She grew up half wild in the Central American tropics, moved back to the States where she continued to haunt favorite treehouses, and eventually settled in a real house on the California coast. Never far from nature, she earns her keep as a wildlife biologist, and lives in the boonies with her wife and a beloved assortment of animals. In addition to the Franco series, Trautman is also the author of *Spirit of the Valley* and *The River Within*. She welcomes you to stop by and say hello at www.baxterclare.com.

Bywater Books

THE MIRROR AND THE MASK
A Jane Lawless Mystery

Ellen Hart

"a tale full of complex plot lines, fast-paced action,
and characters skilled in deception"
—*Library Journal*, Starred Review

Minneapolis restaurateur Jane Lawless is at a turning point.
Thanks to the tanking economy she has scuppered her plans
for a third restaurant, and her long-distance romance is on the
skids and likely over. Opting for a big change, she takes her
good friend A. J. Nolan up on his standing offer to train her as
a private investigator.

Jane's first job seems like beginner's luck. All she has to
do is find Annie Archer's stepfather. Jane tracks down a likely
match—a man who has made a small fortune in real estate.
While she's happy to close her first case, she finds it hard to
reconcile the difference between PI work—finding what
people pay you to find—and uncovering the truth, especially
when clues in this seemingly simple case point to more
threatening family secrets than where Annie's father has
been hiding out.

Ellen Hart's *The Mirror and the Mask* is another riveting
mystery filled with the deceit and psychological intrigue that
fans have come to expect from an author at the top of her
game.

Print ISBN 978-1-61294-043-4

Available at your local bookstore
or call 734-662-8815
or order online at www.bywaterbooks.com

Bywater Books

THE CRUEL EVER AFTER
A Jane Lawless Mystery
Ellen Hart
"Buttressed by distinctive characters and a splendid
Minnesota setting, the well-constructed plot
builds to a satisfying conclusion."
—*Publishers Weekly*

Jane Lawless is nearly dumbstruck when her ex-husband Chester reappears in Minneapolis. After their divorce he swore he would never return and left Jane with enough money to open her first restaurant. Now he's back and penniless, or as he would prefer to say, between fortunes.

But Chester is never without an angle to make more money. This time he is selling a priceless artifact recently looted from the Baghdad Museum. When he wakes up next to the dead body of his buyer with no memory of what happened the night before, Chester panics and flees the scene. Later he returns to cover his tracks only to find that someone has already taken care of that for him, but at what price?

The Cruel Ever After is filled with the intrigue and cunning that makes Jane Lawless one of the most absorbing series on shelves today.

Print ISBN 978-1-61294-044-1

Available at your local bookstore
or call 734-662-8815
or order online at www.bywaterbooks.com

At Bywater Books we love good books about lesbians just like you do, and we're committed to bringing the best of contemporary lesbian writing to our avid readers. Our editorial team is dedicated to finding and developing outstanding writers who create books you won't want to put down.

We sponsor the Bywater Prize for Fiction to help with this quest. Each prizewinner receives $1,000 and publication of their novel. We have already discovered amazing writers like Jill Malone, Sally Bellerose, and Hilary Sloin through the Bywater Prize. Which exciting new writer will we find next?

For more information about Bywater Books and the annual Bywater Prize for Fiction, please visit our website.

www.bywaterbooks.com